D1457797

THE DEVIL'S KISS

The glittering world of pampered, young Roslyn Darby falls apart when her beloved father is murdered and their beautiful Ceylonese home burnt to ashes. To escape the Sepoys' rebellion Roslyn flees to England, her only possession a ruby pendant reputed to have mysterious powers.

Her journey is filled with dark horrors and danger but grey, misty Yorkshire seems even more sinister. For as Roslyn loses her heart to the arrogant Greg Radcliffe, the pendant's malevolent powers seem to possess her and threaten to destroy her love forever.

THE DEVIL'S KISS

The Devil's Kiss

by
Sally Blake

Magna Large Print Books
Long Preston, North Yorkshire,
England.

British Library Cataloguing in Publication Data.

Blake, Sally
  The devil's kiss.

  A catalogue record for this book is
  available from the British Library

  ISBN 0 7505 0396 3

First Published in Great Britain by Macdonald Futura Publishers
Ltd., 1981

Copyright © 1981 by Jean Saunders.

Published in Large Print 1992 by arrangement with the copyright
holder.

Printed and bound in Great Britain by
T.J. Press (Padstow) Ltd., Cornwall, PL28 8RW.

CHAPTER 1

A shimmering heat haze danced over the vast grey-green slopes of the Darby tea plantation. The group of women pickers nearest the boss-house paused momentarily in their task, the wicker baskets slung on their backs from brow-bands weighing heavier as the day became furnace hot. On the lower ranges of the Ceylon hills, before they soared in smoke-hued peaks towards a relentless blue sky, the afternoon air was humid and oppressive. Here the Darby estate sprawled in lush prosperity. The tea-pickers noted, envied or hated the sight of the two figures now on the shady verandah of the white mansion built in the English style, James Darby and his daughter, Roslyn.

James Darby had been a vigorous young man when he came to Ceylon to seek his fortune, determined to let nothing and no one stand in his way. He had already had one bitter disappointment in his life and was out to prove to the world that Yorkshire grit meant exactly what it said.

The mysterious East had always fascinated

James. Ceylon in particular, the 'dropped pearl' off the southern tip of India, had drawn him like a moth to a candle-flame. Since his arrival on the island, his ruthless ambition had made him many enemies, but none could doubt his success. Darby had been one of the first Ceylon planters to risk experimenting with tea bushes instead of the long-established coffee. The new plantation was already flourishing when the devastating coffee blight swept through the country in 1869, destroying the entire crop eventually.

Now, ten years later, the Darby plantation was one to be reckoned with. It stood in the region between Colombo on the western coast and the central town of Kandy, set like a little jewel in the hills.

Into this country of ancient custom and Buddhist rites, Roslyn Darby was born. A beautiful, fair-skinned baby, she had grown into a lovely and desirable young woman, her hair a glorious rich dark brown with tawny highlights, and eyes of a lustrous deep blue. After years of being caressed by the tropic sun, her fair skin was now the colour of warm honey, but had never lost its delicate English texture bestowed on her by her mother. At almost eighteen years old, Roslyn Darby was a beauty, and with a voluptuous shape that made more than one young man lust after her. James adored her, and kept a watchful eye on who was invited to the Darby mansion on the occasions when he entertained lavishly.

It was these two Europeans, still fair-skinned by Ceylonese standards, though James' had coarsened and darkened after more than a quarter of a century in the East, who were the objects of the tea-pickers' discontented stares. The booming sound of the afternoon tea gong, followed a little later by the appearance of the boss-man with the air of a king surveying his domain, and the rippling laughter of his daughter, never failed to irritate their dust-laden throats even more.

At four o'clock every afternoon, James and Roslyn took tea on the verandah of the Darby mansion, the blistering heat dispelled a little by *punkahs* to give them a semblance of a breeze. James' Yorkshire heritage still made him cling to certain rituals remembered from his boyhood, and four o'clock tea was one of them. He was a tall, gaunt man now, and habitually wore loose cotton clothes in defer-ence to the heat.

Roslyn, used to no other climate, looked as fresh as a lotus blossom, despite the fash-ionable imported English gown she wore of cream-coloured sprigged muslin. The British in

Ceylon never forgot their ancestry, and James had instilled the love of patriotism in his daughter, even though it was a far away country to her, cool and green and romanticised by its very distance.

She had learned much about it over the years, though not from her mother. Rose Darby had died on the day her daughter was born, clinging to James' hand and begging him not to be distraught at his little English Rose for leaving him...his wife had never been his true love, had she but known it, but he had felt guilty enough to give his daughter the name of Roslyn, after her mother. Truth to tell, he had loved Rose more in death than in life, for leaving him this lovely and delightful child.

But Rose had begged for other things in the tormented months of her pregnancy. She had hated Ceylon, the mosquitoes and the never-ending heat that sapped all her energy and kept native passions simmering and throbbing like the sound of village drums heard distantly in the night. She hated the parched earth and the vivid blue glare of the sky. She hated the ever-present animal and insect noises, and the feeling that past and present overlapped when the jungle threatened to encroach on Darby land and had to be forcibly hacked away. She had wanted her baby to know about England.

James had hired an English schoolteacher to educate Roslyn until she was fourteen years old, and an Indian woman, Nadja, used to caring for English families, to be her nurse. Nadja was still with them, an old woman now, a friend as well as a servant.

James would have strongly denied that his daughter was spoiled. She had merely been brought up in the manner of the child of a tea-planter. She was his darling, the one person to whom he showed that there was still a tender side to him, and he gave her everything she wanted. She smiled prettily into her father's eyes now, her generous mouth coaxing as ever, her full lower lip pouting just a little. She put one small hand on his arm as they waited for a servant to bring their tea and rice cakes.

'Oh, just once more, Father!' Roslyn's voice had a husky quality to it that would always have the power to twist men's hearts, even if she was as yet unaware of it. She ignored the deferential bow of the houseboy, seeing nothing subservient in it. It was just the way things were.

'You promised,' she went on. 'You know you did!'

'Did I?' James' eyes twinkled at her indulgently, in a way that would have astonished some of his workers, who were more used to his ice-cold fury and the clipped Yorkshire

11

vowels that let fly a stream of English expletives in their direction when the Ceylonese language deserted him in favour of good old Anglo-Saxon.

'You're teasing me,' Roslyn relaxed her slender shoulders, pretending petulance. 'I knew it all the time. If you don't agree to taking me to Kandy for the last day of the *perahera* I shall refuse to go through the list of guests for my birthday ball. I don't care if the Honourable Mrs Fitzwallace ends up sitting next to Sri Rajni, even if she *will* die with fright!'

James laughed. No one dared to speak to him the way Roslyn did, nor would he allow it from anyone else. He leaned back in his wicker chair, letting the fragrant scent of the frangipani flowers tantalize his nostrils. The drone of humming-birds; the turquoise flash of king-fishers on tamarind trees; the aromatic scent of eucalyptus all added to his contentment. Now and then the brilliant blue-green eyes of a peacock's feathers would fan out, to give them a spectacular display among the lawns and gardens that were landscaped with spraying fountains on little stone statues to give the illusion of coolness to the day. And to James, a breath of home.

'All right,' he said now. 'Tomorrow we shall

go up to Kandy with the rest of the masses, though I'd have thought you'd seen enough of it by now. One elephant is very like another...'

'How can you say that?' Roslyn's face became animated, her deep blue eyes sparkling as she remembered yesterday's trip to Kandy. 'Nadja was nearly frightened out of her wits when the second elephant turned in the line to trumpet at her. But the bearer held on well, and I told her she should feel honoured and that it was bound to have some mystic meaning!'

The whole of Ceylon seemed to converge on Kandy for these ten days in August each year when the *perahera*—the procession of the tooth relic—took place.

'How can any place be other than blessed, little Missy, when Kandy's temple contains the replica of the right eye-tooth of our beloved Buddha?' Nadja's voice would throb with reverence and conviction whenever she related the old tale.

But it was the excitement of the festival that drew Roslyn's interest. Bejewelled elephants, their *howdahs* decked with flowers and silks, their riders glitteringly dressed in ceremonial garb, would line up near the entrance to the temple. The leading elephant would bear the golden casket containing the tooth relic through the crowded streets, to the acclamation of an adoring audience. And at night, the *perahera* would resemble something from the Arabian Nights, as it was illuminated by a thousand torch-lights.

And at the end of this year's celebrations, it would be Roslyn Darby's eighteenth birthday. There was to be a ball at the Darby mansion, to which would be invited British officers and other notables with their wives and daughters, as well as the elite of Ceylonese society.

James Darby laughed into his daughter's sparkling eyes, an affectionate gleam in his own as she coaxed him.

'Yes, we'll see the end of the *perahera*, my love! And we must think about seating arrangements for supper at your birthday ball too. Though I've no doubt you've already decided which lucky young man will be your escort for the evening!'

Roslyn pursed her soft lips at his teasing. She could have her pick of the young men on the island, but there was not one eager suitor who appealed even remotely to her passionate nature. They were either too gushing or too insipid; too swarthy and running to fat from good living, or glistening pink with sweat if newly arrived from England and embarrassingly aware of it. There was not a single young man of her acquaintance who could stir her senses one jot. As for the planters' sons...she dismissed them scornfully.

Perhaps she may have looked more kindly on her would-be suitors if there was not already imprinted in her mind the image of her ideal lover...Roslyn's cheeks grew warm at this point in her secret daydreaming, and James could not help but notice the sudden rise and fall of the superbly shaped breasts beneath the cool low bodice of her gown. To him she had never looked lovelier. A rose ripe for the plucking...he was not a poetic man, but his Roslyn would make the dourist Yorkshireman wax lyrical and want to give her the moon. And on this special birthday, James Darby planned to give his daughter the most precious gift in his possession.

The devil's kiss, they called it. It was a perfectly cut ruby, a fabulous stone of glorious, glowing depth of colour like smouldering red fire. It had been given to James in his early wanderings by an Indian prince when James had saved his life. The prince had insisted on rewarding him, and the reward was beyond the young Englishman's wildest dreams. The ruby's value was unquestionable, as was the legend behind it, and like all Eastern legends was neither to be dismissed lightly, nor to be scoffed at by a foreigner.

'I give you the devil's kiss, friend Darby,' the dark young prince had solemnly intoned on that far-off day, 'in grateful thanks for my life. If you look, you will see that it is pear-shaped like the country of your dreams, but it is not a gem of Ceylon. Their rubies are light-coloured like the fruit of the raspberry, while this deep-hued gem is pure Siamese. See how the colour catches the light, my friend, as if to rival the sun. Take it in good health, and may fortune follow you.'

The gem had been handed to James as ceremonially as an English knighthood. He had been awed by the occasion, for which he was totally unprepared, and by the splendour of the glittering ruby as it lay on a bed of white silk.

'Why do you call it the devil's kiss, your Highness?' He forced his voice to break through the tongue-tied silence with which he'd been stricken.

The young nobleman leaned towards him with a rustle of costly silks and dazzling gems. The prince's black eyes had glowed like coals and the usual sing-song intonation told James the prince had an ancient tale to tell.

'This ruby has magical powers, friend Darby. See how it glows. It has all the fire of a warm and passionate woman. Guard it well. While it is yours, you will prosper. The ruby bestows love and protection on the owner, but listen well to this, my friend.'

The voice dropped even lower, the tone almost mesmeric. James had been entranced by his surroundings, the simple belief in the young prince's voice, and the gleaming ruby in his hand.

'When the ruby is warmed by the skin, it can give premonitions of danger. It may deepen in colour and cast a mirage into the mind. It may be a vision of time past or time still to come. Heed it well. It causes a sensation of burning on the skin when danger threatens, maybe no more than a prickle or as fierce as a clutching hand. Because of this, the ruby is known as the devil's kiss.'

James had kept the precious ruby safe in his possession for more than twenty-five years. Few people knew of its existence in the Darby mansion. Whether his prosperity was due to its protection he wouldn't speculate; his Yorkshire bluntness assured him his good fortune had come from hard work and hard mastery. During the last weeks, he had made several journeys to the finest jeweller in Colombo, and the ruby was now mounted in a beautiful gold-encrusted setting as a pendant to grace Roslyn's slender golden throat. If any gem could do justice to his daughter's beauty, it would be a prince's ruby.

It was to be James' greatest gift to her, and one of which she had no idea as yet. James was filled with joyous anticipation of her reaction. He had shown the jewel to her on rare occasions during her childhood, planning for this day in his mind, though he had never revealed the old legend to her. But Roslyn should know of it. He would write it all down for her. He knew how her romantic nature would delight in the tale, and the devil's kiss should be hers on her eighteenth birthday. James never once gave heed to the fact that once the gem passed out of his possession, he would no longer be under its protection. Such thoughts ascribed too much importance to a legend.

Roslyn had been engaged in pasting dried flowers in her scrapbook when the gong sounded for afternoon tea on that blisteringly hot August afternoon. Pasting, and leafing through the earlier pages which contained a young lady's collection of mementoes: dinner invitations and dance-cards; a child's first fan, embroidered with tiny seed-pearls; a silhouette of her mother's profile; a piece of silk from a favourite sari; her father's own printed cards that had grown in grandeur as the Darby tea estate expanded; the pencil sketches...

Roslyn's soft mouth curved into a smile. She traced a delicate finger around the face in the pencilled portrait, as if tracing the skin of a flesh and blood lover. And there were more pencil sketches of this same young man in her father's study drawer, together with a similar number of a younger man. These two that were now in Roslyn's possession, sent last year and only last week, had stirred something deep inside her. She had eagerly awaited the annual packet from England this time and begged for the sketch to add to her mementoes.

Every August, sooner or later a packet would arrive from England for Roslyn's father, containing a long letter and the two sketches. Until the previous year, she had merely glanced at them at James' request, and noted that the young men had strong faces, rugged as well as handsome, particularly the older one. But she had been unable to summon up much interest in the two Englishmen living in some remote Yorkshire farmhouse who were her kin. But time had changed all that.

From the time she had attained seventeen summers, as Nadja so quaintly phrased it, little Missy Roslyn had become a woman. She had blossomed into a sensual beauty with fine child-bearing hips and softly-rounded belly, a dipping waist and glorious honey-coloured breasts with rosebud tips. On the occasions when Nadja had moved silently about the bathing-room when little Missy had been attended to by a serving-girl, she had been struck by the young lady's golden beauty as she emerged from the scented water of the bathtub to be swathed in warm, lint-soft towels. The soft pearls of water caressed the fabulous contours of the honeyed skin, as Roslyn rose from the blue-tinted bathtub like a mermaid from the sea. The cool damp tendrils of her long dark hair matched a glistening dark triangle below the rounded belly. To Nadja's simple Indian philosophy, little Missy Roslyn was ripe and ready for a man.

If Roslyn herself sensed it lately by the restlessness that sometimes gripped her emotions, she did not fully recognize the new sensations stirring inside her. She only knew they became more forceful when she gazed at the pencilled face of the Englishman, and that the feelings were pleasurable to her. And this latest portrait of Greg Radcliffe had caused her to catch her breath for a moment when she had gazed on it for the first time, as if to reassert the wanton desires insidiously filling her mind for the last twelve months. She had almost begged James to let her have the sketch.

'They're sent for me, you know!' He had teased her when she had tried to disguise the eagerness in her voice. 'What would a young lady in Ceylon be wanting with the sketch of a rough Yorkshireman?'

Roslyn had laughed back, her voice breathy, her cheeks fiery. 'And what would Aunt Hester think if she knew you would rather keep him away from me?'

James had given in as usual, his hard eyes gentle with pleasure at the familiar use of Hester's name on Roslyn's lips. Roslyn would never know her, but it pleased him to keep Hester's name alive between them. It brought her closer to him...and he had not always been the hard man he was now. There had been a time when he was as young and passionate as any virile young man...

Roslyn knew the story, of course. James had never intended to tell anyone of his hurt, or that he'd once been vulnerable enough to feel the wild pangs of a frustrated love, to have his adored Hester courted and snatched from under his very nose by his own cousin, Thomas Radcliffe, while he had been frittering his time away from the family farm in his restless youth.

James had always felt the family intruder, living at the Radcliffe farm under sufferance when his own parents had died. But he was kin, and that counted for a great deal in Yorkshire farming country. They had lived in uneasy peace until he and his cousin Thomas had both fallen in love with the same fair-haired young lady, and tempers had exploded violently because of it. James had gone off in one of his rages after they had quarrelled to the extent of a fist-fight, and when he'd come back, sufficiently cooled down to talk sensibly, he'd found Hester already affianced to Thomas. His fierce pride wouldn't allow him to beg her to change her mind. If he tried, and Thomas intervened, he feared he might very well kill his cousin.

That was the initiative he needed to push his adventurous spirit across Europe into India, and finally to Ceylon. Thomas' treachery was intended to be a secret kept locked in his heart for ever—until the letters started coming. The second one arrived soon after the first, because it had taken a long time to track down a wandering Englishman with no particular purpose in mind, and once he had read Hester's tearful words, he didn't have the heart to tear them up, and neither could he forget her.

The letters revealed Hester's desperate unhappiness with Thomas Radcliffe, and her free admittance that she had married the wrong man. She still loved James and always would, but she knew her duty was to Thomas now, for she had made her choice. In Hester's mind the choice had been sacred and never to be refuted. Besides, there were now two sons...the first pencil sketches, at which Hester excelled, had fallen out of the envelope.

James had looked at them hard and long. They were children then, with an innocence about them that reminded him instantly of Hester. They were Hester's sons...and therefore dear to him, he realized slowly. He brushed aside all thought of Thomas having sired them with the ease with which he trod on spiders. Hester still belonged to him.

If he'd been as ruthless at that time as he'd grown to be over the years in Ceylon, he'd have gone storming back and claimed her for his own there and then. But by then he was just beginning to build a good life for himself, he'd met and married Rose because she'd vaguely reminded him of Hester. And though Rose was now dead, he had his lovely little Roslyn. One sweltering night long ago, when he'd drunk too much imported Scotch whiskey, James had poured out the whole story to his little round-eyed daughter, who had been enchanted by the sheer bitter-sweet romance of it all.

'...please don't ever write back to me, dearest

James,' Hester had begged in that first passionate letter. 'Thomas still has a temper as violent as your own, and my life would be intolerable if he knew I had written to you. It is enough for me that I send you a letter once every year with a sketch of my boys, and pray that it will reach you. I remember all your talk of India and the East, and I am sending this letter to the East India Trading Company. I will continue to do the same every year, James, if they are forwarded on to you. If they are sent back, I will know that either you do not wish to hear from me, or—but I won't even consider the possibility—that you are dead. I can't bear to think of it, when it is because of me that you left your own country.

'Love my boys a little if you can, James. If things had been the way they should have been, they might have been our sons. I know it is wicked and shameful of me to think that way, but I don't forget the love we shared. How could I? I still love you, James...'

Roslyn's young eyes had filled with tears at reading such beautiful, tragic words. Her poor father...and her poor Aunt Hester.

Over the years, Roslyn's interest in her father's yearly letters from England had waned. Until the time Greg Radcliffe's pencilled features had suddenly epitomized everything desirable in a young man to her awakening eyes.

Greg had an arrogant, proud look about him that sent a shaft of excitement through her veins. She doubted that he had posed for his mother's pencilled sketch. There was too much of an air of impatience about him. His eyes were dark and brooding, with bushy, well-shaped brows; his hair too was dark, and more unruly than a gentleman's should be; he had a strong masculine nose above a very sensual mouth. Roslyn had studied it so often she felt she would know its shape blindfolded if she were to explore a hundred mouths with her fingers. In her most wayward moments, she had even imagined kissing it. And as often chided herself for her foolishness.

'Little Missy dreams of the Englishman,' Nadja's knowing old voice would grow as caustic as it could when she caught Roslyn gazing at the sketches in her scrapbook. 'What use are such dreams? There are many fine young men who would willingly wed little Missy. Have you not seen one to whom you could give your heart? Not even one of the fine British officers who could cause its beats to quicken?'

No, none of those. Only a fantasy lover who was half a world away and did not even know of her existence...

25

Roslyn sipped at her cup of finest Darby tea and let her gaze roam around the regimented lines of fragrant tea bushes. The smoke-hazed hills beyond reared up like guardian sentinels. She had known no other home but Ceylon, and yet lately she had become aware of the same restlessness that had brought her father here so many years ago.

There was a stillness about the island at this time of day. Even the perpetual birdsong seemed to be muted; the animal calls half-hearted; the rustle of trees almost non-existent in the langorous heat. Yet beneath all its stillness, life throbbed and pulsated in thicket and jungle, in meandering rivers and sun-baked plains. Especially in Kandy at this very moment...Roslyn's momentary inexplicable feeling of unease disappeared as she remembered the *perahera*. She left the white wicker tea table, moving across to the wooden fencing around the verandah with the effortless grace she had unconsciously adopted from the Ceylonese that was so alluring on a European. She leaned against it, breathing deeply of the sweet-scented frangipanis.

'Do you ever want to return to England, Father?' The words were out before she really thought about them. She twisted round to look at him when he didn't answer.

'I shall never return,' his voice was strangely mournful, as if his destiny was already planned for him.

'I think I should like to see it with you, just once...'

'You must go to England when I die,' he told her suddenly. 'Yes, I should like to think you trod the paths I used to know. To walk the cool green Yorkshire dales in the early morning, with the dew around your feet and an easterly wind to take your breath away is something you must experience for yourself.'

She had covered the distance between them, kneeling on the matting floor of the verandah at his feet and hugging his knees to her breast.

'You're not to talk of dying! Not for years and years and years! And when I go to England, you will take me!'

James laughed at her confident words, but a little chill ran through him like the touch of the east wind on the Yorkshire moors. As if suddenly realizing he was not invincible, and one day his Roslyn would be alone. Though surely not for long. She was too lovely for that. Some man would love her and care for her and give her babes. The cycle would begin again. And he would not be here to see it.

He got to his feet. Some devil of depression

27

was getting into his bones today. It would quell his brief gloom if he attended to the matters he'd been promising himself he must do, putting down in writing the legend of the devil's kiss for Roslyn's enjoyment. And something not so pleasant. A letter to his cousin, Thomas Radcliffe, acquainting him of all that had happened to James Darby in the last twenty-five years. A man had an instinctive need not to be entirely forgotten by his own family. Finally, he would at last write to Hester, and surely this letter would not incense Thomas Radcliffe, for both of them were to be dispatched after his death, however far away that may be.

He left his daughter scanning through the list of guests to be seated at her birthday ball. She hadn't even noticed that she said 'when' she went to England, and not 'if'. But the thought ran through her mind that if Greg Radcliffe were to be included in the birthday invitations, there would be no doubt whatsoever who her escort for the evening would be.

CHAPTER 2

Roslyn woke early the next day, vaguely aware that something pleasant lay in store. For a few seconds she remained still, watching the slivers of sunlight stream through the slats of her window shutters. Outside she could hear the morning calls of the peacocks, and then she felt the blast of heat as a serving-girl folded back the shutters on her open window and let the full force of the morning sun rush in.

Then she remembered. It was the final day of the *perahera*. And James was taking her to Kandy to join in the last frantic festivities. She threw aside the gauze mosquito net shielding her bed. The night had been impossibly hot, and she knew James would not be ready to leave the estate until he had made his inspections and left orders for his managers. It would be late morning before they could start the journey, and an hour's ride in the two-wheeled carriage over dust roads before they joined in the celebrations. But she knew of old that nothing would dissuade James from attending to his duties first. She would have to contain her impatience a little longer.

'My bath, Meera,' Roslyn informed the young serving-girl who stood awaiting her wishes.

'Yes, Missy Roslyn.' The girl glided away on her soft flat slippers to prepare the fresh-scented water in the bathing-room alongside Roslyn's bedroom. It would take a little while before the perfume of attar-of-roses drifted through the adjoining door to tell her the bath tub was ready.

As Meera disappeared through the door, Roslyn became aware of an inexplicable irritation towards her. She moved with the sinuous grace of all Ceylonese girls, her simple house sari of a soft cream fabric emphasizing the smooth brown skin that gleamed with health. Meera was pretty, with doe eyes and hair the colour of ebony. Although she was only fifteen, she was already bethrothed. Meera was still a child in years and yet infinitely wiser in the ways of the world than Roslyn herself. Even if she had not experienced the full intimacies of the marriage-bed yet, Meera knew how it felt to be desired for herself and her feminine charms—and not because of her father's wealth, because Meera's father had none. She had been courted and asked for according to custom, and would soon spend every night in her husband's arms.

It was perfectly ridiculous, but Roslyn Darby felt a sudden stabbing envy of her own serving-girl. And it made her even more tetchy, because she who had everything that money could buy was still lacking in certain knowledge. The realization made her sharp with the girl when she stood waiting for Roslyn to enter the bathing-room.

'Well? Is it ready?' she snapped.

'Yes, Missy Roslyn...'

'Are your fingernails trimmed? They scratched me the last time. Show me!'

Meera silently held out two small brown hands, palms down. She must have done something bad to displease the little Missy Roslyn, but for the life of her she could not think what it was. Yes, the nails had been trimmed. Roslyn stared at them, and the thought rushing into her head was of those same brown hands caressing a lover. She mentally shook herself. She seemed to be in the grip of some madness today.

Roslyn rose from the bed in her cambric nightgown and brushed past the girl. Meera's face was as impassive as ever. If her mistress chose to be angry with her, then she was at fault. She moved softly behind Roslyn to the bathing-room, where the blue-tinted bathtub

31

stood in the centre, invitingly wafting the sweet scents around the room. Roslyn pulled the nightgown over her head and tossed it carelessly to the floor. The girl helped Roslyn into the bathtub before retrieving the nightgown and placing it on a stool.

The water was pleasantly lukewarm, soft and caressing. Roslyn leaned her head back against the shaped headrest and eyed the docile serving-girl, her eyes downcast as she soaped her small hands in preparation for the washing ritual. Roslyn had never bathed her own body in all her life.

Seconds later she closed her eyes blissfully as the gentle hands of the Ceylonese girl palmed her shoulders and arms and the long smooth line of her throat. Then down over the honeyed breasts and around their rosy tips with the rich pampering lather, and on to her belly. Featherlight strokes were all that was needed in the softened water, and finally Roslyn stood up to let the ablutions conclude.

It slowly dawned on her that the rapturous sensations that had assailed her in the bathtub were comparable with the feelings she had experienced so often lately, when dreaming by day or in the secrecy of the night about Greg Radcliffe. She looked down at herself, seeing that her nipples had hardened, and for the first time ever she was conscious of her body's nakedness in front of a serving-girl. She turned her back on Meera and told her to hurry up with the towels. When she had been patted dry, she waved her hand.

'Away,' she said. 'And ask Nadja to attend me.'

Nadja was the only woman of the household Roslyn 'asked' rather than commanded.

Usually it was Meera who helped her to dress, but today was different. Today Roslyn wanted to study her own form in the long mirror of the bedroom. She was almost eighteen years old, yet she was ignorant of the ways of love, or the closeness of spirit that came from loving. Back in her room, she let the cocoon of towels drop to the floor and gazed at her golden reflection. Was she beautiful to a man? To her father, yes...and there had been others who had stumblingly told her so. But not with the masterful urgency her passionate nature demanded.

Hesitantly, Roslyn let her hands skim lightly over the curves and hollows of her body. It was good to be touched, she thought tremulously. It was pleasant to feel the caress of the bath-hour, but even so, it was not a seemly pleasure because it was between herself and a serving-girl. Something instinctive told her

33

there must be more...

Nadja arrived silently from her quarters to find her mistress standing naked, gazing at her beautiful, seductive body with all the curiosity of an inquisitive puppy. She picked up a towel and wrapped it round Roslyn's smooth shoulders, with a murmur of protest at such impropriety. Roslyn slowly turned to face the old woman, spreading her arms wide with an expression of helplessness. The sheer innocence of the action, revealing herself to Nadja's eyes in a cloak of white lint, moved her deeply.

'I fear there is something missing from my education, Nadja,' Roslyn's voice was less sure than usual. 'All these years of learning, yet suddenly I feel I know nothing. I know nothing about *men*. Tell me about men, Nadja!'

The Indian woman's face beamed. So her little Missy Roslyn had finally become a woman. It took more than the number of years after all. It took a certain need...and it was time for the final instruction. Roslyn took the smile to be teasing, and for a moment was a child again, stamping her foot.

'Why do you laugh? Is it such a secret? You were once a bride, but perhaps it is so long ago you forget the ways of love! Would you rather I asked Meera instead...?'

Nadja bristled. It would be demeaning for

little Missy to obtain such information from a servant of lower house status than herself. Besides, the girl Meera was not yet wed. Her knowledge should not be complete.

'A woman never forgets the ways of love, little Missy,' she said softly. 'And if you wish to know them, it is for me to tell you.'

'Well then! Tell me what I need to know to—to please a man!'

Now why had she said that, Roslyn thought crossly? A man should please *her*. Eastern women were content to be the playthings of men, but she was of English stock and in England things were different. Her father had always told her so, but he had never explained himself; in matters such as these, discussion between them was taboo.

And as she listened to the old woman's words, she acknowledged that it was better so. Such things were women's talk.

Nadja's tuition was simple and explicit, told in the same sing-song way she would have related a childhood fable. But this was no fable...Roslyn's eyes grew wide and dark as she discovered the mysteries Nadja unfolded to her. By then she had curled up on her bed inside the cool white towel, her dark hair tumbling over her shoulders before its pinning, already dry in the heat of the day. Nadja, seated on a low stool at her side, thought she had never looked lovelier than she did then, with the growing awareness in her lovely eyes and the promise of passion trembling on her soft mouth. Nadja, who was distantly acquainted with the ways of the harem as well as a brief married love, instructed her charge fully.

'And—does it not hurt—this breaking of the maidenhead?' Roslyn whispered. The old nurse's hand closed over hers reassuringly.

'Perhaps, for a moment. But who can count a moment's pain against a lifetime of love? As long as love is there, little Missy, the pain will be as fleeting as the brush of a butterfly's wing. And a woman should be proud of the pain. It is her gift to her husband. It tells him of her purity. It is his triumph and her submission.'

Roslyn's head was whirling by now. It was frightening and yet thrilling, but Nadja's words gave great dignity to the deflowering. It was also disturbing to consider this idea of submission. She had not thought of that in connection with love. Her thoughts moved on to where they lingered so often of late.

Would Greg Radcliffe know all these things? A man presumably knew them by instinct. Would he be gentle in such a situation? Would that so-sensual mouth arouse a woman with its kisses? What would his hands be like—their shape, their tenderness and strength, their touch? And all the rest of him that Roslyn had never seen in the pencil sketches—was he tall, broad, as arrogantly sure of himself as his face suggested? Did his dark eyes come alive with passion as well as anger? Did they deepen with pleasure when they looked into a woman's eyes? And the maleness of him...?

Her breath was coming faster as Roslyn realized with a little shock that she had been mentally translating all that Nadja had told her in relation to Greg Radcliffe. Greg, who was no more than a dream to her...was she really going mad? Too much sun, too much heat...too much time to think these deliciously shuddering thoughts...

'Little Missy, I have upset you! I should not have told you so much all at once—' Nadja's distressed voice pierced her jumbled thoughts.

Roslyn shook her head quickly. 'It is right that I should know these things.'

She heard the distant shouts of the tea-pickers, and through her window she could see the women were already at work on the tiered slopes of the plantation. If she were not ready soon her father would have one of his rare moods of annoyance with her and not take her to Kandy after all. She slipped off the bed and gave her old nurse a quick hug. Nadja had been a substitute mother to her, and was much loved.

'Will you help me dress quickly, Nadja? And then you will accompany us to the *perahera* for the last day, won't you?' she wheedled. 'Father will pretend to be bored with it and want to come back early, but you can persuade him otherwise.'

She could have insisted Nadja came, but her respect for the old woman went too deep for that. And Nadja smiled ruefully, knowing little Missy could persuade James Darby to do anything without help from anyone!

The road towards Kandy took them through spectacular scenery of tumbling waterfalls and rocky gorges, along the fringes of jungle and plantations of banana and coconuts. The sun blazed down on the shaded vehicle carrying its three occupants along the busy road; the gaunt features of the tea-planter in his habitual loose cottons and the wide straw hat; the old Indian woman with her grey knotted hair and brown leathered skin, the customary sari looped over her shoulder; between them, fresh and cool, was James Darby's lovely daughter, in a blue gown of finest English cotton, embroidered with little eyelets. In her hand she held a matching parasol over her pinned tawny hair, from which little ringlets escaped alluringly.

The excitement from those already in the town quickly reached out towards those still approaching it. The sounds of throbbing drums, of thin wailing music, the noise of elephants trumpeting into the air and of people laughing and shouting, combined with the rumble of wheels on the dust roads and the singing of birds. The road led down towards the lake in the centre of the town, and a kaleidoscope of colour met their eyes as the Darby carriage made its approach. Roslyn's heart leapt with excitement as she saw the procession of elephants winding its way through the adoring masses.

There was a place where for a few rupees they could leave the carriage safely in the charge of native boys. It was an extortionate price to pay, but James would have tossed the coins to the scrabbling children anyway. He paid his workers so little, yet he enjoyed making a show of generosity. They joined the jostling throng of people in the streets, straining for a good view of the entertainment.

Near the lake was the Temple of the Tooth, not as grand as might have been expected. It was an octagonal building with a tapered roof and surrounded by a moat. On this glittering

August day, the elephants plodded along serenely, their little eyes gleaming in the sunlight, their backs adorned as ever with the dazzling displays of riders and treasure. Ceylonese dancers twisted sinuously among them for the entertainment of the crowds; cymbals clashed in ever-deafening dins; conch shells made good substitute drums for the cheering onlookers; soothsayers intoned dire warnings or sold good-luck charms to eager buyers; young boys did a roaring trade in wood apples and bananas, rice-paper cups of coconut milk and the potent drink of arrack, fermented from palm juices. Sometimes too, a sidling native boy would offer betel nut, the mild narcotic chewing substance that stained the mouth and teeth blood red. Occasionally, a brown hand would hold out a selection of semi-precious stones, still in their newly-panned state with the traces of clay clinging to them, in the frenzied desire to make a quick rupee at the *perahera*. In the teeming streets zircons and amethysts, topaz and moonstones, even sapphires and garnets changed hands with no questions asked.

There were times when Roslyn was forced to press a dainty lace handkerchief to her nostrils or take a whiff from her bottle of smelling salts as the day grew ever hotter, and the mixture of smells became heightened. Rank and spicy, fetid and suffocating, sometimes heavy with perfume and musk, the unmoving air hung like a pall. There were times when she had to turn her head sharply away from the sight of snake charmers with their hooded cobras weaving hideously near the crowds for their screaming excitement. Cobras were much revered in Ceylon, and by Buddhists in particular, because of the old legend that told of Buddha meditating outside his cave, and the cobras spreading their hoods about him to give him shade. Such legends only made Roslyn shudder.

'These goddamned natives stink to high heaven.' James Darby suddenly lashed out his arm at two young boys clad in loincloths who seemed to be clambering all over him trying to get a better view. It was such a small incident, and unfortunate that a group of the boys' relatives were standing nearby, large swarthy young men, out for excitement and spoiling for a fight. They were intoxicated on betel nut, and quick to take offence at the bad-tempered Englishman shouting abuse at the boys. It was the goddamned Darby-wallah —the words screamed round the group like a wave of charging buffalo. The Darby-wallah who paid poor wages for long hours and hard labour, and despised his workers as if they were less than the dust of the earth.

Suddenly there was a mass of brown bodies pressing so hard against Roslyn and her father she could hardly breathe. Fear was knotting her stomach as she looked into the leering brown faces. No devil masks on them, but they were all devils to her at that moment, teeth bared, the whites of their eyes gleaming as the betel nut flamed their passions.

Her father was shouting abuse in words she did not recognize, but the gist of them was very clear. Nadja seemed to have disappeared, thank goodness...there were clutching hands prodding her thighs and her bodice...she was almost sobbing with terror. No one helped.

'Father!' She suddenly screamed as she saw the streak of blood on his cheek.

'It's all right. I got the bastard,' he yelled back. 'Stay close to me, Roslyn. Nadja has gone for the military—'

Within minutes, it was all over. The appearance of a dozen army officers sent the group scattering, but before any could be caught, they had twisted away and been swallowed in the crowds. Roslyn leaned against her father, trembling. The threats from those dark throats had not escaped her, and James Darby had made more enemies this day.

'It's all right, darling,' James said harshly.

42

His arms held her close. 'We'll get out of here as soon as you've recovered and find a shady place to sit awhile.'

Nadja appeared as if by magic with a cloth wrung out in cool water to dab on James' cheek. One of her many cousins had a humble house in Kandy she told him, and would be honoured if they would allow him to give them some refreshment.

'I sometimes think Ceylon must be populated with your cousins, Nadja,' James gave her a brief smile and said they'd be pleased to follow her if they could make their goddamned way out through these hordes. Roslyn bit her lip, knowing the storm of anger inside her father still raged. He was king of his plantation, but here he was just another foreigner watching the ancient customs of an old civilization. Why could he not see that he antagonized people by his roughshod ways? Roslyn sometimes feared for his safety. Even now, he was elbowing his way through the crowds with imperialistic arrogance, unheeding the mutters that echoed after him. She held on tightly to his hand until they were away from the main crush of people and approaching the edge of the town, in one of the narrow back streets where the tiny huddled houses of the poorer classes stood, made of part-timber, part-bamboo, with a

43

thatch of palm. Nadja apologized profusely for the meagre home of her cousin, but to Roslyn at that moment it was like a little oasis of coolness and calm.

They were offered tea by the cousin Kaspin, and his wife Oon, who were embarrassingly honoured to have such important personages in their poor house. And if they would honour them still further, there was more than enough curry and rice for all. The gloomy interior of the house, with its rush matting and modest bits of furniture, the spicy smell of curry clung to everything.

Roslyn's first instinct had been to refuse, but she suddenly realized she was ravenously hungry, and her father was already accepting the offer. They sat on cushions on the floor and thanks were offered to Buddha before Kaspin nodded for the food to be served.

It was surprisingly good, as was the tea that followed. *Darby* tea, Kaspin assured James solemnly. James laughed, his good spirits restored.

When they left, it was to see the sun a glowing red ball low in the sky and the sudden onset of night about to begin. Roslyn knew nothing of the twilight that James told her happened in England, and the gradual deepening of light to dark. Here darkness fell almost in the twinkling of an eye, and they heard a great roar of cheering rise from a thousand dusty throats as the *perahera* suddenly took on a magical, breathtaking quality.

Flickering torch-lights illuminated the entire town. The tricksters were still there, the dancers still enacted their frenetic rituals, but now there were more subtle enticements on offer as well. Perfumed Ceylonese girls, in silken saris, bodies oiled and gleaming, arms and ankles chinking with gold chains, writhed in and out of potential clients willing to pay for their charms. They added extra glitter to an already fantastically glittering scene. The adornments of the elephants extended over their heads to the beginning of their trunks, so that only their little eyes peered through the slits in the ornate, gilded fabric. Jewels caught the lights of the torches and dazzled the eyes wherever they turned.

Roslyn's eyes suddenly focused on her father, a little distance away from her now, and saw him smiling down into the provocative face of a young Ceylonese girl with thrusting breasts and tiny waist. His arm was circling that waist and he was mouthing something to the girl. She couldn't catch the words, but she could lip-read them clearly enough.

'How much?' they said. The girl laughed and

gave an answer, and the next minute Roslyn saw him drop some coins between the girl's breasts, where she shook them sideways to nestle safely in between. It shocked her. He had left her and Nadja in the care of two army officers of their acquaintance, while he said he was going to find some cordial because the fierce curry had burned his throat. Now, she watched him take hold of the young girl's hand and disappear with her into the crowd.

'It is the way of things, little Missy,' Nadja's voice was suddenly in her ear, and she saw the old nurse had seen the little transaction as well as herself. She looked at Nadja blankly.

'She offers her body for money as one would offer a bag of rice in the market,' Nadja said matter-of-factly. 'For a few rupees, a man may have his fill of her and do as his desires tell him. It is the oldest profession of all.'

Roslyn was not completely naive about these matters, but never before had she connected her father with such activities. She had never considered his need for a woman, since she had only learned of the ways of loving that very day. She remembered Nadja's sing-song voice that morning at the Darby home, weaving a tale of enchantment out of the love a man bore for a woman, when that woman was his beloved wife. The idea had been romantic and heart-

46

catching. Now it had been besmirched by the passing of money between her father and a whore. Roslyn's eyes blurred as she felt the sharp sting of tears, knowing she would never feel quite the same deference towards him again. She had looked on him as a kind of god all her life, and it hurt to discover he was only human after all.

It was a good while later before James returned. The officers had no objection to escorting Roslyn Darby about the streets of Kandy, even if the old biddy of a nurse stuck to her side like glue. But she was out of patience with both of them, and glad when James finally made his appearance, looking flushed and well-satisfied, and blustering about his whereabouts.

'You'd think it was asking for gold dust to try and get a drink of cordial in this place,' he grumbled. 'I got swept along by the crowd and then ran into some of the other planters, so we spent our time chin-wagging once we'd hunted down a few drinks.'

'It's all right, Father,' Roslyn avoided looking at him. 'We've been enjoying the pageantry, and the officers have been good company.'

They preened themselves, a little surprised as Miss Darby had seemed not even to notice they were there.

'Have you had enough yet, Roslyn?' James went on.'

'More than enough,' she murmured.

He looked at her hard for a moment and then shrugged. The vagaries of women...and then he smiled to himself. There were some who were less complicated than others, and the last hour had been enjoyable. He wished the officers goodnight, and escorted the two women to the carriage square. When they reached their own conveyance, the young native boys scrambled down, having discharged their duties of keeping guard and feeding and watering the horses, and receiving a bonus for their diligence. Somehow their shrill voices as they gabbed in quick native dialect to James sent a chill through Roslyn.

The group of young men whom he had incensed earlier on had come looking for his carriage, meaning to destroy it, but the boys had insisted that this was not the Darbys' carriage and the men had gone away. They waited hopefully for more coins and were not disappointed. James lit the carriage lamps as Roslyn and Nadja climbed in and set the horses in motion immediately. He was more disturbed than he admitted.

It seemed an endless journey home. James and Roslyn were wrapped up in private thoughts.

A yellow moon rode high above them, lighting their way. Fireflies flickered among the undergrowth as they passed, and tall coconut palms rustled in the warm night breeze. In the distance a herd of wild elephants could be heard thudding through the jungle, and nearer at hand there was a constant scuttle of smaller animals and insects.

Roslyn was never afraid of noises. It was silence that unnerved her, but it was rare that the country was silent. All the same, there was a feeling of unease about James tonight that was quickly transmitted to her, and she was never more glad to see the lighted Darby mansion, cool and white, fringed in its lovely grey-green setting of the plantation.

'I think I shall go straight to bed, Father,' Roslyn said at once. 'Nadja...'

'I wish to speak with Nadja in my study,' James said abruptly, as the old nurse, patient as ever, waited for instructions.

Roslyn stared at him.

'Shall I send Meera to you, little Missy?' Nadja murmured.

She would probably be sleeping, but if Missy Roslyn sent for her, she would come.

'No,' Roslyn snapped. 'I shall manage for myself. Goodnight, Father.'

She sped across the marble floor to the elegant

staircase and up to her own room, restraining herself from banging the door behind her with a great effort. Today had started so beautifully, and somehow now it seemed to be all in shreds. Nothing was the same anymore. The world was not a simple place in which to live, but one where deception and hatreds simmered beneath the smooth surface. Once the ripples started to move, who could tell what storm might be unleashed?

Roslyn sat down abruptly on her bed, angry with herself. She was starting to think now as Nadja would. She crossed to the window and pulled the shutters, shutting out the night. The room was lit by the rosy glow from her oil lamp. She tugged at the back fastenings of her blue gown, tearing it in her frustration when she was unable to reach the fastenings easily. Somewhere during the scuffle in Kandy her matching parasol had disappeared, probably trampled underfoot by the crush of people or a parading elephant.

Tears of sheer frustration and tiredness sprang to Roslyn's eyes. She stripped off the remainder of her undergarments and tossed them to the floor, thankfully sliding into the coolness of her cambric nightgown. She turned the lamp down to its lowest point, so that there was just a glimmer of light to throw the softest shadows about the room. Pulling the mosquito net into position, she lay wide-eyed on the bed for a while, letting the tumultuous jumpings of her heart subside.

There was nothing wrong, she told herself. She was safe now. She was home. But she couldn't sleep. There was too much tension inside her. Finally she padded across the room to fetch her scrapbook, riffling through the pages to transport her mind to other things. And eventually arriving at Greg Radcliffe's portrait.

Roslyn stared at it for a long time. In some strange way it represented home in a way her familiar surroundings failed to do tonight. She was still gripped by the numbness she had felt when she had seen the lascivious look in her father's eyes as the little whore tantalized him with her breasts. The numbness had stayed with her throughout the journey home. She realized now that there had been a deep fear inside her that her father's fall from grace in her eyes might have wiped away every trace of her own desires. But the feelings were still there.

She traced the contours of that unknown face as if touching his skin. There was still the unbidden little thrill his image could evoke, still the pounding inside that was such a new and vibrant sensation, the longing to know his touch and his kiss. All the sweet and beautiful feelings still clamoured to be known.

Roslyn bent her head and touched her soft lips to the paper. It was foolish, of course. It was a young girl's dream of love that could never be fulfilled, but perhaps after all, in a world populated with hatred and lust, it was safer to put her trust in dreams.

CHAPTER 3

James Darby faced Nadja, where he'd asked her to sit, across the width of his desk. Now that she was here, he wasn't at all sure what he intended to say. But say something he must. The feelings of unease that of late had invaded his mind were too strong to be denied. And he had been in the East too long to ridicule them. He'd had a good run of luck, but he doubted if even the devil's kiss could protect him against the menace and threats he'd encountered that day. And it was Roslyn's future he was most concerned about.

'You are devoted to my daughter, are you not, Nadja?' he began clumsily, and then found himself apologizing as he saw the sudden hurt in her old eyes. 'Oh, forgive me. That was a stupid thing to say.'

'Yes, Sahib,' she agreed with quiet dignity. 'And you know I would protect her with my life, for what it is worth.'

James nodded. The humility of these people! Sometimes he loved them, at others he despised them. But he knew Nadja's loyalty to him and to Roslyn was unquestionable. He had trusted her many times in the past, and he must trust her now. He walked across to the safe in the corner of the study and unlocked it, bringing a long jewel case to the desk.

'I want to show you my daughter's birthday gift,' he said. 'She has no idea what it is to be, so tell me if you think it will please her, Nadja.'

He opened the clasp of the case and pushed it across the desk towards the old nurse. Inside, on a bed of white silk as James had first seen it, the Siamese ruby glowed like fire, its pear shape, like the island of Ceylon itself, lending itself perfectly to the exquisite setting and gold chain the jeweller had used for the pendant. The rich colour of the gem seemed to eclipse all else in the room, and James heard the old woman's sharp intake of breath.

'It will please her, Sahib,' she spoke with

her usual understatement, but James did not miss the note of awe in her voice.

He laughed, satisfied with her reaction. And then his laugh faded as he passed one long finger lightly over the ruby's lovely surface. James was not a deeply superstitious man, but he did not choose to take the ruby in his hand and let it be warmed by his skin. If there were visions to be seen of good time past or bloody time to come, he preferred not to know about it.

'There is a story behind it, Nadja,' he said now. 'And one that I wish to tell you so that you are fully aware of the implications in my giving this ruby to Roslyn. I have written it all down for my daughter, but I do not wish her to know the full story unless it becomes necessary. I have put it and other important documents in this leather bag.'

He rose and pulled the bag out of the safe to show her. Nadja remained silent, her instincts telling her to listen carefully and not to make comment until required.

'I shall give you a duplicate key to my safe, Nadja. No one else has my full trust, so guard it well, as well as you guard my daughter. If the time should ever come when you need it, then take the bag and Roslyn to safety.'

It hardly seemed to be himself talking, James

thought. He wasn't usually given to fancies or premonitions, and he could no more imagine this old woman fleeing with his daughter into the night than he could imagine flying to the moon. But she nodded, her face impassive.

'I will do as you say, Sahib. And I will not fail you.'

James suddenly felt he was being melodramatic and slightly ridiculous. He turned his eyes back to the ruby, lying in all its lovely splendour, and quickly related the tale the young prince had told him. He made light of it, but when he had finished, he realized that the Indian woman was breathing hard and that her old gnarled hands gripped the sides of the chair.

'You take a great risk, Sahib Darby,' she was more agitated than he had ever seen her. 'The ruby should remain yours until you die, as was intended. Did you not understand that?'

'It will still be in my family, Nadja.' Her intense gaze irritated him now, and seeing her obvious apprehension, his own lessened. He was once more the no-nonsense Yorkshireman. He replaced the leather bag and the cased pendant securely in his safe and brought out a key on a leather neck-thong.

'The duplicate key,' he said. 'And now we had better both get to our beds, or the day

55

will be on us before we are ready for it.'

Nadja, ever submissive, rose at once. Before she retired to bed, the key to James Darby's safe was securely around her neck, where it would remain. It would never be required, unless...she prayed fervently that that day would never come.

The preparations for Roslyn's birthday ball occupied all her attention over the next few days. She supervised while Nadja attended personally to the deliciously silky gown she was to wear, pressing its folds and ruches to perfection, tweaking out the little puffed sleeves and the bewitching hint of a bustle. The neckline was deep and showed the swell of her breasts and the tantalizing valley between them. Her tawny hair would be worn in a top-knot, but with ringlets tumbling over her creamy shoulders. She had half-guessed that her gift from her father was to be jewellery of some sort from his hints that she should not choose a gown of too deep a colour. Something light, he'd said vaguely, and with a décolletée bodice. Something on which a necklace would look well ...he was never very good at disguising veiled hints from Roslyn.

She smiled now as she remembered. She was trying on the new gown for the final alteration to the ruching, which hadn't been quite to her liking. Nadja went off to fetch some more pins and Roslyn smiled again at her reflection in the long mirror. She looked beautiful and she knew it. If only there was to be someone at the ball to appreciate it in the way she desired. Impulsively, she opened her scrapbook to where the rugged face of Greg Radcliffe looked broodingly back at her. She propped the book up against the mirror and preened herself in front of it, twisting this way and that as if for his approval.

'Well?' she spoke softly to the picture. 'Will I do for you, Greg Radcliffe? Because you will do very well for me!'

Suddenly elated at the thought of the evening ahead, Roslyn picked up the open book and waltzed around the room with it in her arms, laughing at herself and at the dark eyes of Greg Radcliffe. If she blurred her own a little, she could almost imagine the image was real...

'Missy Roslyn, what are you doing?' Nadja's disapproving voice stopped her spinning at once, and Roslyn swayed giddily for a moment, annoyed at being discovered in such an undignified action. 'Such foolishness in a young lady! There will be plenty of young men anxious to dance with you at the ball, and this Englishman is far better forgotten.'

'Why should I forget him?' Roslyn's brows

drew together in a frown. Her mutinous expression was very like her father's at that moment, Nadja thought. Especially when she tossed her head like that. Roslyn threw down her book and suddenly caught sight of herself in the mirror. Her cheeks were flushed, her eyes sparkling, her breasts heaving. She looked like a girl who had just embraced a lover.

She avoided Nadja's keen glance, lifting her hand to lift the weight of her tumbling hair from her shoulders. It was an unconsciously provocative gesture, and one that arched the slender curve of her waist. The silk of the gown felt cool and seductive on her skin.

'Am I not fortunate in not needing corsets, Nadja?' she wheedled a little flattery from her nurse. 'The ladies newly-arrived from England must be near to fainting to wear them in this heat. Imagine being pinched and pulled to make yourself look presentable!'

'You are fortunate in many ways,' Nadja said a little tartly. 'Including your father's indulgence of you!'

She was thinking about the jewelled pendant James Darby was to give his daughter for her birthday. As she knelt with the pin-box and adjusted the hip line of the ballgown, Nadja was filled with apprehension. The ruby with its protective powers had been for James and James alone. Its powers would continue to the next owner, but James himself would be vulnerable. And in Ceylon he had many jealous enemies.

Roslyn was watching her old nurse. 'Nadja? What have I done to displease you?' Her voice was small and entreating now.

Nadja's brief irritation vanished. Roslyn hated to be out of favour with anyone. She wanted always to be loved. She could be wilful and cold on occasion, but her nature was normally passionate and warm-hearted, and like most people, Nadja responded to it at once.

'Nothing, my sweet one. It is just the tiredness of an old woman. You will be the belle of the ball, which is how it should be. There will be no need to dream of an Englishman who is far away. Promise me you will not waste your thoughts in this useless manner, little Missy.'

Roslyn bent and kissed the old woman's cheek.

'I will promise to try,' she said airily. 'But dreaming of faraway people and places is in my blood, Nadja. If my father hadn't been a dreamer, he'd never have come to Ceylon in the first place!'

Roslyn knew well enough that it was wise not to pursue the matter further, and she let Nadja retire to her own quarters to do the final stitching on the cream gown.

Outside, the lawns and gardens of the Darby mansion were being hung with paper lanterns, sweet-smelling sachets of dried flowers and herbs were scattered among the trees to add to the already scented surroundings. The kitchen-hands were preparing a fine selection of both English and Eastern dishes for the favoured guests who would arrive for the dinner preceding the ball. More guests would attend later in the evening, when the musicians took their places and the dancing began in the great marble-floored hall. James had spared no expense and wine would flow like water.

The tea-pickers and the estate labourers, watching the exterior preparations while they toiled in blistering heat, with the boss-man riding around the plantation or striding among them as cuttingly brutish as ever, felt the simmering resentment burn more brightly within them. It was close to boiling point.

An hour before the first guests were due to arrive, Nadja stood back and admired the vision of loveliness in front of her. She and Meera had attended the little Missy, bathing, perfuming and dressing her, and the result was perfection. The cream silk gown shimmered each time Roslyn moved, with a subtle seductiveness. She was a little princess, Nadja thought. Roslyn's rich tawny hair framed her exquisite face, and the lovely golden skin fleshed out over the bodice of the gown. No other woman in the Darby mansion would come within a mile of her loveliness, Nadja mused with quiet pride. And Meera, too, was glad that her vigorous young lover, who had sometimes glimpsed the golden beauty of her mistress and teased her about her desirability, could not see Roslyn tonight.

'Your father will be waiting for you in his study, little Missy,' Nadja said. And instantly the cool goddess became an animated child again, as her eyes glowed with anticipation and she clapped her hands gleefully.

'At last! The mysterious birthday gift he's made me wait all day to receive! Have you seen it, Nadja? Tell me!'

'I would spoil your father's surprise, little Missy, and you should not ask me!' Nadja protested.

She smiled genially. Roslyn paused only to snatch up her pearl trimmed fan and the dance card to trail from her arm before she whirled out of the bedroom and sped down the stairs to tap at her father's study door. Meera began the task of tidying away Roslyn's discarded clothes and the bath towels and looked at Nadja curiously.

'Do you know what this wonderful gift is to

be, Nadja?' She did not bother to hide the sarcastic note in her voice. Missy Roslyn had not been really civil to her for days now, and she was tired of the old nurse's mysterious hints. Nadja looked at her severely.

'I do, and you had better keep a more humble tongue in your head, girl,' she said sharply. 'I have not missed your sullenness lately. Missy Roslyn is to receive a splendid jewel from her father.' She saw no reason to be reticent now, since Roslyn would be already receiving the pendant. Nor did she intend going into any detail about it. 'It is enough for you to know that it is very precious indeed, and was given to Sahib Darby by a prince of my country.'

Nadja had a haughty dignity about her now that angered the Ceylonese servant. This was *her* country, and this grey old biddy spoke as if she did Ceylon a favour by being here. But she did not dare to answer back. The nurse had a higher status than Meera, and she was already out of favour with her mistress. She would rebel by stealing out of the house when all the festivities were under way. No one would miss her and she could spend the time more enjoyably in her lover's arms. His family was kin to those in Kandy who had told of the unpleasant incident at the *perahera* involving the imperious James Darby. She would inflame them even more by telling them of the precious jewel given to Sahib Darby by an Indian prince that was to be Missy Roslyn's birthday gift. It would make a good tale with a little bit of embellishment, and the added haze induced by the betel nut could loosen many tongues. Meera's spirits rose.

Roslyn leaned back against the closed door of her father's study and waited for his reaction to her appearance. She was not disappointed. He felt a tightening in his throat and a rush of warmth in his blood at the vision in front of him. He slowly walked towards her.

'I have never seen you look so beautiful, my darling,' he said. 'No young man will be immune to your charms tonight!'

She gave a low soft laugh, and he wondered uneasily if he should be saying something more about the way those vigorous young men might react when they saw her and held her during the dancing.

'Oh, please don't keep me in suspense any longer, Father,' Roslyn cried. Excitement sparkled in her eyes. 'How much longer must I wait for my gift?'

He laughed. 'Not one moment longer, sweetheart!'

She followed him across the room to his desk,

where a long jewel case lay. Roslyn smiled, knowing she had guessed correctly that it was to be a necklace.

She waited with lips parted in a smile as James opened the lid of the jewel-case, and then the smile changed to a sharp gasp of pleasure and awe. The pendant lay invitingly on its bed of white silk, the ruby blood-red and dazzlingly perfect. It took her breath away. She recognized the gem from long ago when her father had shown it to her as a little girl, but she had forgotten it over the years. She had never thought to see it again like this, magnificently set in gold on a glittering neck-chain...James picked it up from the case, and instantly it glowed like red fire as the light caught its facets. He held it in his hand for a moment, the first time in many years, for he had let it lie untouched in the case since collecting it from the jeweller in Colombo.

A strange shudder ran through James' palm. His skin prickled as if licked by tongues of fire. For a moment his vision seemed to blur and redden, and clamouring noises filled his head...voices, and screams, and the throb of native drums...just before the vision faded there was a great silence and a black emptiness, and then the day was as it was before. He stood by his desk in the study of the Darby mansion, the devil's kiss in his hand, the gold chain dangling over his wrist, while Roslyn gazed at it in sheer delight.

'Oh, Father, it's so beautiful,' she breathed ecstatically. 'It's the prince's ruby, isn't it? The one he gave you for saving his life!'

'That's right,' James said huskily. He moved behind her and fastened the chain securely at the back of Roslyn's neck. He bent and kissed the clasp at her nape, feeling the deliciously perfumed ringlets tickle his cheek. Roslyn pressed the pear-shaped stone against her throat, feeling its warmth from James' hand, a tremor of delight running through her. And something like a little shock where it hung so unfamiliar against her delicate skin. She felt quite dizzy with emotion.

'Just feel my excitement!' Innocently, she pulled James' hand towards her and lay it against the swell of her left breast, where her heart pounded. The ruby lay between his palm and Roslyn's skin, and he jerked his hand away as if he'd been stung, as the sudden noises surged into his head once more and the prickling began to spread to his fingers.

'I hope you're not going to ask every young man at the ball to feel your excitement, my love!' He admonished her more teasingly than he felt. A sudden thrill of fear, a sensation practically unknown to James Darby, coursed through him. And a feeling that all the fury of the East was weighing down heavily on him at this moment because he had dared to flaunt a prince's legend and give the devil's kiss away. It was nonsense, of course...superstitious nonsense...and his daughter glowed as brightly as the jewel itself.

'And I hope you've brought me up to know better than that!' she teased him back. 'But I must see how the pendant looks, and you have no mirror in here.'

She looked back as she reached the door, her eyes soft with love.

'Thank you, Father. I shall never forget today.'

James gazed at the closed door. The words had been sincerely meant, but to him they had a prophetic ring about them.

Roslyn hoped the two women would be gone from her room. She was rarely alone except for sleeping, and this time she wanted to be by herself, just to admire the glowing ruby against her skin. Her room was empty, and she stood in front of the long mirror, all vanity in her own appearance gone as she saw the real effect of the gem. It was the ruby that was the true beauty, she thought with an odd humility, with none of the flaws that human beings were cursed with. The ruby was almost dazzling as it flashed in the glow of lamplight. She narrowed her eyes against its fiery brightness for an instant, and the words were almost torn from her lips, soft and low.

'Why can't you see me now, Greg Radcliffe?' they whispered. 'Would I not please you?'

She felt herself sway slightly to left and right, in the sinuous movements of the Kandyan dancing-girls. Her body seemed to have a seductive motion of its own, writhing and undulating in provocative postures, sensual and inviting. For a few heady moments she was back in Kandy again at the festival, but this time she was part of it, one of the bejewelled dancing-girls with glittering gold and silver decorating their bodies, jewels through their noses and the sheen of silk caressing their skins. She was alive with the music, wanton with the excitement and the desire on the young men's faces...her head throbbed with the pulsing drums that pounded in time to her heartbeats and the frenzy of the dancing...it stimulated her to an almost hypnotic rapture...it was the world she knew, hot and alive. It had nothing at all to do with a remote farmhouse, grey and bleak, on top of a windswept moorland wreathed in cold English mist...the sudden searing through her senses of its image was so forceful it made Roslyn stumble against the side of her dressing-chest. She was breathing heavily, her face flushed, eyes wild, as she tried to regain her composure.

She sat down on the edge of her bed and passed a trembling hand across her forehead. Had she danced in that abandoned way...? Surely not! She did not know how...nor could she have seen the Yorkshire farmhouse where Greg Radcliffe lived with her English kinsmen ...she had somehow conjured up its likeness from the tales she had heard from her father so often in her childhood. And the drums that had seemed to be all in her head...

She could hear their dull throb now, out there in the darkness. It was a sound that was often heard during the Ceylonese night, its message palpating round the island faster than any bearer could deliver. As for these shameless feelings aroused in her by the unknown Englishman...Nadja was perfectly right. She should put them out of her mind immediately. They frightened her, because never in all her wildest dreams had she believed they could appear to be so real. Like a mirage in the desert...

When she had calmed herself, Roslyn went back downstairs. The first carriages were arriving. She could see the bobbing lights as they approached the wrought-iron gates to the Darby mansion and hear the rattle of wheels on the dust roads. The drums still throbbed incessantly, but she closed her mind to them. They were nothing to do with her. And once the fine ladies and gentlemen started entering the house, Roslyn became the centre of attention, her delight in her birthday celebrations eclipsing all other thoughts from her mind.

CHAPTER 4

The sparkling chatter in the Darby mansion as the evening wore on almost smothered the hypnotic drumming, until it became less of an intrusion and more of a rhythmic accompaniment to the succulent feasting and drinking, and then to the start of the dancing and the arrival of the ball guests. There were about sixty all told, and the whole scene took on a fairy-tale quality, with the beautiful English ballgowns and the splendid regimental uniforms of the officers vying with glittering saris and Ceylonese officials, darkly handsome in silks and braided evening attire. The paper lanterns swung softly in the warm breeze, lighting up the estate with a soft glow, accentuated by the intimacy of oil lamps and candelabra inside the house. Tantalizing scents drifted in from the gardens of herbs and eucalyptus and frangipani, and couples strolled around the fragrant walks, cooled by the refreshing fountains they paused to admire.

The first waltz of the evening was begun by Roslyn and James. He held out his arms proudly, and she went into them as if she glided in a dream. As they whirled, the colours all around them blurred and mingled, elating her. This was James' kingdom, and tonight she was the undoubted princess, the most beautiful lady in the room, as had been whispered to her so many times already. Loved and admired, as James never had been. As she danced with her father, his arm held firmly around her waist, she felt a brief sadness for him. He had so much, and yet it all meant nothing without love. He had *hers*, she thought fervently, and always would have.

James smiled down at her. She was very lovely, his Roslyn.

'Remember what I told you, my darling,' James heard himself saying. 'If anything happens to me, go to England, to your family.'

'Please don't spoil my birthday by talking of

such things, Father,' Roslyn begged him.

'Just remember.' His voice was intense, and she nodded, keeping the smile on her face but feeling a sudden chill run through her all the same. The only part of her that wasn't momentarily cold was her throat where the pendant rested. If she didn't know it was impossible, she'd have said her skin was almost burning beneath its pear shape...

As the music stopped, the couples moved away from the centre of the floor. Roslyn was suddenly aware that there was a change in the atmosphere, and just as she realized the drums had stopped, there was a shrill scream from the garden. Everyone crowded towards the long open windows and the verandah, as more screams followed. Tongues of fire were leaping around the tea bushes on the lower slopes. The ground was tinder-dry and, in the light from the flames, the watchers could see a wall of dark-skinned natives with flaring torches and wads of brushwood in their hands. Black smoke was already soaring skywards and it took no more than minutes for the fire to get a raging hold on the plantation.

James let out a roar of anguished fury. Everything he'd lived and worked for was shrivelling in front of his eyes. For a few minutes there was stark horror and disbelief among the ball guests, and then a sudden stampede as the breeze fanned the flames, blowing them fast and furiously towards the house.

He started shouting orders to the servants, but they had either fled at the first scent of fire or stood in numbed fear.

'Get buckets of water, you fools,' he roared at them. 'Soak the boundaries of the garden before it reaches the house. *Move*, damn your eyes!'

'It's no use, Darby,' the officers were shouting just as wildly. 'The whole place will be an inferno in no time. An army of buckets would never hold this lot back. We'll have to abandon the area. The only thing to do is get the women to the carriages and away from here. The fire will have to burn itself out. Thank God it will meet the river before it does any more damage.'

James was almost beside himself with rage as the company surged towards the back of the house like a brilliant tidal wave. The women were sobbing with terror, and there was a great trampling and whinnying from the courtyard where the carriages waited as the horses sensed the danger.

'Won't any of you stay and help me?' he almost screamed out.

'Father, can't you see it's no use?' Roslyn's teeth chattered with fear as she pulled at his arm. 'They're right, and we must go too. We'll all be killed, if not by the fire, then by those men out there—'

The bloodcurdling yells convinced her the drums tonight had been for one purpose only. She had heard enough tales in her life of the natives drumming up a frenzy to get revenge on someone they hated. She should have realized it sooner. Tonight it was her father they wanted, and if they didn't get away from here, native honour wouldn't be satisfied until James Darby was dead. She felt rising fear as she grabbed at his arms. He was standing as rigid as a statue.

'They won't drive me out, by God,' he roared. 'I'll get the buckets myself—'

'For heaven's sake, man, don't be a fool.' One of the few Ceylonese officials still remaining caught his arm. 'Your daughter is right. Get away while there's still time.'

Facing the house, the once-lush plantation was already a sheet of fire, the outer fence of the garden seemed to shrivel and blister as soon as it was touched by the relentless flames.

The Ceylonese gave a smothered oath and turned to Roslyn. 'Come. And be quick.' He had to shout above the noise.

'No.' Roslyn screamed. 'I won't leave my father. Where are the servants?'

'My dear,' he was shaking her now, 'everyone has fled.'

'Then go and join them, you old fool,' James bawled at him in red-eyed fury. He threw off the restraining hands and stormed through the house to the kitchens, yelling the servants' names at the top of his voice as he shouted for buckets. No one answered. He reappeared with containers in his hands and rushed out to the fountains, scooping up water and flinging it towards the flames. It was completely futile.

It seemed impossible that all this had happened in so short a time. Roslyn's mind was stunned and bewildered with shock. The stench of burning was in her nose and her mouth, and it stung her eyes so badly they watered constantly. She was choking with the smoke, but she couldn't let her father do all this alone. She couldn't let him die alone. Even though it was useless and she knew it...she rushed out to the garden to take up one of the buckets and do as he was doing. It was like tossing a pebble in the ocean for all the difference it made.

There were dark shapes silhouetted against the orange flames: Grotesquely leering faces that wished the Darby-wallah dead. And her father was answering them back, screaming abuse as was his habit; even though he knew he was no longer king, and the Darby tea estate that had flourished for so long was in ruins.

'Get out of here, Roslyn,' he suddenly turned and roared at her. His face was blackened by smoke, and only the whites of his eyes glared frighteningly. 'Find Nadja. Where is the stupid woman? Find her! Tell her to carry out my wishes. I'll be obeyed, by God!'

Still thundering out his orders, James caught the gleam of the devil's kiss on his daughter's throat, and a sudden calm swept over him for a brief moment. She would be safe. She had the protection of the ruby's power, but he had done for himself. Though not by giving it away! He wouldn't give in to the belief of these heathen devils at this late hour. It was because he had dared to show them who was boss-man. His contempt overpowered his fear, and he felt a flood of relief as he saw Nadja's squat figure hovering in the open windows. Where the devil had she been? The old duck was in the habit of taking sleeping draughts these days, so perhaps that explained her absence until now. Certainly, she looked dazed enough.

'Take her, Nadja,' he hollered. 'Remember my instructions.'

Through the orange mist in front of James'

eyes, he saw that the old nurse held his leather bag tightly in one hand and a dark shawl in the other for Roslyn. She hadn't failed him, thank God. She was the only one who hadn't. He was beginning to feel light-headed, and he could hear Roslyn sobbing. Nadja was tugging at her arm...

'Go *on*! I'll catch up with you. Head for the river'

Roslyn hesitated and then gave in to Nadja's urgings. She was gasping for breath now, and couldn't understand how her father was still standing upright by the fountains, framed by the raging fire that seemed to be crumpling everything in its path. Most of the natives who had started it had fled, but there were still a few shouts to be heard, and then she saw to her horror that the upper storey of the house was alight. Flames surged out of the bedroom windows and she gave a strangled cry as footsteps could be heard running down the stairs with whoops of crazed excitement.

'Come quick, little Missy,' Nadja croaked. 'Your father will follow. Come *quick!*'

Roslyn realized those inside the house had started looting. She gave one last despairing glance towards her father, and then allowed herself to be dragged around the side of the house hidden within the shadow of the verandah from those inside, and to flee with Nadja into the darkness. Her heart was thudding with terror, the breath tight in her chest as Nadja flung the dark shawl round her shoulders. It kept out the worst of the blistering heat, and disguised the once-shimmering cream silk of her lovely gown, now dusty and torn.

Had they stayed a moment longer, they would have seen the rioters come charging out of the house with Roslyn's trinkets and jewels in their hands, excited beyond measure at the night's work; and the sight of James Darby, like a demon possessed with the flames licking all around him. For a moment they paused, hearing the running footsteps leaving the house, undecided which quarry to follow first. James made up their minds for them by roaring insults.

They swarmed over the verandah towards him. It was a black onslaught from which he knew there was no escaping. But they would not have him. When they were almost on him he twisted round and ran headlong into the greedy enveloping flames...

Once the officers at Roslyn's birthday ball had got their ladies to safety, they alerted every able-bodied Britisher they could muster, and rode back to see what help they could give at the Darby estate. But it was too late. The house was burning furiously by the time they arrived, and charred native bodies lay strewn about the courtyard and gardens. Of James and his daughter there was no sign whatsoever. They could only assume and hope that both of them had got away. James had had his faults, but he was still one of them, and as for the lovely Roslyn...more than one officer hoped it would be *his* sanctuary she sought...

Roslyn and Nadja lay motionless in the long waving grass alongside the river for a long time. Too exhausted to move, and terrified that if they made a sound the rioters would come swooping down on them. Roslyn was still stunned with shock. This wonderful evening that had begun so gloriously had turned into a nightmare from which there seemed no escaping. She and Nadja clung to each other in the darkness as raucous animal noises screeched or howled from the tangle of trees. There was always the additional horror that the furry scuttle of a tarantula would touch their skin, or a thread-like leech fasten itself to them for a tasty meal. Nocturnal birds flapped angrily at these humans disturbing them, and fireflies and glow-worms made it appear that a thousand brilliant eyes watched their stumbling progress.

'Do you think my father got away?' Roslyn finally stammered through dry parched lips.

She stretched her painful limbs. The pounding of her heart had lessened a little, but there was still a sickness inside her that would not leave her. Something terrible had happened to James. She was convinced of it. If she closed her eyes her mind was instantly filled with the sight of the burning plantation, and the acrid stench of smoke was in her nostrils. Her teeth would not stop chattering, no matter how hard she clenched them.

'I think we must not hope too much, little Missy,' Nadja said carefully. 'I fear too that once it becomes daylight we shall be easily seen, and if the rebels have not had their fill of...' she nearly said blood, but quickly changed her mind, '...revenge, they may come looking for you. They will know by now, of the ruby pendant from the servants' ready tongues, and it will be compensation for them if Sahib-Darby escaped their clutches.'

'What shall we do?' For once Roslyn felt incapable of thinking for herself. She had been so used to giving orders and having them obeyed, yet now all she wanted was for someone to lead her by the hand, away from the terrors that surrounded her. And she trusted Nadja, as she had always done. Her eyes were huge and dilated as she looked into the smudged face of her old nurse in the rustling, whispering darkness.

'I have a cousin who will shelter us until we find out what has become of your father, little Missy,' Nadja told her. 'It is a poor home, but we will be safe there.'

Nadja was right. They must reach the cousin's house before daylight. She would be too easily spotted in the ballgown, and even the thought of those half-crazed creatures swarming towards her made her shudder violently.

'How much farther, Nadja?' she said falteringly.

'Some distance towards the sea,' Nadja nodded vaguely towards the west. 'I cannot tell in miles, little Missy, but we should start now. First, we must cross the river. Fortunately it is shallow at this point, but we had better keep hold of each other's hand all the way across.'

She wound James Darby's leather bag higher around her neck so that it should not sink beneath the water. They stepped cautiously down the bank and into the cool water. It might have been refreshing had they not both been conscious of the possible presence of crocodiles and lizards, and Roslyn felt as if she had been holding her breath for an eternity before they reached the other side safely. Her fingernails had dug little half-moons into Nadja's weathered palm, but the old nurse was silently uncomplaining.

Roslyn stumbled through the shoulder-high grasses on the other side of the river, her ballgown sodden, filthy and clinging to her skin, and snatched by clawing fingers of spiny bracken. The nightmare went on, until she began to wonder if this cousin's house really existed at all, or was Nadja unwittingly leading them round in circles?

'How much farther?' she sobbed the words out of a dry throat. Surely she could smell an acrid burning again? The terror gripped her as she swivelled her head round. Behind them the river gleamed darkly in the pre-dawn hours. A red glow lit the sky a long distance back. Roslyn jerked her head away from the sight of it, knowing it was all that was left of her home. But the scent was stifling her...she swayed with horror remembering those leering black faces...

'There, little Missy! The home of my cousin Bahu. He will shelter us.'

Roslyn blinked the stinging tears from her eyes. One among a small group of scattered hovels on the edge of a village, the building

81

was made of bamboo with a crude thatch of palm for a roof. The smell was coming through the slits between the bamboo stems that served as windows, and behind it was the glimmer of a light.

'Bahu wakes early. He works with the boys in the village gathering fruits for the market in Colombo.'

Roslyn felt her nostrils pinch together as Nadja called out her cousin's name softly. He answered immediately. Roslyn could barely see him in the gloom of the interior, lit by a stump of a smoking candle in one corner. Nadja spoke to him in quick native dialect, and the man ushered them in at once.

'He speaks no English,' Nadja told her quietly. 'But he is honoured for you to rest in his house, little Missy. You will be quite safe here. Bahu bids you welcome.'

Roslyn ached with the tension inside her and the effort of trying not to breathe too deeply. As her eyes became used to the gloom she saw there were crude bits of furniture in the room, and a bed of sorts along one side. There was matting made from coconut fibres on the floor and strips of it hung from the roof to make rough room dividers.

'What's that awful smell?' she whispered to Nadja. The cousin was motioning her to sit, and she perched on the edge of the bed, disregarding the fact that her sodden gown would soak through the thin covering. She was used to others attending to such details as cleaning and laundering and mending her clothes.

'It is the dung-fire,' Nadja said quietly. 'Bahu does his cooking over it back there.' She nodded to where the man had disappeared through a strip of coconut matting. 'He was preparing his breakfast, and he offers us some, little Missy. It will give you strength.'

It would probably kill her, Roslyn thought wildly. Seconds later Bahu came back with two wooden dishes for his guests, in which was hot rice and pieces of some kind of blackened bread. Nadja accepted gratefully and began to eat at once. Normally she would have waited for her mistress to begin first, but perhaps she sensed Roslyn's dismay. Roslyn was ravenously hungry. To her delicate digestion, used to the best that James Darby could provide, the food was brackish and almost inedible, but she forced down as much as she could. The cousin ate his own breakfast with noisy enjoyment, washing the lot down with a bitter drink which Roslyun and Nadja both refused politely. Instead, they asked for water, which Bahu brought in a leather container and poured into crudely-fashioned cups. Roslyn realized that it probably had to be brought from the communal well in the village, and shivered, thinking she would never take anything for granted again.

It was suddenly daylight, the sunlight streaming through the slits of bamboo like golden slivers across the humble interior of the hovel. Roslyn saw Bahu properly for the first time. He was a short, powerfully-built man, not much younger than her father, Roslyn guessed. She wondered, fearfully, if Bahu too had been one of those who hated James Darby. But evidently not, because after a few minutes of their conversation, in an incomprehensible dialect, Nadja turned to her.

'We will rest here this morning, little Missy. Bahu will find out what he can about your father and if he is safe.' Roslyn lifted the damp weight of her tawny hair from her shoulders as the tears stung her eyes again. Already the humid heat of the day seared through the bamboo hovel, and the stench of the dung-fire was becoming putrid. The sounds of the Ceylonese village morning were raucous and noisy, both human and animal, and nothing like the protected world she had known. The cool green dales of Yorkshire called to her with the allure of an oasis in the desert, as did the sudden longing to be with her own kin. Her eyes blurred a little.

'My father is dead,' she said flatly. There was a dull acceptance in her voice. She did not need to be told it for a fact. She had seen it all as if in a mirage...

'Bahu will find out the truth, my sweet one,' Nadja said quickly, but she kept her eyes lowered. There was little doubt in her own mind, Sahib-Darby had almost surely perished but, until they knew for certain, it was her duty to give the little Missy hope. 'And we will try to sleep while he is gone.'

The man left them a little later, after showing them into the rear of the hovel, where another crude bed stood alongside one wall. Nadja indicated to Roslyn that she should lie down, while she curled up on a straw-filled cushion on the floor. It never occurred to Roslyn to argue, though she eyed the bed with distaste. She sank down on the bed, curling herself up into a tight ball and closing her eyes so hard they hurt. She had refused to remove her gown, and it still clung damply to her body. She thought she couldn't possibly sleep, but she was so utterly exhausted that she drifted into unconsciousness almost immediately.

When she awoke she could hear voices through the matting curtain. Nadja and Bahu were conversing in that strange dialect again. Away in the distance, the constant beat of drumming throbbed on the humid air. Were they beating out the triumphant news that the Darby-wallah was dead, Roslyn thought bitterly? She called Nadja's name and the old nurse appeared at once. Roslyn only had to look at her face to know.

'You don't need to tell me,' she said tiredly. 'My father is dead. I have known it in my heart.'

Nadja took her in her arms and rocked her silently. But Roslyn felt too stunned for tears. It was as if there was an ice-cold band around her emotions, despite the heat of her surroundings. And then she was aware that Nadja was talking to her urgently.

'We must get away from here, little Missy. Bahu has heard that there is talk of the ruby. Sahib-Darby chose to die in the flames rather than be killed by his attackers, and they are still seeking revenge for the wrongs they felt they suffered at his hands all the years. They may not harm you, but they will hunt you down for the ruby.'

Roslyn hardly heeded her words. Of course she would get away. Not to the mountains or the safety of some other British-owned plantation or the military, but to England. To the cool green dales of Yorkshire. The music of the words ran through her mind like a recurring melody in the midst of a nightmare. She had no idea of how she would get there. She had never had to think for herself in all her life. But now she gripped the old woman's hands, her eyes feverish in her face.

'We will go to England, Nadja. It is what my father wished, and I wish it too. We will go to my Yorkshire family, and I will see this Englishman on whom you think I wasted so many foolish dreams!' She hesitated suddenly, seeing the old troubled face in front of her. 'Nadja—you would not desert me now?'

'Of course not, little Missy. We go to England if that is your wish.' She managed not to betray the trembling the thought gave her. She had promised to follow her little Missy to the ends of the earth, and so be it. She prayed to be given strength to complete the journey. 'We will eat soon, and then Bahu will return to his work. There are things I must give you while we are alone. Once it is dark, I will go with Bahu to a reliable woman to obtain a more suitable dress for you, little Missy.'

Looking down at its tattered hem, no one would believe it was a ballgown, Roslyn thought. But Nadja was right, of course.

'Bahu will find out what he can about a ship

bound for England,' Nadja went on. She spoke as calmly as if it were a short ride in the Darby carriage around the plantation. It was best not to let her thoughts race ahead to the hazards that lay in front of them. Best just to continue serving the Sahib-Darby's daughter as she had always done and would do until she died.

The smell of the dung-fire was rising to Roslyn's nostrils again. She felt as if her body and her clothes would never be rid of it, but a little later Bahu called them to eat some brown tamarind berry soup, heavily spiced. Roslyn forced it down. It was as hot as fire with Bahu's own peculiar flavourings, and her eyes watered. She loosened the shawl from her shoulders and she saw Bahu's eyes take in the beauty of the ruby pendant as it rested against her breasts. He rattled off some words to Nadja.

'Bahu thinks it wiser if you remove the pendant, little Missy,' Nadja told her. 'I would trust him with my life, but there are others, even in the village, who would kill for it.'

A shiver ran through Roslyn. She agreed that later she would do as Nadja said. Now that the first searing shock was lessening, she was curious to know what things Nadja had to give her when they were alone. She had guarded the leather bag she carried so carefully since they had fled from the Darby plantation, and yet to Roslyn's knowledge Nadja's possessions were few and simple. They retired to the inner room of the house where they had slept, being a fraction cooler in the shadow of the waving coconut palms outside.

'I think I will leave you alone with your father's bag, little Missy,' her first words startled Roslyn. So it was her father's bag. She should have guessed. 'I will try to clean Bahu's house for him as a small payment for all he is doing, while you read your father's words.'

She went silently out of the inner room. Bahu had already returned to the fields, and Roslyn was alone. She ran her hand over the soft leather of the old bag, feeling a lump in her throat, and then she opened it to take out the various items inside. Her heart lurched sickeningly as she saw her father's will. She put it on one side. There were three other large envelopes, not old and yellowed, as was the packet containing the will. They had been recently written. It was as if her father had had some premonition of all this...

There was a letter addressed to herself. The other two had the names she had heard in the past on her father's lips. The cousin with whom he had fought so bitterly over the love of a woman—Thomas Radcliffe. The other had the scrawled name of the lady herself—Hester Radcliffe, who had once been James Darby's sweetheart. Roslyn ripped open the envelope addressed to herself.

'I intend giving you this letter on the morning after your birthday, my darling,' Roslyn read, 'because you are now the owner of the prince's ruby, and as such you must know of the legend behind it.'

There followed the same legendary tales the young prince had related to James all those years ago. As Roslyn read them she became aware that she was not so much seeing them as hearing them, spoken in the soft boyish yet dignified Indian tones in which they had been narrated to her father, and that the touch of the devil's kiss on her flesh was warm. Not prickling as if in warning, but welcoming, as if acknowledging that she was now its rightful owner and that it would serve her well. And raised as she had been, in the shelter of an English home in the midst of an ancient land where old superstitions were sacred, Roslyn knew better than to dismiss such feelings. And she realized at once what a sacrifice James had made in bestowing this gift on her. Had he not been such a hard master, his cruel end may not have happened. As it was…without the ruby's protection he had perished in flames as bright as the jewel's fire.

She blinked back the tears as she came to the end of the letter.

'Go to England, Roslyn, if only for a visit. I also wish the other letters you see here to be sent, but only after my death. Do this for me, darling...'

She would not send them. She would deliver them herself, Roslyn thought chokingly. Her decison had been the right one. She realized something else now too, that strange burning sensation she had felt when she had worn the ruby pendant at the ball...it had already begun to work its magic on her, had she but known it then. It was warning her; giving her premonitions of the danger to come; just as it had conjured up the images of her father's crazed walk into the flames...and once, the misty image of a Yorkshire farmhouse among the rolling moors and dales of England...Roslyn never doubted the magic of the devil's kiss for an instant.

Roslyn opened James' will and cried bitter tears over it. What James had to leave her, the Darby house and the entire tea plantation, was now a smouldering ruin. After her grief, a feeling of blind panic stole over her. She was completely alone but for Nadja, and had nothing but the tattered ballgown in which she stood, and the valuable Siamese ruby, which would be a target for theft of every robber and rogue on the island of Ceylon from now on.

Roslyn unfastened it with trembling fingers from around her neck. The gold chain slid into a little heap in her hand, from where the ruby winked dazzlingly up at her. Bahu was right—it would be better off her person, but where...

She felt inside the old leather bag, and as she had hoped, there was an inner pocket deep inside. She slipped the pendant inside her father's letter and pushed it down as far as it would go in the pocket. As she did so, she felt something else there and pulled out a wad of money and a tightly-bound bag of rupees. The notes were unfamiliar, until she realized they were English money. Hot tears filled Roslyn's eyes again, for at least she was not entirely destitute, even though she had no idea of the value of the currency. A message in her father's hand told her it was put there as a safeguard should the need for flight become urgent.

He might have premeditatedly planned the whole thing, Roslyn thought tremulously. Or maybe he too had had a mirage of the mind, so that he was not entirely unaware of his destiny...or hers.

CHAPTER 5

Bahu found out that there was a cargo boat leaving Colombo for England in two days' time. As with most of the cargo boats, a few paying passengers were acceptable as an extra bonus for the captain. Bahu promised to take Roslyn and Nadja to Colombo under cover of darkness the following night and told them the boat would leave Ceylon early the next morning. A few more rupees had assured Bahu of the loan of a bullock cart for the journey.

The bag of silver coins would not last forever, thought Roslyn, as she sat alone, waiting for Nadja and Bahu to return. But it did not matter, she was prepared to spend all she had. Once on board the boat, she would undoubtedly be able to pay for their passage in English money. The thought made her spirits soar a little, and helped to deaden the unspoken fear she felt at being so completely on her own. It was such a rare and nerve tingling feeling.

She sat on the edge of the bed, the shawl loosely draped round her shoulders. It was still unbearably hot, but fear made her cold. Fear ran down her back and between the hollow of her breasts in little rivulets of sweat. Those drums still vibrated through the night, somewhere in the dark, like an insistent reminder that they hadn't done with her yet. The sudden surge of rain thudding down on the thatched roof and the moan of the wind through the palm trees made her catch her breath. It blew in through the gaps in the bamboo stems of the walls and the candle went out with a little hiss. She had no idea how to relight it, and she remained where she was, tight with apprehension.

The rain was a sudden torrent that splattered in through the walls with a pleasant coolness, but Roslyn was in no mood to appreciate it, nor the value it would have on the parched earth or dust-dry crops. Why could it not have come one day sooner, so that the fire would not have got such a hold on the Darby tea bushes, and her father would not have perished?

Suddenly the drumming outside stopped. Except for the downpour of the monsoon rain, there was no other sound. Birds had stilled their squawking, and the animals that roamed the jungle and the river banks had sought shelter. There was a sudden gust of rain blowing in as the door was opened and then pushed shut.

'Bahu?' Roslyn said in a strangled gasp, 'Is that you? Nadja?'

It was neither. Roslyn felt despair washing over her as she heard the laboured breathing of another human being in the room. A voice spoke in a guttural male cadence in a dialect similar to Meera her serving-girl's. She could follow a little. The man seemed to apologize for disturbing Bahu and his woman, but the rain had forced him inside...

His assumption made Roslyn forget the fear she felt. 'I am not Bahu's woman,' she snapped.

She did not know whether the man understood English, but her old air of authority gave her a small feeling of dignity. She heard the man's breathing quicken with interest. He spoke in halting English.

'Not—Bahu's—woman.'

There was a sudden flare of light in the man's hand that was almost as quickly extinguished. In those few seconds they glimpsed each other, Roslyn saw a muscly man of indeterminate age, wearing rain-soaked Ceylonese garb, long brown legs gleaming with moisture. He saw an unexpected golden vision in front of him, with luscious breasts, a young and lovely face surrounded by dishevelled brown hair that gave her the look of a wanton; a bedraggled gown

95

that had once been beautiful. It all added up in the traveller's mind to a street whore, and as such was fair game for anyone. He was astute enough to guess that Bahu was not here...Now he realized the gods had been smiling on him through the storm-clouds. He knew very few English words, but the whore would understand...and Bahu was generous enough to share her...

'White woman,' he leered through the darkness. *'Bed!'*

Roslyn gasped, angry rather than frightened. How dare he suggest such a thing? No filthy native was going to lay his hands on her...the next second she felt his hands reaching for her breasts and heard the tearing of her bodice. He cupped them together, his breath becoming rasping in the unexpected delight of this encounter, and then she was flung down on to the uncomfortable bed and pinned there.

She opened her mouth to scream, but was forced to twist her head away from the man's fetid breath. She struggled furiously, and he realized she was not acting in the ways of a street whore. By then he was too lust-bent to stop, and the back of his hand dealt her a stinging blow across the cheek. It almost stunned her. She felt him fumbling at her skirts, felt them being pushed roughly aside, and the tip of something hot and hard being thrust against her unyielding flesh. It pierced her with an agonizing pain, and then the coupling was feverish. He was excited by her virginity and the need to get away from here as soon as possible, in case Bahu had been saving her up for himself. He finished and hauled himself off her, leaving her just where she was. And Roslyn heard him lunge out into the night.

She lay without moving. The tears ran down her cheeks and into her neck. Her breasts were sore from the man's rough treatment. Her thighs were bruised where he had wrenched them apart, while the tenderness between throbbed and ached as if he had pierced her very soul. She had heard about such men who used women. Nadja had warned her of them.

That wasn't love, Roslyn's mind screamed out. It was hateful, hateful...and the most precious gift that had been destined to be given to her husband had been cruelly lusted away from her in this place she had thought of as safe. She tried to think rationally and calmly, but the shame of what had happened overwhelmed her. It hadn't been her fault, and yet she felt utterly defiled.

She could not bear to tell Nadja. Nor Bahu. It was too shaming. She sensed that the man would not come back in case she did confess, and it would remain her painful secret.

The ruby! Where was its protection when she needed it? Roslyn thought angrily. Where its warning...? She felt beneath the bed to where the leather bag had been hidden, and gave a sigh of relief to find it there. Maybe the devil's kiss *had* protected her. The man could have killed her. And there had been a kind of premonition that all was not well. She felt completely exhausted, and the events of the last two days suddenly became too much for her dazed mind to accept. She dragged the thin bedcover over her torn gown and her bruised body, ignoring the bloodstains on them both, and fell into a state of unconsiousness.

'She sleeps peacefully, poor child,' Nadja said softly to Bahu when they returned later. The rain had forced them to remain in the next village until it stopped as suddenly as it started, in the way of monsoon downpours. They had borrowed the bullock cart one day early to bring them back through the quagmire that would be steaming with humid heat with the coming of dawn, and parched again within a few hours of blistering heat.

Nadja put the parcel of everyday clothes in the inner room and went to share a meal with her cousin. She would not attempt to waken Roslyn. There were traces of tears of the little Missy's flushed cheeks, Nadja noted, assuming she had been crying in private for her father. Nadja understood the need for privacy and would ask no questions.

It was brilliant daylight when Roslyn awoke. Instant recollection rushed back to her, and her eyes remained tightly closed as the sick shame filled her mind. When she moved her legs she felt soreness where the man had scythed into her. Her breasts were tender. There was temptation to burst into a fit of weeping and call Nadja to rock her as she had done so often when Roslyn was a little girl.

But she was no longer a child. And there was too much of James Darby's character in her to give in to helpless weeping. James always told her it was wasted effort to cry over things that couldn't be changed. And nothing could ever change the fact that she was no longer a virgin. Roslyn flinched as the words spun into her mind, but they were the truth and she had to accept them.

'You look more like your old self this morning, little Missy,' Nadja's voice jolted her from her thoughts. She managed a small smile. If Nadja only knew what had happened.

'I'm well enough,' Roslyn murmured. 'Is

there some water for me to wash, Nadja? And did you find a dress?'

It was more important than the old nurse realized, and when she had brought a small bowl and rough towel, and the brown cambric high-necked dress that was approximately Roslyn's size, Roslyn waved her away.

'I will manage for myself, Nadja,' she said. 'Could you find us some breakfast?'

It would be rice again, she thought with a grimace. It was the monotonous diet of the villagers, rice and curry. But she was glad when Nadja did as she said. Roslyn bundled the stained and torn gown into the paper that had contained the more modest day-dress, and after washing herself she slid the brown dress over her head and began to feel more human again.

The neckline was high and so Roslyn decided to wear the ruby pendant beneath it, thinking it would be safer on her person than in the leather bag, however deeply hidden. She preferred to feel the weight and coldness of the stone against her skin...

It seemed an endless day with nothing to do but stay inside the safety of the little house with its dung-fire and curry smells clinging to everything. The longing for sweet, clean, fresh air became almost unbearable, but there was none outside either. The day steamed relentlessly until midday after the rain, and then it buzzed with flies and mosquitoes and the drying vegetation. But at last it was evening and once it was dark Bahu helped the two women into the bullock cart and it clattered away from the village towards Colombo.

It took several hours to reach the city. There were rocky peaks that threw strange shadows in the moonlit darkness; vast swamps of rice-paddies and waving King coconut trees alternated with each other, and occasionally a ghostly dome of a *dagoba* loomed up whitely in the distance. Nadja was very quiet on the journey to the coast and for the first time Roslyn thought of the enormity of what she was expecting Nadja to do. For Roslyn, going to England was an adventure, at the end of which she would find a home and kinsmen. Whereas Nadja was leaving the land that had been home to her for many years, not with any feeling of discovery, but as a servant. And she was old, and frail...Roslyn suddenly felt uneasy. Perhaps she was asking too much of Nadja. In the darkness of the bullock cart, she sought for Nadja's hand and held it tightly, as she had done so often when she was a child looking for comfort. This time she was the one hoping to transmit some of the confidence she was far from feeling herself right now.

'Will it be too much for you, Nadja?' Roslyn murmured. 'Am I being cruel in asking you to accompany me? You must tell me—'

The old hand curled round hers.

'My home is wherever you are, little Missy,' Nadja said simply. 'It was your father's wish as well as mine that I go with you, no matter how far.'

'But *so* far,' Roslyn was still uneasy. 'Father told me it would take many days to reach England by boat.'

'Are you trying to tell me you do not want me to go with you, little Missy?' the sharp dismay in Nadja's voice halted Roslyn's words. 'Without you what would I do?'

Roslyn threw her arms round the nurse with her old impulsiveness. 'And what would I do without you, Nadja?' she said fervently.

It was true. Nadja had taken the place of mother, sister and counsellor so often over the years.

Roslyn's eyes drooped as the rhythmic motion of the plodding bullocks lulled her into a light sleep. She dreamed of the welcome she would receive from her Yorkshire relatives. She knew Aunt Hester would love her because she was James' daughter. Thomas Radcliffe must surely have regretted the violent quarrel that had separated himself and his cousin so many years ago. He would be glad to know how James had prospered...Roslyn stirred restlessly, refusing to consider that she might be unwelcome...

She dreamed instead of the two young men, Greg and Francis. The younger one, Francis, had rarely come into her thoughts, though she had seen as many sketches of him as of his brother. It was always Greg, Greg who had occupied her waking and sleeping dreams as he did now. She had never thought to see him in her lifetime, and now she was on her way for the greatest journey of her eighteen years, and she was impatient to know him at last.

The night-time hours were pleasantly cool as they journeyed west, and there was the tang of salt in the air as Bahu finally brought the bullock cart to a halt. Roslyn had slept more soundly than she had expected. She had lost so much...but she still had her life and her youth and her beauty. Remembering James' own zest for life, she knew she still had much to be thankful for.

There was a great bustle of activity as they neared the wide harbour at Colombo. Tall masts jostled and creaked as the boats were made ready to put to sea. Along the coastline stood warehouses and office buildings, and near the harbour the great silvery dome of a church.

Bahu pointed to a boat ahead and spoke rapidly to Nadja.

'That is the cargo boat, little Missy,' she told Roslyn. 'Bahu will go to speak with the captain on our behalf. He begs us to wait here.'

Wild horses would not have dragged Roslyn on to the boat until she was sure that they had been accepted as passengers. The port buzzed with the noise of native labourers and seamen, and she was suddenly nervous. She and Nadja would probably be the only two women on board the cargo boat. It did not look very large, but it would no doubt have a crew of hardened men. She shivered.

It seemed an age before Bahu came back. The ladies were to go aboard and meet the captain.

They walked carefully up the gangplank, feeling it rock beneath them. The harbour was protected from the surf beyond by long fingers of stone stretching out to sea, but the unfamiliar motion of a boat was still enough to make their stomachs turn. Roslyn had rarely seen the sea, and had never set foot on a boat before. It was still dark, so they were unaware of their immediate surroundings, or of the vast emptiness of the expanse of ocean they would cross.

Roslyn noted with relief that, visible in the glimmer of light from the dockside, the cargo boat flew a British flag. Then the captain would be British too. He might even talk with the flat clipped accents of Yorkshire, like her father.

Bahu led the two women down a short flight of steps to a small cabin. He told Nadja this was as far as he could take them, and that Captain Webber was expecting them. He kissed Nadja with emotion, and it was obvious he never expected to see her again. He bowed gravely to Roslyn, but she grasped him warmly by the hand. She knew very well that without Bahu's help they might easily have perished. When he returned to his bamboo house, he would find the remainder of her father's rupees waiting for him.

Roslyn tapped nervously at the cabin door and heard a strong voice bid her to enter. Nadja followed one step behind, and stood silently as the rugged-faced captain rose at their appearance and motioned Roslyn to be seated.

Captain Peter Webber hid his surprise as he looked at the two women in front of him. It had been difficult to comprehend the native's words, but he understood it to be an English lady who wished for passage, and her old servant. These two were not quite what he had expected. He could see that the young one had an air of class about her, despite the cheap dress she wore. She was beautiful, in spite of the haunting sadness in her lovely dark blue eyes, and the tension in every fibre of her body. The old one...Captain Webber wondered briefly if she would even stand the journey.

'So you want passage to England, Miss...?' he said abruptly. He was too canny to let sentiment stand in the way of business. That the young woman was eager to leave Ceylon was clear to him, but the first essential was to be sure she had the passage money as the native fellow had intimated.

'Miss Radcliffe,' Roslyn said quickly. She had decided to use the family name. Darby was too well-known. Even this cargo boat might be carrying chests of Darby tea to London...She read the Captain's questioning look correctly.

'I have money to pay for our passage, Captain,' she said with dignity. She drew out some of the white banknotes from the pocket of the brown dress.

Captain Webber nodded as he took the money. Instinct told him the girl had no idea of its worth. He felt a sudden protectiveness towards her. He had a daughter about her age back home in Lambeth, whose future was assured in the service of some titled gentry. Menial though the job might be, his Beth had none of the anxiety of this young lady. And if it had been his Beth who was desperate to leave the country for some reason, he'd have been glad to know it was on a boat such as this one, with a fatherly captain and a trustworthy crew. He let his weathered face crease into a smile as he put the notes in a tin box.

'The money will be more than sufficient, Miss Radcliffe,' he told her gravely. 'And if you will allow me to take care of it until we reach Tilbury, I will give you any remaining from your victuals and cabin quarters when we dock. You'll be needing no money while you're on board.'

Roslyn gave her assent. The relief of being almost on her way was overwhelming, as was the sudden kindliness in the captain's face. She was aware of the pendant's touch against her skin as she turned to smile at Nadja. The devil's kiss...but there was no sensation of burning, only a gentle spreading warmth, as if to assure her that she had reached safety at last. There was nothing to fear here. As if to underline her thoughts, Captain Webber spoke again.

'As you know, this is primarily a cargo boat, Miss Radcliffe. We carry tea and coconuts and some spices namely cinnamon, pepper and nutmeg. No doubt you'll be familiar with the aromatic smells if you've lived on Ceylon for a while.'

'Oh yes, I'm quite familiar with them all,' Roslyn's breath caught a little in her throat. The unmistakable scents, especially of the fragrant tea, had made her head swim with poignant longing for her father, but she looked steadily at the captain.

'We don't normally carry passengers,' he went on, 'and have a small but valued crew. We have no trouble on board the *Sea Maid*, so you have no need to be afraid, although you are the only two ladies here, and indeed the only two passengers this trip. You will be treated politely, and meals will be served in your cabin. Apart from that, you are free to use any part of the ship that you wish, as long as you keep below should the weather blow up rough. For safety's sake, you understand.'

It was as if he knew exactly the right words to say to put aside the gnawing fears that had sometimes beset her, Roslyn thought tremulously.

'Thank you, Captain Webber,' she spoke a little huskily, not wanting to burst into tears in front of a stranger.

The captain spoke into a speaking tube, summoning someone called Vickery. 'Vickery will show you to your cabin, Miss Radcliffe. You'll find it a bit cramped, but it's the best we can offer. I hope you will not be too uncomfortable.'

The longer he spoke with her, the more sure he was that Miss Radcliffe was used to finer things, despite her unprepossessing appearance. If for no other reason than the way the old Indian woman stood so patiently behind her in the way of long-serving maids. And the fact that the young woman saw nothing unusual in it. There was a tale to tell here, Captain Webber thought sagely, but it was none of his business as long as the fares were paid...

A seaman tapped at the cabin door. He was of the same stance and countenance as the captain, and cast a filial eye over the taut young woman obviously desperate to reach England. Unconsciously, Vickery echoed the captain's own thoughts as he ushered the two women along dark passages to the tiny cabin they would share for the long sea journey ahead. They could be glad they had picked on the *Sea Maid* and not a ship with a lust-minded crew, threatening terrors closer at hand than the sharks and swordfish or the hazardous coral reefs beyond the coastline ahead. Vickery left them, saying he would bring them food at seven o'clock the following morning, by which time they would have set sail from Colombo and be heading westwards to the Arabian Sea.

Roslyn was so exhausted she could hardly find strength to nod her head to thank him. All she wanted was to sleep...she looked around at the cabin. It was dark and gloomy, lit only by a glimmer of light from an enclosed lantern fixed firmly to the wall. It was hardly bigger than the size of the clothes closet in her room at the Darby mansion. She looked dumbly at Nadja, whose arms opened wide and folded her to her thin chest.

'Come, my sweet one,' Nadja whispered. 'We have each other, and we are alive. We must be thankful. You have been so brave. Don't let your spirit desert you now.'

'Oh Nadja, how can I bear it...?' she wept.

'You will bear it, little Missy, Sahib-Darby wished you to go to England, and you have not failed him. I think we had both better try to sleep now, and try to forget the last few days for a while.'

She would never forget, Roslyn thought passionately. Never as long as she lived. And she was beginning to realize that the secret she had vowed never to tell was praying more and more heavily on her mind. Her savage rape had been pushed to the back of her mind in the urgency of her flight, but now the flight was over and there would be endless time to shudder and weep over the vile thing that had been done to her. Let Nadja think all her tears were for her beloved father...

She felt Nadja's body heavy against her, and then the old woman's rigid self-control returned as she still held Roslyn in her arms. Roslyn realized how appallingly weary Nadja must be, and swallowed back her own tears as she looked around at the two narrow bunks, one on top of the other. It was obvious she could not expect Nadja to climb into the top one, so that must be hers. They had no nightwear. Nothing at all except the clothes in which they stood. But Roslyn's heart warmed as she remembered the captain's kindness. She took the leather bag from around Nadja's neck and gently told her to have the bottom bunk, while she climbed awkwardly into the upper one. The motion of the ship made her momentarily dizzy, but she closed her eyes tightly and forced down the surge of nausea.

CHAPTER 6

Though the *Sea Maid* had steam propulsion, she still clung to the added security of sails, billowing to catch the smallest breeze on the burning air. The days at sea were dazzlingly blue, followed by blood-red sunsets. Daylight hours were filled with entertainment by shoals of fish in the clear turquoise waters of the Arabian Sea; golden-scaled pirau and gleaming swordfish, and the ever-present triangular sharks' fins. Farther out, they would glimpse the shooting spray of basking whales in spectacular displays.

Nadja chose to stay in the cabin for much of the journey, groaning and tossing in an uneasy sleep.

One morning Roslyn knocked on Captain Webber's door. She had rehearsed her words carefully.

Captain Webber motioned her to sit down, marvelling as always at the golden beauty of the comely young woman that showed even through the crumpled clothes she wore. Nothing could detract from the fine tilt to her head and that glorious dark hair.

'You'll have guessed that my nurse and I left Ceylon in haste, Captain,' Roslyn began. Her chin was high, inviting no questions, and the captain merely nodded. 'I have no idea as to our route, and am only vaguely acquainted with the geography of the world away from Ceylon. If we are to call at any ports on the way might I be able to purchase some nightwear and perhaps a change of clothes for my nurse and myself? And I wonder if it were possible to arrange for a letter to be posted to England?'

Her voice shook a little as she finished speaking. The idea of contacting her Yorkshire relatives before her arrival had been worrying her for some time. It would be a great shock for them to see her when they knew nothing of her existence. She had not wanted to post the letters her father had written, but to deliver them as he had wished. Neither had she cared to write to her father's cousin Thomas, since the two men had parted under such bad circumstances. It would be upsetting for her to write to Aunt Hester with such tragic news...so that left Greg. It always came back to Greg...

Captain Webber was opening a drawer in his desk and spreading a map out in front of her. He was glad the young woman was taking an interest in her whereabouts and in her appearance, and that the haunted look in her beautiful eyes was beginning to fade. He stabbed his forefinger at the pear shape of Ceylon, and drew an imaginary line westwards across a vast blue area on the map.

'We'll be putting in at Aden to pick up some supplies. I can arrange for Vickery to escort you to a suitable establishment for the things you require, though I doubt if it will be very fashionable. There is a posting-house there as well. With luck, a letter will reach England before we do.'

'It does not matter about fashion,' Roslyn murmured. She had never expected to hear herself saying those words. 'And where do we go after we leave Aden, Captain?'

Captain Webber traced their route. Through the Red Sea and the Suez Canal and so into the Mediterranean. And finally to the English Channel and the Thames at Tilbury where the *Sea Maid's* cargo was to be unloaded. His matter-of-fact summary made Roslyn catch her breath. The vast distance and the realization of a different culture were just beginning to make sense to her. She was British...but to these Yorkshire relatives she was going to appear completely foreign...

'All those oceans!' she said tremulously.

'Thank the stars we can go via Suez now, and

not the long way right around the Cape of Africa, my dear!' He saw her sudden nervousness. 'You write your letter and we'll see it's safely posted. To your family, I take it.'

'Yes. My family. My...my brother,' she invented jerkily, since anyone seeing Greg's name on the envelope would notice it was the same as the name she had assumed. 'I want to ask him to meet me once we arrive in London. When is that likely to be, Captain? And is there a suitable inn where I may wait for my—my brother?'

Captain Webber smiled reassuringly. He had taken a liking to his young passenger. Something had crushed her spirit recently, but there was great strength and determination there, and tenderness and passion too, as he'd seen from her caring attention to the old nurse. He admired those qualities in a woman. He couldn't say exactly when they would dock at Tilbury. So much depended on wind and current, but it would be approximately six weeks from the day they had left Colombo.

'As for a place to stay, I suggest the Black Boar as a suitable inn, Miss Radcliffe. It's clean and respectable, and I'm acquainted with the landlord. I'll see that you and your companion are delivered there safely when we dock.'

Roslyn's eyes threatened to fill with tears at his rough, kind voice. As she stammered out her thanks he rummaged in his desk for writing materials for her.

Some time later Roslyn sat on deck beneath the rough canopy the crew had rigged up for her comfort as protection from the boiling sun. Even so, her golden skin was deepening still more in its rays, and the tawny highlights in her lustrous dark hair were picked out like stranded gold. The sleeves of her brown dress were pushed up over her elbows to reveal her slender arms, the top buttons discreetly unbuttoned at the throat. In the hollow between her breasts the ruby pendant nestled as always, hidden from sight, but comfortingly there. She had had no reaction from it ever since stepping on board the *Sea Maid*, and she trusted its protection implicitly.

On that first night on the cargo boat when she and Nadja had been so exhausted, she had been too tense to sleep properly, and had woken in a fever of terror almost every hour at the memory of all that had happened. She had clung to Nadja as if she was still a child, lulled by the ever-soothing, sing-song voice.

'Don't be afraid, little Missy. The ruby will protect you, never doubt. All the gems of fire have magical powers, but this one is even more wonderful. A prince's ruby will take you to your heart's desire...'

'Supposing it is stolen? What then, Nadja?' Fears she was unable to suppress tumbled in and out of her mind. Perhaps even now she would not reach Greg after they had come through so much...Nadja's creased lips were cool on her fevered brow.

'A talisman that is a gift bestows only love and protection on the owner, little Missy. But a talisman that is stolen brings only disaster. It is the way it is written.'

Roslyn was trying desperately to think of the words to write to Greg Radcliffe. There were already two abortive attempts crumpled at her side. With a sigh of frustration she picked them up and re-read them, trying to salvage some way of stating the facts in the tone she wanted, neither too emotionally as in the first letter, nor too coldly as in the second...

Roslyn stared out across the endless turquoise ocean to where it merged into the blue of the sky. Her eyes hurt with the dazzle of sunlight, glinting like silvery knives where the bows of the boat forged a steady passage through the water, its engines throbbing dully and rhythmically below. Nadja was asleep in the cabin, and Roslyn closed her eyes for a while, putting off the letter-writing until she could find the right words.

But her brain would not stop mulling it over, and she shifted restlessly in the sticky heat. There was barely a breath of air to move the sails, which were of no use in this area except to afford the crew a little shade. The sun was directly overhead, and Roslyn knew she would be better off down below out of the heat. Her delicate skin prickled...with a start she realized the prickling was concentrated in the patch of flesh beneath the devil's kiss.'

Her eyes flew open. As if she had been transported into space, she became aware that the scene in front of her was no longer a vast blue ocean. Her whole vision seemed to be clouded as if a swirling mist spiralled around her. She was suddenly cold where seconds before she had been so hot, and only the patch of flesh beneath the pendant burned deeply in her chest. James' words came sharply to her mind.

'...the ruby can cast a mirage into the mind...a vision of time past or time still to come...'

The swirling mists surrounding Roslyn appeared to part a little, so that they still remained on the edge of her vision, but the central image was fractionally clearer, as if she looked through a smoke-haze at the scene presented to her. Everything was grey in colour; the large sprawling farmhouse and the undulating hills in which it lay. The curl of smoke from the farmhouse chimney was grey, as were the ghostly faces that now swam alarmingly in front of Roslyn's eyes. Faces that had no real shape or features, but were grotesque in their floating imagery, with no bodies attached beneath them to give them form.

She did not recognize any of them, nor did she want to. The entire greyness of the mirage, if that was what it was, was so alien to the brilliance and colour of her former surroundings in Ceylon, it stunned rather than frightened her. And then a voice spoke alongside her. The mirage vanished as quickly as it had appeared.

Everything was as it had been before. The *Sea Maid* forged smoothly westwards through the Arabian Sea, while distant whales spouted white spume into the air. The sun dazzled overhead, and Vickery stood at her side with a cool drink in his hand for her, a troubled look in his eyes.

'Are you ill, Miss Radcliffe?' He noted the strange pallor in her sun-kissed cheeks and the touch of dampness on her brow. 'This heat is not good for young ladies—'

'I'm perfectly all right, Vickery, thank you,' Roslyn said quickly. She took the drink with a grateful smile and felt its coolness trickle down her dry throat. 'I'm really quite used to the heat, but when I have finished my letter I'll go down below for a while.'

The man nodded. He had unconsciously assumed the role of protector. Roslyn shivered, wondering if she would ever be in need of real protection. The first vision the devil's kiss had conjured up had disturbed her profoundly, though she could not imagine the Yorkshire countryside being anything like the horrendous greyness she had glimpsed. If indeed, that was what it was...James had always spoken of England as being green and gentle and fertile, and he spoke with the nostalgia of a remembered and much-loved homeland. Roslyn pushed the sudden unease out of her mind, retrieved her writing materials, and concentrated on the letter to Greg once more. And at last it was done.

'Dear Mr Radcliffe,' she read back,

'My name is Roslyn Darby, and I am the daughter of your father's cousin, James Darby. My father has recently died in Ceylon, and he wished that I should contact his only relatives in England, namely your family. I trust my visit will not be an inconvenience to you, but I bring letters from my father to your parents.

I expect to arrive in England during the first week of October. I am sorry I cannot be more precise, but I will stay at the Black Boar Inn at Tilbury until I hear from you. If it is possible for you to meet me and my elderly nurse there, I would be very grateful, as it will be my first time in England and I'm sure will be very strange to me. I look forward very much to meeting you and my English relatives, and hope my letter is not too much of a shock to you. One last thing—I will be known at the Black Boar as Miss Radcliffe, your sister. I will explain my reasons when we meet, and beg you to forgive the small deception.
With warm good wishes,
Roslyn Darby.'

She frowned, trying to view the letter through Greg Radcliffe's eyes. Would he be angry or amused or merely curious? She had no way of telling. She was undecided about her last phrase—should she send 'warm good wishes', or was that a shade too intimate? With an exclamation of impatience, Roslyn folded the letter and pushed it into its envelope before she could rip it in half to join the others. Then she rose a little stiffly and made her way down to the cabin.

It was no cooler below, Nadja still muttered in her sleep, and Roslyn felt a stab of alarm as she looked at her. Nadja seemed to have shrunk in the week since they had left Ceylon. In the narrow bunk she looked old and shrivelled, and Roslyn sponged her forehead. When the old nurse seemed more relaxed in sleep, Roslyn climbed into her own bunk after removing the brown dress, and lay in her undergarments in the stifling heat.

The rise and fall of her breasts revealed the fiery brilliance of the ruby, contrasting with the white cambric petticoat and the deep golden hue of her skin. The ruby was cool on her flesh now. She cupped it in one hand and looked deep into its pure perfection, as if willing it to speak to her.

'Don't hate me, Greg,' she hardly realized the whispered words had left her lips. She closed her eyes tightly and pictured his face. She pictured his hands as they turned over the letter written in the strange feminine hand, and imagined the small frown that would pucker his brow, and the pursing of his lips...

'...please want me, Greg...'the words were less than a sigh trembling on a breeze as she drifted into a trance-like sleep, while the *Sea Maid* droned steadily on in the burning heat of the tropical afternoon.

By the time the *Sea Maid* dropped anchor at the port of Aden, Roslyn felt quite at home on board ship, but she was eager to go ashore and make her purchases, and see that the letter to Greg went safely on its way.

It felt odd to be walking on solid ground after the constant motion of the deck. Vickery called a native boy with a hand-cart to carry the ladies, while he strode alongside. Nadja looked frail and said little as they traversed the short distance to the bazaars.

'This will be the establishment you require, Miss Radcliffe,' Vickery indicated the place. 'There are many rogues about eager to steal English money, but you will be quite safe here, and I will wait outside until you are ready.'

The choice was dismal, catering only for lower-class dresses, such as she wore now. There was an even poorer selection of nightwear, but she and Nadja chose the best they could. European wear was obviously not sought-after.

The only clothes of any consequence in the place were a few Indian saris of gossamer silk, heavily embroidered with gold thread, and with accompanying gold-coloured wrist bangles and anklets. A sudden nostalgia swept through Roslyn. Probably never again would she see the exquisite garments that had been such an every-day sight to her in Ceylon. She fingered the shimmering blue gauze of one of the saris, feeling its sensuous texture against her skin.

Why should she not buy one for a keepsake, she thought recklessly? She had sometimes worn one at home. It would bring back a breath of Ceylon, even if she could just look at it occasionally.

'It will be beautiful on you, little Missy,' Nadja said gently, as if she could read Roslyn's thoughts.

That decided it. Roslyn paid over the English money, counting out the change carefully, and took her purchases out into the bright sunlight again. It was doubtful whether anyone in England would ever see her in the sari, but it didn't matter. It was enough that she owned it.

Vickery instructed the boy to take them to the posting house. It was a short distance along the busy street with its glaring white buildings and crowds of turbanned natives and dark-clad women. Roslyn wasn't sorry to be back on board the *Sea Maid* once more, knowing the letter was safely on its way to England. Nadja had approved of the action when she told her what she had done.

'It is best that he meets you, my sweet one.

You will need someone to lean on once you arrive.'

Roslyn might have said that she had Nadja for just that purpose, but it was becoming obvious the old woman was failing daily, and would need a long rest once they reached England. Roslyn was sure from her father's description of her Aunt Hester, that Nadja would have every care from that lady at least. In the cool sweet green of England Nadja would recover her strength...

The days merged into weeks of monotonous sameness. Roslyn found that even blue sea and sky could pall, and the glimpses of city and desert and the gleaming minarets of Alexandria could stir an interest that was almost fervent. The passage was smooth with one exception through the Bay of Biscay, where the small cargo boat was pitched and tossed in pounding seas. For the two passengers it was sheer torment in the tiny confines of the cabin, with both of them suffering from sea-sickness and clinging to each other. The weather finally calmed and Captain Webber told them the last stretch of the journey lay ahead.

Nadja shivered constantly in the cooler temperature. It was far colder than either of them was used to, but Roslyn was young and could adapt more easily. Nadja slept huddled up in blankets and shawls, and still she shivered. It was early in October now, and in England the nights were cold with an occasional hint of frost.

Nothing was going to cast a cloud on Roslyn's spirits on the morning Vickery brought their breakfast to the cabin and told them they were steaming along the English coastline. She sped up on deck without bothering to eat, eager to see this green country at last...she saw very little through the dark sea mist of early morning, only a hazy shadow that was England. But it didn't matter. It was enough that she had arrived, and she could hardly contain her impatience for the rest of the day until they were tied up at Tilbury Dock. She thanked the captain for his kindness and a safe passage, and collected the remainder of her money.

'Good luck to you, my dear,' he said gruffly. 'Vickery will walk with you to the Black Boar if you can wait a while longer while he attends to his duties. It will be safer to go escorted.'

It was several hours before Vickery was ready for them, but Roslyn was now filled with apprehension and content to wait. The dockside was filthy and stinking, and the seamen shouted harshly to each other in a variety of accents she didn't understand. It was dusk by the time they left the *Sea Maid* for the last time, and a cold breeze blew in from the waterfront as they hurried along the uneven cobblestones through a maze of tiny streets and alleyways.

Vickery pointed out a swinging inn sign above a busy courtyard.

'I'll see you installed, Miss Radcliffe,' he said stolidly. 'They don't have too many ladies staying here alone, but Captain Webber's compliments to the landlord, and he'll see that you have a quiet room at the back away from these hoitys.'

Roslyn knew instantly the kind of 'ladies' who frequented the Black Boar as she saw the laughing-eyed girls in the courtyard, ogling the newly-arrived seamen with coins jingling in their pockets. She had seen that expression before, on the face of the Kandy whore...it all seemed like centuries ago now.

The whole area was gloomy and Roslyn swallowed her dismay. Captain Webber, after all, had assured her it was clean and respectable. She clung to the fact that Greg would soon take her away from this place into the cool green countryside. Greg would come, she repeated over and over...

Soon she and Nadja were ensconced in a small room at the back of the inn. Roslyn caught sight of herself in the cracked mirror above the wash-bowl. Her appearance shocked her. She would indeed be safe here. No man in his senses would look twice at the unkempt, dowdy reflection that looked back at her. Her once-beautiful hair was dried and coarsened by the strong sunlight, her skin was darkened and there were shadows beneath her blue eyes. She had lost weight, and the cheap dress hung on her. She could have wept, but a hoarse bout of coughing from Nadja filled her with sudden shame for her own vanity.

A hasty look round the room had shown one large bed and a lumpy sofa.

'You must have the bed, Nadja,' Roslyn insisted. It should have warned her how ill the old nurse was when she made no objection and allowed Roslyn to undress her. Nadja slid between the coarse sheets without a murmur. She was asleep almost at once, breathing noisily and shallowly.

Roslyn went back downstairs to ask the landlord for a hot meal to be sent up for them both in one hour. The florid-faced landlord looked her up and down. For two pins he'd tell the scruff to take her old Indian and get back on the street. He wasn't too sure whether the chit herself didn't have a touch of the tarbrush...but there was something in the tilt of her head that stopped him snapping back at her. Besides she'd paid for a week in advance, which was something. If she'd stolen it, it was no concern of his.

He growled. 'This ain't no charity house, miss. 'Tis extra for victuals…'

'I don't ask for charity,' Roslyn spoke scathingly. 'See that the food is nourishing, and please send up some more blankets. It's freezing in that room.'

''Ere, this ain't the Ritz, me fine lady…' He found he was talking to himself.

Roslyn's head throbbed. The inn was thick with smoke and the smells of ale and cheap scent, and she had to fight to keep back the tears. Nadja's breathing laboured on. The candle flickered in the draughts from the window, and Roslyn tucked the blankets more firmly round the old nurse, who didn't stir.

For three days and nights Roslyn stayed in the room with Nadja, only venturing downstairs to ask for food or more candles. She was unused to sickness, and believed implicitly that once Nadja got accustomed to the cold climate of England, she would recover. But there was no sign of it yet and slowly it began to dawn on Roslyn that Nadja could die. Then she would be completely alone in this cold grey country that was not at all how her father had described it. Outside a constant drizzle of rain streaked the grimy windows. Roslyn knew a sudden panic as she drew the curtains across to shut it out. Where was Greg? The thought trembled inside her. Why didn't he come...?

Roslyn's legs suddenly gave way and she sank on to the lumpy sofa in a bout of despair, brought on by agonizing doubts and sheer fatigue. She should never have come...even though it had been her father's wish...A sudden sharp longing for her father swept over her. She wept as if her heart would break, and only dimly did she realize later that there was someone rapping on her door. She shivered as she went to answer it, numb with cold. It would be the serving-girl, she thought...

Roslyn's face filled with hot, painful colour as she threw open the door and looked up into a face she recognized instantly. The strong, arrogant face of Greg Radcliffe with its rugged features showed no sign of pleasure, and his dark, brooding eyes swept over her incredulously. The sensual mouth Roslyn had so often romanticized about was set in a hard straight line, his expression contemptuous. Roslyn instinctively moved back. How unattractive she must appear to this fine gentleman in her stained and crumpled dress, her hair awry, her faced swollen with weeping.

'Well? You know who I am, I suppose?' Greg's voice was sharp with impatience at the stunned look of this noddle-head who had brought him here. He'd half-expected it to be a ruse, an attempt to extract money from distant relatives, but if that were the case this daughter of James Darby was in for a rude shock, because there was no money...He'd come out of annnoyance and curiosity, and because his mother had been so obviously affected when he'd shown her the letter from Roslyn and begged him to bring her home to Yorkshire, saying she would try to explain things to his father. Someone had better explain it to *him*, Greg thought grimly, as the girl flinched at his tone.

'Are you going to ask your "brother" in, or do I call the landlord and tell him he has an imposter under his roof?'

CHAPTER 7

Roslyn found her voice. Behind Greg she could see the young serving-girl approaching with a tray of food. The small diversion gave her a moment to recover from the shock of seeing

Greg at last. Her heart had momentarily stopped, but now it thudded painfully.

'Please come in,' she stammered, and turned to the serving-girl.

'Leave the food on the table...'

'I've to wait for the money, miss,' the girl said obstinately. Her eyes approved the fine gent's tall, muscular figure in long travelling coat and boots. She wondered what the connection could be between him and the scruff. Before Roslyn could fumble for the coins, Greg had tossed the money to the girl and kicked the door shut after her.

'Was this ordered for my arrival?' he spoke sarcastically, picking up one of the meat pies and sinking his teeth into it, his eyes never leaving Roslyn's face.

'It was for my nurse and myself,' she seemed unable to control the stammering.

'I gathered that much, but my use of it would be greater than hers at the moment by the looks of things, Miss Darby—or am I supposed to call you Roslyn, since we are supposed to be brother and sister?'

Roslyn couldn't touch her pie. Her nerves were stretched taut. This was her prince, about whom she had dreamed for so long, weaving so many loving fantasies about him in her mind that she had half expected him to sweep her into his arms the moment he arrived. Her foolish dreams crumbled into ashes. She had dreamed of a lovers' meeting, not these long cold looks from a stranger. Looks that made her feel less than nothing, she who had travelled halfway round the world to be with him.

Although he acted so coldly towards her, Roslyn was still aware of his magnetism. But a white-hot fury was superceding all other emotions in her now. Was this how the English welcomed their kin? She had told him exactly who she was in her letter. He knew her father had recently died, and if for no other reason, she'd have supposed his own mother might have intimated something of her own connection with James Darby, and that would have softened him towards her. There was no hint of it in his manner. Could it be that his own father had taken a blind rage at being reminded of his old rival after all these years and forbidden Greg to bring her to his house? Was Greg merely here as his father's messenger to see her on her way with a few shillings? The possibilities raced through Roslyn's mind like quicksilver.

'My name is Roslyn,' she said tightly. The room was suddenly spinning in front of her as she fought to keep control of herself. 'I have thought of you as Greg for so long, I trust you

133

will have no objection to my continuing to do so.'

He looked at her a little blankly. She seemed to sway in front of his eyes, and suddenly his arms moved automatically to stop her from falling. She felt tense in his arms, her body lithe against him. The realization that there was a warm, curvaceous shape beneath the cheap crumpled dress the girl wore surprised him. Greg propelled her gently towards the sofa and sat her down before he unfastened his travelling coat and threw it aside, sprawling down beside her, glad to relax after his long journey. His eyes were still hard and unyielding, but his voice was less caustic.

'You'd better tell me exactly why you've come, Miss Darby—Roslyn—and how you could have known of my existence as long as you imply, when I knew nothing of yours until a few days ago.'

She sat on the very edge of the sofa, thankful that the dizziness was passing. She was nervous. Greg could sense it as her body arched in the soft candlelight. The cheap dress was tight across her full breasts. Their tips stood out visibly as if she was in fear of him. The sight moved him, despite his mistrust. Behind her head, the candle spluttered on the bed table, throwing dancing lights through her tangled dark hair. In no way could she be called a beauty, Greg thought, but there was a certain look of wantonness about her that could almost attract him if she didn't smell so appallingly. Perhaps in any other circumstances...

'How much has your mother told you?' Roslyn said in a strained voice.

'Very little,' he said shortly. 'She was profoundly disturbed when I showed her your letter. My first reaction was that it was some kind of hoax. If my father had not been away on business, I would have handed the matter over to him. As it was, my mother wished that I should come to fetch you home as she wished to meet you.' He ignored the sudden glisten of tears in her eyes. 'I understand that she and your father were once very close, but whenever she tried to tell me more she had to resort to the smelling-salts. I have heard mention of a James Darby over the years, but since it was a name that usually reduced my father to a state of apoplexy, neither my brother nor I asked questions. We merely assumed him to be the black sheep of the family and best forgotten.'

'He was never that!' Roslyn burst out. Bright spots of colour heightened her pale face, and her blue eyes flashed angrily at him. Her chin lifted proudly, remembering James Darby's king-like position in Ceylon. Who were these

135

Yorkshire farmers compared with him...?

Good God, Greg thought, with a surge of irritation rather than interest—the girl could be quite stunning. He glanced towards the bed as the ragged breathing became momentarily noisier. The old woman lay close to death if he wasn't mistaken. He doubted if the old woman would stand the journey to Yorkshire in the carriage.

'Explain it to me then,' Greg said flatly. 'We Yorkshire folk are wary of inviting folks into our homes before knowing anything about them.'

Roslyn's anger fled, seeing it from Greg's viewpoint and wishing desperately his mother had told him everything before he came to London for her. But if Aunt Hester had been so affected by news of James Darby's death, it almost certainly meant she would have a friend in her, and the thought warmed Roslyn a little. She told Greg all she knew, speaking hesitantly at first, about the past in which they had had no part, yet which had brought them together. She could see the mixture of emotions on Greg's face, particularly when her voice faltered and shook as she spoke of her father's death and the flight through the night to Bahu's house. The one thing she could not relate was the shame of being raped.

'Then you have known of my brother and myself since you were a child?' Greg said incredulously.

For the first time Roslyn let her face relax into a small smile.

'Oh yes. Your mother—Aunt Hester as I have always thought of her—captured your likeness so perfectly. I cannot speak about Francis yet as I have not seen him, but in her sketches of you there was always the proud look, and the impatience. I always imagined that you could not sit still too long to pose for her...' she finished in embarrassment as her tongue ran away with her. 'I'm sorry. That must sound extremely personal coming from a stranger.'

Greg leaned towards her, his hands taking hold of her cold ones and enveloping them in their warmth. His face changed completely as he too smiled. Little creases fanned out at the corners of his eyes, and the sensual mouth opened wider to reveal strong white teeth. The smile broadened his long face, and the suddenness of it sent little shock waves running through Roslyn. He was every bit as charismatic in reality as he had been in her dreams, she thought tremulously. Every bit and more...

'But we are not strangers, are we?' he said simply. 'Not any more, at least. And tomorrow morning we will leave for Yorkshire if the old woman is fit for travelling. Have you sent for a doctor?'

Roslyn looked at him helplessly. It had never occurred to her. She had never had to think of such things for herself. She shook her head wordlessly. Greg strode to the bed, pinching his nostrils together at the stench exuding from it. He was no doctor, but he knew there was none born who could help here. It was like looking down at a shrivelled old prune to look into Nadja's brown face. But he did not tell Roslyn of his thoughts. He turned and picked up his travelling coat.

'I suggest you get a good night's sleep, and leave thoughts about a doctor until morning,' he said, his face impassive. 'And if you should need me for any reason, I am in the room next door. Goodnight, Roslyn.'

Her eyes filled as she heard the door click shut behind him. The voice was not yet warm towards her, but neither was it as unfriendly as when he arrived. She felt as if she had been starved of all emotions but fear for weeks past now, and it was very comforting to know that from now on, Greg was there when she needed him. She crept across to the bed where Nadja hardly made a bump in the bedclothes, bending to kiss the crumpled old face as it slept on.

'Greg is here, Nadja,' she whispered. 'He will take care of us now.'

As if she heard and understood, the old nurse gave a long sighing breath in reply. Roslyn turned away, and for the first time in days she dragged a comb through the tangled mass of her hair and splashed cold water over her face, hating herself for appearing so unkempt to Greg at their first meeting. Her appearance was a world removed from the way she had always been so immaculately attired in Ceylon. She felt a sudden longing for him to see her as she had been then—dressed in silken gowns, her hair burnished and soft, her skin pampered and fragrant with perfume, the beauty of the devil's kiss enhanced by the swell of her breasts. Her cheeks suddenly burned at the wayward thoughts rushing into her mind. She threw down the comb and crept into the blankets on the sofa without bothering to undress. Tomorrow she would wear the other dress. At least it was cleaner than this one, even if it was more suited to a humble working girl than a lady…she could not bear for Greg to see her as little better than a slut…

In the bedroom next door, Greg Radcliffe lay sleepless on the identical bed to the one in which Nadja lay. His eyes were wide open, the enigma of Roslyn Darby bothering him more than it should. At first sight he'd thought her a ne'er-do-well, caught unawares by his arrival before she could tart herself up. But even without the story of her father and his mother, which was too easily proved on his part to be untrue, he'd have seen that she was used to better things. There was an air of breeding about her, and an arrogance that almost matched his own.

The moment when he'd caught her in his arms he'd been surprised at the voluptuousness of her figure. The hideous dress had hung on her, so that she might have been any shape beneath it. But there had been a pleasurable pressing against him of womanly curves, and when she'd sat so tense on the sofa, her breasts had strained tight against the cheap fabric of the dress.

What a blow it would be to his father if he were to come home with this Roslyn Darby and showing more than a kindly interest in her. His thoughts ran on. For months now, Thomas Radcliffe had been urging Greg into an alliance with a young lady of their acquaintance, Louise Judd. Louise was a sophisticated beauty who lived in York, about thirty miles south of the Radcliffe home, and had made it blatantly obvious that she would not be averse to a marriage between them. She was an elegant young woman who would grace the best houses in the country, and her father was rich enough to bestow a handsome dowry on her. Such riches would help restore Radcliffe Manor to its former glory, Thomas had hinted more than once to his son, but such hints only made Greg more determined than ever that his life was not to be manipulated. He admired Miss Judd, but he had no desire to marry her, or anyone. It might be amusing to let his father sweat a little in pretending a sudden attraction to this honey-skinned Roslyn Darby...he and Thomas were more often antagonistic towards each other than filial, and Thomas made no bones about the fact that he preferred his more pliable son Francis, to the arrogant Greg. He would bristle to the soles of his feet if he thought Greg was even faintly enamoured of the daughter of his old hated rival...

He started as he heard his name urgently called, and a hammering on his door. He threw off the bedclothes, thankful he hadn't bothered to undress in this pig-pen of an inn. As he opened the door Roslyn fell into his arms, her eyes wild and frightened.

'Oh Greg, come quickly,' she sobbed against him. 'I can't rouse Nadja. I thought she was breathing more easily, and when I went to tuck her in, I got frightened. Oh Greg, I think...I think...'

He half-held her up as they both moved back to the other room. One look at the old Indian woman confirmed what he had expected. She was undoubtedly dead. He could hear Roslyn's teeth chattering beside him. He covered the woman's face with a blanket and gripped Roslyn's arms tightly.

'I can't leave you here with her,' he said roughly. 'And we cannot rouse the landlord in the middle of the night. It will have to be done in the morning—'

'She will have to be buried quickly,' Roslyn said wildly. Her mind could not cope with this new tragedy. In Ceylon burials were hastily arranged because of the heat...Greg grasped her meaning and nodded.

'I will arrange everything tomorrow,' he promised. 'But right now you must trust me, Roslyn. We will leave her in peace with the candle burning and the door locked. She is at *peace* now,' he repeated as she seemed not to understand his words. 'And you must not be alone. My room is next door and you will be safe with me. Will you trust me?'

She looked up at him numbly. She could not take in his meaning. All she wanted was to be taken care of, told what to do. She let him lead her away from her own room and into his. He picked her up as if she were a child and carried her to the bed. It was warm where he had lain, and he slid in alongside her and drew her into his arms. They were both still fully clothed and for Roslyn the contact meant little more than the relief of sharing her grief with another human being and being held and comforted while she sobbed herself to sleep in his arms.

For Greg, it meant something different. As she relaxed in sleep while he still lay wakeful, she moulded herself to his embrace in childlike trust. He was aware of every curve and hollow of her body pressed tightly against him in the bed, and unconsciously he let his hand roam over the dip of her waist and the alluring curves of her buttocks. He had had occasion to visit a bawdy-house from time to time, but the couplings there had always been swift and businesslike. There had never been an aftermath of sweetness, lying here with a soft warm girl in his arms...and even though there was an aura of unwash about her, nevertheless Roslyn's body scents were warmly earthy and sensual.

Almost without realizing what he was doing he moved back from her a fraction and felt her soft breath on his cheek as she slept from sheer exhaustion. He had told her she would be safe with him, and so she would be...but he could not resist touching that soft dewy mouth with his lips, just to taste its sweetness...nor to stop his hand from brushing her breasts and gently squeezing the fullness of them. He lay as unmoving as he could against her body, fighting to control the sudden urge to possess this golden girl in his arms.

Roslyn could not think where she was for the first seconds when she awoke. She was in a bed instead of on a sofa...memory rushed back at once, and she gave a little moan of grief. She was quite alone, and she only dimly remembered Greg comforting her in his own bed. Her cheeks reddened, but he had been so gentle...acting exactly like the brother she had pretended he was. She had dreamed he kissed her and felt a swift shame for other, more erotic dreams that had followed. Greg had not touched her in the way that hateful man had done in Bahu's house on the night of the monsoon. If Greg had tried to harm her she would have felt the warning of the devil's kiss on her skin, and she had felt nothing of it. The only heat that had suffused her body had been the spreading warmth of a pleasure completely new to her.

Roslyn started as he came into the room now. He brought a cold draught with him as if he had been out of doors, and his first words confirmed this. He had been out early and been busy, she discovered.

'The landlord does not wish it known there has been a death here, Roslyn' he said, his voice deliberately brisk to distract her from grief. 'I have arranged for her body to be taken to the funeral home nearby. A burial can be done this afternoon. I have told the landlord we will vacate the inn when we leave for the funeral home. We will need to make several overnight stops on the journey to Yorkshire, but I thought you would rather leave this place than stay another night here.'

'Oh yes!' She was almost weak with thankfulness that Greg had seen to everything so quickly and efficiently. She was still deeply shocked at Nadja's death and unable to think properly. Greg was speaking again.

'Do you have another dress to wear? If you wish, I can send the serving-girl to purchase a more suitable travelling outfit. It will be colder in Yorkshire. She is about your size, I think.'

He avoided letting his eyes linger where his hands had wandered during the night.

'I would be grateful for that,' Roslyn said at once. 'I have only thin clothes with me. There was no time to bring my own things, and I feel ashamed of these rags.' She bit her lip for a moment. Nadja was dead, and she concerned herself with the way she looked... 'Something dark, please, Greg. I have two loved ones to mourn now...'

He went to instruct the serving-girl, disregarding the landlord's grumbling mutterings that one way and another these two seemed to have taken over his establishment. He had his own dark suspicions as to whether they were brother and sister, come to that, but if the gent wanted to amuse himself with the scruff it was no concern of his.

'Before you go for the clothes, girl, will you see that a tub of hot water is sent to my room for Miss Radcliffe to bathe, please?' Greg added. 'And while you are purchasing the clothes, some new undergarments had best be added to the list. Something suitable for a young lady. You'll know the things to choose.'

Yes, she was about Roslyn's size and shape, Greg thought, studying her dispassionately for a moment. The girl turned to do his bidding, her waspish reply that she wasn't here to do for the likes of the scruff completely forgotten in her reaction to the intense stare the gent

gave to her bosom. It sent a flame of excitement through her veins as she went to stoke
up the fire beneath the cauldron of water for
the young woman's bathtub. That one could
light her fire any time he liked, she thought,
and she'd be only too ready to help him stoke
up...

A while later, she dumped the tub in the
bedroom where the scruff sat aimlessly on the
edge of the bed, looking into space. She hauled the cauldron of water behind her and tipped it in the tub, finally throwing towels and
washing-cloth beside Roslyn. There was soap
by the water-jug, she told her curtly. The scruff
seemed to have lost all her hoity-toity airs, the
girl thought sourly. Perhaps the gent had been
too much for her last night...she for one was
certain they were not brother and sister, and
this one looked as if she didn't know what had
hit her. Amateurs...

'The gent said you'd be wanting a bath,' she
snapped. 'I'm off to get your things now.'

Roslyn hardly heard her. The warm water
made a little humidity in the room, and the
sudden longing to soak her limbs in its caressing softness was overwhelming. She tossed in
the bar of soap. Its smell was nothing like the
delicate perfumes that used to drift into her

nostrils at home, but as she stripped off the cheap garments she wore and lowered herself into the tub, the sensations were the same. It had been so long since she had been able to relax like this...just to lie in the soft soapy water and let the warmth of it seep into her every pore...she should have pinned up her long hair, but she was used to Nadja or Meera doing such things. She was used to someone else's hands plying her with soaps and perfumes and soft dry towels and attending to her every need.

For agonized moments she lay in the tub with her head back and the tears streaking down her cheeks. The long dark tendrils of her hair curled wetly against her shoulders. And suddenly she leaned her head forward again, hugging her knees and burying her head on them, weeping silently for all that was gone for ever.

The door opened softly and closed again. Greg had expected her to be out of the bathtub. He thought she would be sitting swathed in towels on the bed by now, waiting for the clothes the serving-girl had produced in double-quick time, and which he now held in his hands. He was completely disconcerted to find her still sitting in the bathtub, apparently oblivious to the fact that the water had grown lukewarm, her soft hair falling like a dark curtain around her knees.

She looked up at his approach. She knew she should be overcome with embarrassment at him finding her like this, and that it was the height of indiscretion for a gentleman to see a lady in the bathtub. But such thoughts were farthest from Roslyn's disorientated mind. She looked at him numbly for a moment, the tears still streaking down her cheeks.

'I've never bathed myself in my life,' she whispered. 'There was always someone to do it for me at home. Always someone to do everything—'

'Do you want me to call the girl?' Greg said roughly. Good God, didn't she know what it was doing to him to see her like this, with those golden breasts almost fully visible above the water, their rosy tips just resting on its surface?

'No! I won't have her near me—' her voice stopped.

Greg moved slowly towards her. He dropped the parcel of clothes on the bed and slipped out of his coat, pushing up his shirt sleeves up to his elbows. Roslyn could see the sinewy muscles in his arms, and the fine dark hairs along their length. He never took his gaze from her eyes as he knelt beside the tub and reached for the soap and the washing-cloth.

'Well then, it will have to be me, won't it?' he said. 'Lean forward.'

She did as she was told. He soaped the cloth and rotated it in small circles over her back to where the backbone disappeared beneath the water. He let the water trickle over her skin and thought how beautiful it was. So different from the pink and white beauty of so-called society ladies. As he instructed her, he saw she closed her eyes, almost as if she was in a trance. As if she was quite unaware of him as a person, Greg thought in amazement. She was so used to being waited on in every way, he might have been no more than a servant attending her...

He was filled with the desire to awaken something more in her. With her hair softly curling on her shoulders and the look of unconscious rapture on her face as he pushed her gently back against the bathtub, he was fully aware that Roslyn was not the young fool that he had at first supposed. She was a very lovely and desirable young woman who could stir his senses with an urgency that took him by surprise. He soaped the wash-cloth again, and this time he rotated it around the golden breasts in deliberately sensual movements.

Slowly Roslyn's eyes opened. For brief

150

moments her stunned mind had managed to push out everything that had happened recently. She was once more back in the Darby mansion, lying back in subtly perfumed water in her blue-tinted bathtub, and the impassive-faced Meera was attending her. But Meera's attentions had never affected her like this...they had never made every nerve-end tingle...

She was breathing quickly as she tried to clear her mind. Her cheeks were flushed and Greg's face was very close to hers. With a smothered exclamation he pulled her into his arms and pressed a savage kiss on her mouth. A kiss that went on and on, regardless of the fact that his shirt was soaking wet as he held her close. Her arms wound themselves round him as the ecstasy of the moment poured over her, blotting out everything but her need of him. Nadja would have wished for this, her dizzy thoughts danced on...Nadja had thought her ripe for loving, and oh, how she loved Greg Radcliffe...how she had always loved him...

He let her go abruptly.

'Forgive me, Roslyn,' he said harshly. 'That was a most improper thing to do, and I apologize for it. I assure you I am not in the habit of seducing young ladies I have only just met, nor do I take advantage of them when they are in a distressed state of mind.' Her hands had involuntarily covered her nakedness and he was even more mortified by the look of bewilderment in her beautiful eyes. He turned away from the sight of her and made for the door, turning slightly as he reached it.

'I suggest you learn the art of bathing, for you'll get no such pampered treatment at Radcliffe Manor! I'll wait until you're ready in your own room. Nadja has been taken away, so there's no need to be afraid—neither of her, nor of me.'

He was gone. Roslyn stared at the closed door with stinging tears of fury and humiliation salting her eyes. She was trembling all over. That he had caught her so violently in his arms and kissed her so passionately she could have forgiven! That he had taken on the role of bath attendant for a few moments, for whatever reason...that she could have forgiven, even though she knew perfectly well it was the height of impropriety for a gentleman to come into such intimate contact with a young lady unless they were married.

What she could not forgive was his sudden rejection of her and his cold unemotional manner. Had it meant nothing at all to him? Oh, but it *had*, she thought. She had heard his own quickening breath and seen the look of desire in his eyes. But had Greg for those brief moments thought of dallying with her in the way a man dallied with a trollop, until he had remembered who she was and thought better of it?

The idea was enough to make her numb inside. In her foolish childish dreams of him, she had assumed he would love her instantly, and that such intimacies would be an unashamed part of that loving...but if he could be cold, then so could she. She would never let him see that she loved him. The incident was past, and she had too much pride to let him know she was concerned by it. Miss Darby was above such trivialities, used as she was to every personal attention in bedroom and bathroom.

But her cheeks burned as she stood up clumsily in the bathtub and scrubbed herself dry with the coarse towels as if she would scrub away every memory of his hands and lips.

CHAPTER 8

The rest of the day seemed to pass in a dream for Roslyn. When she presented herself to Greg she might have been a different person from the one he had first seen, dowdy and unwholesome, and different again from the lovely creature he had held in his arms and desired so urgently.

This Roslyn stood before him with her hair scraped up into a knot on top of her head. The dark high-buttoned dress added to the severity of her appearance. Black did not suit her, seeming to take away every vestige of colour from her cheeks. She cared nothing for that, wanting only to be away from this place and the various memories it held.

The small ceremony for Nadja and her subsequent burial in a windswept cemetery where falling leaves swirled and snapped at their faces produced the only emotion Greg saw in her that day. She allowed him to support her as she wept bitter tears for the old woman who had been such an integral part of her life. It was a chapter that was over, and she had no idea what life now held for her. Even with Greg she could no longer feel comforted. There was a barrier between them that she could not cross, and he, assuming she was humiliated by his attentions, did not attempt to cross it either. They were strangers again. The only comfort Roslyn knew was the touch of the ruby pendant, snugly between her breasts. She had lost the two people she had loved most in all the world, but both of them had had implicit faith in the ruby's protection, and she would have it also.

The carriage journey to Yorkshire began as soon as they left the cemetery. Roslyn was thankful to see the back of such gloomy surroundings. She spoke little, and Greg decided to leave her to her own thoughts rather than try to make idle conversation. He had tucked a travelling rug around her knees before they began the long ride north, and she remained huddled inside it until they alighted at an inn for their overnight stop. He helped her down. She was stiff and cold. The air had grown noticeably colder, and she could not suppress a shiver at the misty evening.

But the inn was warm and more wholesome than the last. The rooms were clean, and Roslyn was too exhausted to do other than sleep, more soundly than she had expected. She was strong-minded enough to know she must put the past behind her, however hard it seemed. She had no other choice.

It was several days later when they journeyed through bleak flat countryside that Greg told her was Yorkshire. She had expected to see rolling hills and dales, but he told her that would come later. There were black smoking chimneys and an air of greyness over everything, and the panorama filled Roslyn with dismay. How could she ever learn to love this place as she had loved the colour and glitter of Ceylon? She swallowed back her choking doubts, and listened as Greg pointed out the twin turrets of York Minster, rising majestically into a grey sky. She tried to show some interest, but it all seemed to be a great effort. It was almost as if she listened to someone else speaking with her voice...

'We have friends in York, and it's quite a social centre,' Greg was saying now. 'I daresay you'll find it very different after living in the wilds.'

His voice seemed condescending to Roslyn's heightened senses. She felt her cheeks grow hot.

'You obviously have no idea of the style of living I'm used to.' Her voice was icy. 'My father was not the black sheep of the family as you once implied, nor was he the poor relation, despite what you may have thought from my appearance when we first met. James Darby was king of his empire, and a very respected tea planter. We entertained princes—'

Her voice died away as she realized he was grinning mockingly at her in disbelief. He had stopped the carriage on a ridge of ground from which to see the city of York more clearly, and

156

Roslyn suddenly felt a stab of anger. Who was he, this son of a Yorkshire farmer, she thought scathingly, to doubt her word? There had been princes and others of noble blood who were pleased to accept an invitation of James Darby's. Impulsively, Roslyn's fingers were unfastening the high black dress, and seconds later she had revealed the ruby pendant glowing at her throat.

'I have little left to prove my words,' she said angrily, 'though I trust my father's letters to your parents will do that. But I think even your untrained eyes will not deny that I wear a priceless jewel round my neck. It is a Siamese ruby given to my father many years ago in grateful thanks by a young Indian prince for saving his life. It brought him luck and protection from his enemies for the rest of his life, and it was his most precious gift to me on my eighteenth birthday.' Her eyes suddenly went bleak. 'I did not realize just how precious then, because once it had left his possession he was at terrible risk. And that was the night the rebels burned our home and the plantation, and my father died.'

Her voice stopped. She had not meant to blurt out everything in a torrent of words, nor to tell Greg so much about the ruby. She had merely wanted to prove to him that she was not the hottentot he seemed to think. Nor did she need the social graces of York, instilled in her...Greg had reached forward to inspect the ruby more closely. It gleamed in the rise and fall of her breasts. He took the pendant in his hand, and she was very conscious of his touch on her skin.

'It's beautiful,' he said at last. 'And once again, my apologies to you. Even if I am too much a Yorkshireman to put much faith in fairytales, I appreciate how it must have seemed to you on the night your father died.'

'He was a Yorkshireman too, and he believed it!' She felt obliged to say more now she had started. 'Greg—I would prefer if this was something between ourselves. There's no need for anyone else to know about the ruby, is there?'

'Of course not.' He let it lie in its little cocoon, wishing fleetingly that he could lie there too after this unexpected glimpse of the fiery gem against the smooth golden flesh. The fairytale was best kept from his own father, for one. Thomas Radcliffe would have no time for such heathen nonsense. Greg thought of him for the first time in several days, and wondered uneasily if his mother had managed to soften his temper yet about their unwanted visitor. He did not need to be at Radcliffe Manor to envisage the reaction to her news, nor his father's rage that Greg had departed for London while he was out of the house. It was best that Roslyn knew nothing of that either.

But the little interchange had at least put them on a more amicable footing than of late, and Roslyn knew a feeling of relief that now Greg viewed her on equal terms with himself, and that was the most important thing of all at the moment. Her pride was as passionate as his, and she would not allow herself to think for a moment that though James Darby had not been the poor relation to these Yorkshire Radcliffes, she certainly was. All she had was the ruby, and with that she would never part.

There were not many more miles to travel now, Greg told her, to her intense relief. The night air was so cold it made her catch her breath. Her head ached, her throat was sore, in fact every inch of her ached if she thought about it. She could have wept with fatigue. There was a muzziness in her brain and an emptiness in her heart that she could not have explained if she'd tried. It was the end of the journey, and yet she felt none of the elation she had expected. At last Greg drew the horses to a halt and pointed some distance ahead. They had climbed steadily into the hills by then, and Roslyn was suddenly, stabbingly aware that the ruby was burning against her skin as she followed the line of Greg's finger.

There below lay the reality of the vision she had seen on board the *Sea Maid*. Swathed in a grey mist, the large stone farmhouse that was Radcliffe Manor reared gloomily against the overcast sky. She could not see the foundations which seemed to be floating on a sea of vaporous gauze. There was danger here...the words seemed to be thudding into her brain as loud as her heartbeats...the inexplicable fear numbed her mind and dried her throat so that she could not speak. Greg appeared to notice nothing strange in her behaviour and merely said that the sooner they got inside the better, for she seemed to be chilled to the bone from the way she was shivering. She could have told him, if she had found the words, that it was a chill of the soul, rather than the body, that gripped her.

As they neared the farm, the building took on a more normal appearance. From the distance it had seemed to loom out of the grey mist, but now Roslyn could see it was a handsome weathered stone building. The frontage was kept strictly formal, with lawns and shrubberies softened by evergreens. Greg explained that the business part of the farm was at the rear, where the Radcliffe land stretched up into the hills beyond.

'I'll take you round it and show you your "inheritance",' he said mockingly.

'Not mine!' Roslyn said quickly.

He reined in the horses as they clattered on the cobblestones at the front of the house and looked at her. 'Why not yours as much as mine? You're family, aren't you? And you've come to stay, I take it?'

She wasn't sure whether the words were said with hope or derision, and before she could attempt to find out the door had opened and a sweet-faced woman with greying hair came running out with arms outstretched. There was no doubt at all in Roslyn's mind that this was Aunt Hester, the woman her father had loved so much. The warmth of welcome on her face, and the hint of tears in her faded blue eyes as she clasped Roslyn tightly, was just too much. Roslyn burst into tears herself, clinging to the older woman as if she were a lifeline.

'There now, my love, don't you fret,' Aunt Hester was saying softly in her ear in the same accent as Greg and her father. 'You're home now where you belong, and the best place for you is by a warm fire with some hot food inside you. Your face is fair pinched with cold, and I've no doubt the journey was an ordeal, but we'll hear it all in good time. Come indoors now and rest yourself.'

It was Nadja all over again, Roslyn thought dizzily. The caring and the loving, and the way the older woman supported her and told Greg to bring her things inside and hurry up about it. Everything revolving around Roslyn, and the fact that there was so little to bring indoors did not escape Aunt Hester's notice. There was only the parcel of crumpled clothes which Roslyn would rather send to the poorhouse than touch again, and her father's leather bag...she felt obliged to stammer out that she had had to leave Ceylon in such a hurry she had very little baggage...

'Then our first task must be to journey to the city to buy you some pretty things, my love,' Aunt Hester cried at once. 'I'm sure your dear father would not wish such a lovely lass to remain in mourning for ever, and black is such a gloomy shade for a young person.'

She was leading Roslyn into a cosy, wood-panelled room with tapestry-covered chairs and a wooden settle at the hearth, where a blazing log fire leaped towards the chimney. The mention of pretty things had reminded Roslyn that there was a beautiful silken sari tucked away in her father's bag as well, but she could not imagine wearing such a gossamer garment in this freezing place. Even with the heat of the fire, she still shivered. Greg had not appeared in the room, and she guessed he had gone to find his father to tell of their arrival. She was suddenly nervous of meeting this old enemy of her father's.

Aunt Hester was rubbing her cold hands and shouting for someone called Mrs May to bring hot soup at once. Then she took a good long look at Roslyn, touching the soft dark hair that was falling out of its confined knot by now. Her eyes were still moist and faraway.

'Yes, you're James' daughter,' she said softly. 'You have such a look of him it all but takes my breath away. You and I have a special bond between us, Roslyn. We both loved him, and you had all those years to share with him. Am I right in guessing that he told you the circumstances of our parting, my dear?'

Roslyn nodded, her throat thick. That she could still think of James Darby with such wistfulness after all these years must surely mean that her life with Thomas Radcliffe had been far less than perfect, and that he was indeed the taskmaster she suspected. There were sounds from the passage outside and Aunt Hester gave Roslyn's cold hand a squeeze.

'We will talk about him at our leisure another time, Roslyn,' she said quickly.

The door opened and the three men of the house seemed to fill the remaining space in the

163

room, large though it was. They were all tall men, Greg and his brother Francis, and Thomas, their father. Roslyn knew she would dislike him at once. He was large and florid-faced, with big bushy eyebrows and a scowling mouth. His nose was bulbous, and how on earth the dainty Hester could ever have preferred him to her dashing father, she could not imagine. Perhaps something of her feelings showed in her face, for Thomas Radcliffe glared hard into her eyes and stood deliberately in front of the fire, lifting his coat tails to warm himself and blocking all heat from anybody else.

'So you're the lass who thinks to make a home wi' us, are you?' he barked at her. 'Darby's girl, is it? So the scallywag made an honest woman of somebody. And what happened to your mother? One of your dusky maidens, was she?' he finished on a sneer, his eyes taking in the golden hue of Roslyn's skin, tanned by the sea voyage and warmed now by a red fury at his manner.

'My mother was as British as you, sir,' she said furiously. 'And my father was not a scallywag. You have probably been drinking the produce of his tea plantation these last ten years if you but realized it. My mother died when I was born, but my father and I had the best life any two people could have had together, and I won't hear his name blackened!'

His look of astonishment gave her courage to lift her chin and stare boldly into his eyes. She heard Greg give a low chuckle behind her. Francis said nothing, but Aunt Hester drew in her breath on a small gasp. Clearly, it was rare for someone to oppose Thomas Radcliffe. To her surprise, his rough countenance broke into a guffaw of laughter, and he slapped his sides.

'By God, you've got his spirit, I'll say that for you, lass,' he growled. 'But you can hardly blame a body for thinking you've come here looking for handouts, can you now? Especially looking more like a serving-wench than a tea-planter's daughter. *Tea-planter*, by all that's holy! You'd better be telling us how all that came about, I'm thinking.'

'Not now,' Aunt Hester said quicky. 'Can't you see the child's all in, Thomas? She's shivering with cold, and she needs food inside her and a good night's sleep in a proper bed. There'll be time enough for talking tomorrow.'

Mrs May, who was clearly the housekeeper, appeared in brown dress and white apron with a steaming bowl of soup and thick home-baked bread on a tray for Roslyn, and a similar one for Greg followed.

'Aye well, we'll leave you to it then,' Thomas Radcliffe growled after a few moments. 'As soon as you can get out o' that fancy clobber, Greg, there's work to be done outside. Me and Francis will be getting back to it.'

Roslyn suddenly felt a hand on her shoulder, and looked up into Francis Radcliffe's friendly eyes. He was a younger version of Greg, more fresh-faced than his brother, and she felt her heart warm towards him at his words.

'Since no one around here thinks it necessary to make formal introductions, I'm Francis,' he told her. 'And I'm very pleased to welcome you to England, Roslyn. You'll brighten up this gloomy place, won't she Mother?'

'She will that,' Aunt Hester smiled in agreement.

Roslyn could hear a sudden buzzing in her ears. The hot soup had burned her throat. The firelight leaped and blurred in front of her eyes. The faces swam in front of her. Uncle Thomas florid and suspicious and unwelcoming...Greg, charismatic—sometimes cynical, sometimes unbelievably tender...Aunt Hester, as soft and loving as she'd hoped...Francis, eager to be friends...They all seemed to be crowding in on her as the shivering started up in her limbs again. The bowl of soup slid embarrassingly to

166

the floor and seconds later Roslyn slid down to join it. The last thing she remembered was Thomas Radcliffe's outraged hollering for Mrs May to come in and clear up this goddamned mess, and Aunt Hester crying out to him that he was a brute if he couldn't see the lass was ill...

She was tossing about in a sea of unreality. How long she had been lying in this soft bed, where she alternately shook with cold beneath the heavy blankets, and threw them off as she burned up with the fever that gripped her, Roslyn had no idea. Sometimes she could hear her own voice crying out for her father...for Nadja...and then she would be conscious of a great empty void gnawing at her insides. Sometimes she was lost in a torrent of weeping that left her breathless and weak. The room seemed to be constantly swaying, reminding her of the long voyage on the *Sea Maid*. Sometimes she imagined Captain Webber's kindly face...at others, Bahu's weathered brown eyes assuring her that all would be well, or another, a face she could not see because of the darkness...the touch of him; the smell of him;. the violation she had suffered as he ravished her...

Her head would thrust back and forth on the

pillow as her mind rebelled against the memories she had fought so hard to suppress. There were other images that softenend the weeping to a muted despair...she was the lovely Miss Darby, admired and cossetted wherever she went.

She wore a soft blue dress and matching parasol, and beside her was her elegant handsome father, and her ever-attentive dearest Nadja. All the jewels of Ceylon could not compare with this jewel of the Darby estate, nor all the gold-encrusted saris of the native dancers vie with the fair beauty of the English girl. If James Darby was king, then she was his princess, adored and pampered, the world at her feet, and on her eighteenth birthday the possessor of James' costliest gift...

Throughout her delirium and the hallucinations that were so real, Roslyn would snatch at the ruby pendant, babbling that no one must remove it...it was her protection...

'There, there, my love, no one will touch it,' a woman's voice came and went. 'Don't you fret now. You just get well—'

'You don't understand,' Roslyn's eyes were wild as she gripped Hester Radcliffe's hands. 'It has magical powers...'

Hester had heard the tale so many times, by now, as had all the members of the Radcliffe household. So much for Roslyn's desire to keep the knowledge between the two of them, Greg thought, as he paid his customary visit to the sickroom one dark evening. She was a pale shadow of the lovely girl she must have been, her skin blanched by the weeks of illness. They had all taken turns in sitting with her, apart from his father, but it was Greg's name she had called out time and again in her delirium. Greg's hands she had clung to most fervently, and Greg's touch that seemed to have the power to calm her fevered babblings. Through it all, they had learned much of her background, jumbled though it seemed at times. James Darby had indeed made good in Ceylon, and his daughter was used to a far more luxurious way of life than she could expect at Radcliffe Manor.

Francis had been increasingly fascinated by the garbled tales Roslyn told. There was a waywardness about him that would have found a kindred spirit in James Darby. When Roslyn recovered, Francis had no doubt she could be urged on to tell him more, and Thomas Radcliffe would be even more angered to think his old rival could instil such interest in his son, even from the grave.

The doctor assured them that she would recover. She was young and strong, but he admitted that the young woman's illness was as much of the mind as the body. The cold climate had brought on a bout of pneumonia, but she seemed to be suffering from shock as well, and only time and gentle nursing would rid her of whatever memories assailed her. Greg was well aware of some of those memories...he could only guess at the others, when the look of horror came over Roslyn's lovely face and the head-twisting began...

It had been almost a month now since the night of her arrival, and in that time she had never been really lucid. It was clear she still dreamed she was in Ceylon. At other moments, when she grasped at Greg's hand and breathed his name, he could feel the relaxing of her tension and see an almost languid look replace the terror. A look as if she held the hand of a lover. It embarrassed and yet stirred him. He was nothing if not a man, and the sight of this golden girl, her dark hair sread out on the pillow, so obviously made tender and gentle by his approach, could start a fever of desire within him as naturally as breathing.

She was cooler tonight, he thought. His hand brushed the softness of her brow, and on an impulse he leaned forward and touched her soft mouth with his lips. When he removed them, it was to see that her eyes were wide open. They watched him with the limpid blueness of recognition for the first time in weeks, and he saw the flutter of the pulse in her throat, where the ruby gleamed in the lamplight.

'Welcome back, Roslyn,' he said softly. 'You certainly know how to make a spectacular entrance, don't you?'

She moved her head to look slowly round the room with its close-drawn curtains shutting out the bleakness of the winter's night; the soft lamplight throwing flickering shadows over the comfortable furnishings and on to Greg's face and the hand she held so tightly. She removed it with a murmur of unease.

'Have I been very ill?' Her voice was thin as she questioned him. Involuntarily her fingers touched the ruby, as if to reassure herself of its presence.

'Yes,' Greg answered, 'but the doctor said today he thought the worst was over, and it seems he was right.'

'I'm hungry!' She realized suddenly that her nightgown was very revealing and pulled the bedsheet up a fraction. Greg laughed as he saw the movement. How pointless her modesty, after the time they had spent at the Black Boar Inn at Tilbury, and these weeks of thrashing about in her fever, but it was a sure sign of returning health and normality.

'I'll inform my mother and Mrs May that you've come back amongst the living, Roslyn.' He stood up to leave her. A short time later his mother came into the room with cries of thankfulness that Roslyn had recovered at last. She brought a warm shawl with her to put round Roslyn's shoulders and helped her to sit up in the bed, plumping up the pillows behind her back.

'I'm so sorry to have brought you so much trouble, Aunt Hester,' Roslyn said tremulously. It was the first time in her life she had apologized in such a way, but the circumstances here were very different from home...*this* was home now, she reminded herself, however strange it felt...Hester took her hands in her own.

'My love, I think of you as my own daughter,' she said simply. 'And you're to treat Radcliffe Manor exactly as you would if you had lived here all your life. Your father would have wanted that, I know, and after all, this was once his home.' Her voice had softened at the mention of James. 'Perhaps you'll feel well enough to get up tomorrow, and you can take a proper look at the place he used to love so well. This, indeed, was his old room. It has a marvellous view of the moors, though you would see little of it tonight.'

'While you have been ill, I have been busy, Roslyn.'

She reached into a little drawer in the bed table and drew out a card folder. Inside was a pencil sketch. Roslyn's eyes filled with tears of joy as she looked at it. It was her father's likeness, but not as she had known him. This James Darby was a young and eager-faced man, with a passionate look in his eyes. Hester had sketched the face of a remembered lover, and Roslyn warmed to her still more.

'I suggest you keep it in the drawer,' she was saying, 'at least when Thomas is about. He still smarts at the mention of your father's name, even after all these years. But it will be a little memento for you to keep, and I hope it pleases you, Roslyn.'

'Oh, it does!' she said fervently. Indeed Roslyn was feeling better by the minute, and some hot nourishing food brought up a little later by Mrs May did even more to restore her spirits. She knew she would be weak from lying in bed, but tomorrow she determined to get up and acquaint herself properly with Radcliffe Manor. The thought that she was here in her father's room and in his loved home sent a glow of pleasure running through her.

Hester watched with satisfaction as the girl ate every bit of the food and enjoyed a glass of Thomas' best wine. He was not aware that she had asked for it to be brought to Roslyn, but what he didn't know couldn't hurt him, Hester thought mildly.

'I have something else to show you when you're strong enough, Roslyn,' she said now. 'Do you remember on the night you arrived I said we'd go to York to see about some new clothes for you?'

'I remember—'

'Well, since the best tonic for a pretty young girl is trying on new dresses, I have arranged for a selection to be sent to the house instead. They are hanging in the closet there for you to try on as soon as you feel up to it. Any that you like can be altered to fit, and we'll soon have you looking the bonniest lass in the county.'

Roslyn threw her arms round the older woman. 'Thank you for being so kind to me,' she said huskily.

'Why shouldn't I be? I love you for your own sake, even if you didn't remind me so much of your father. It's not hard to be kind to people we love, Roslyn.'

Roslyn's youth and natural resilience made the horrors of her illness recede rapidly. That night she slept soundly for the first time, with none of the tormented dreams that had so beset her since her arrival in Yorkshire. She awoke refreshed to find a young girl in the room with a jug of washing water, who went to pull back the curtains and told Roslyn her name was Ellen. Her accent was so pronounced Roslyn could barely understand her, but she asked if the girl would help her wash and dress. Ellen stared at her sullenly.

'I was only to bring the water, miss,' she said doggedly. 'Nothing was said about owt else, and me place is in t'kitchen by rights, not waiting on folks!'

To Roslyn, used to having her every whim gratified, the words were nothing short of insulting.

'I wish you to help me,' she said imperiously. The girl glared back.

' 'Tain't me job, miss, and Mrs May will have me hide if I don't get back to t'kitchen. There's towels and soap on t'side.'

She marched out of the room, leaving Roslyn gasping. No servant had ever spoken to her like that before. If this was the way things were conducted in Radcliffe Manor, she considered it very lacking in social graces. Was she not then to have a lady's maid? She stayed exactly where she was for a while, but there was no sign of anyone else approaching. Finally she stepped carefully out of the bed, feeling her head swim a little at being upright, and walked across to the casement window.

She almost reeled back in shock. A marvellous view of the moors, Aunt Hester had told her, seen from the room her father had loved...Roslyn looked out on a wintry scene. The moorland stretched away into the distance. The first snows had lightly powdered the whole countryside while she had been ill, and a bleak white vista met her eyes, undulating skywards until it met overcast greyness. The scene was only broken by the smudgy yellowish outlines of sheep, and the stark black leafless trees that were scattered sparsely across the moorland.

Roslyn pulled the shawl tightly round her shoulders as she shivered. She had never seen snow before, though James had told her of it. It was soft and cold to the touch, but as children he and Thomas had had wonderful games in it, rolling ecstatically down the slippery hillsides and tossing snowballs into each other's faces. The snow made the cheeks glow and the appetite enlarge, James had said nostalgically, but to Roslyn the first sight of it only made her shudder. How could anything be thought exciting that stripped away every sign of colour from the countryside? And how could it ever become green and verdant again she thought in bewilderment.

She moved away from the window. So far she had seen none of the green and pleasant land her father had described. She turned to the wash-stand and after she'd splashed her face and neck and limbs with warm soapy water, she felt fresher.

In the closet she saw the selection of dresses Aunt Hester had ordered. There were several warm ones in rich glowing colours, and others that were more frivolous and suitable for after-noon tea...she thought at once of the wide shady verandah at the Darby mansion, with its fragrance of eucalyptus and frangipani, and the hot dusty air, and swallowed back the lump in her throat.

Her aunt had provided all the garments necessary to a young lady's wardrobe, Roslyn saw with grateful eyes. She pulled on a dress of deep russet wool, which fitted her quite ade-quately, restoring some of the glow to her pale face. She held the others against her eagerly, enjoying the touch of the soft fabrics again after the drab clothes she'd been forced to wear.

It never occurred to her to offer payment for the clothes. She had no money save the English notes James had provided, and she doubted whether they would be enough. In similiar circumstances, James would generously have provided all a distressed relative needed, and Roslyn saw no need to embarrass the Radcliffe's by mentioning money. She might have been less complacent had she heard the conversation between Thomas and his wife when the clothes had been delivered.

'Have you gone mad, woman?' he'd roared. 'This chit arrives from nowhere, and because she's your fancy-man's lass, you think you can run us into debt! I'll have none of it, do you hear? You can send the things back where they came from, and her with them!'

'No, I won't, Thomas.' Hester rarely stood up to him, but in this she was adamant. There was more than an ounce of truth in Thomas's suspicion that she had an added fondness for Roslyn because she was James' daughter, but she was fond of the girl for her own sake too. It was good to have another woman in the house, someone young and pretty...and Hester still had some money of her own in a bank account in York that had been left her by her father. It was hers to do with as she wished, and until now it had been left untouched. She would buy Roslyn's clothes herself...

Her announcement only incensed Thomas the more.

'If you've money to spare, you'd do best to

hand it over to me,' he spluttered. 'Haven't I made it plain enough how things are? We've made a serious loss this year, woman, and if things get any worse, the Lord knows what will happen. One disastrous year of bad weather and crops lost, the sheep dying or rustled and the tenants' cottages falling down about their ears because there's no money for repairs—and you can talk of spending money on some lass who thinks she's too good for the rest of us—'

'Maybe she is,' Hester's face was as red as his. 'She's James' daughter, not yours! And if things are as bad as you say, the small amount of money I have would go nowhere, so I'll do as I please with it.'

Thomas glared at her, his bulbous nose like a beacon in his florid face. 'I think the girl has bewitched you,' he snapped. 'I'll wager Greg won't want the encumbrance of her when he weds the Judd lass, and the sooner that comes about, the better!'

He stumped off, while Hester wilted. It was not often she offered any resistance to her husband's plans. He was a boor and a bully, and her one prayer was that Greg would not be manipulated as easily as she knew herself to have been over the years. Hester hoped desperately Greg would not marry Louise Judd and bring her to Radcliffe Manor. She was a beautiful young woman, but so sophisticated she unnerved the gentle Hester...and besides, she had to admit to a growing hope that there might be someone else on Greg's horizon now. She had not missed the way Roslyn had clung to his hands in her delirium, nor the way Greg was the only one who could calm her when the fever was on her...it would be the culmination of something that should have happened a long time ago. Hers and James' love for each other re-enacted in their children... and she knew her son well enough to realize that the more Thomas pressed for this marriage between Greg and Louise because of the handsome dowry Louise would bring, the more Greg would resist. The thought heartened her.

Hester went to Roslyn's room to find her parading in front of the mirror in the russet-coloured dress, and her face broke into a delighted smile. Her womanly intuition had told her this was the best therapy for a young girl. And maybe when Greg saw how Roslyn was blossoming hourly, her dearest wish would come true. Hester laughed at herself, knowing they were perhaps foolish dreams.

'I feel I've been stagnating up here, Aunt Hester,' Roslyn told her. 'I'm still a little weak, but I want to see everything!'

Hester laughed. 'Then so you shall, my love. But I think you had better confine youself to the house for a few days yet, or the doctor will be on my tail. We don't want to risk a relapse now that the bloom is back on your cheeks.'

'Greg said he'd show me the countryside.' Roslyn could not resist speaking his name, and the extra tinge of colour it brought to her lovely face was not lost on his mother. At least half her desire seemed possible, she thought elatedly. Roslyn was certainly not averse to spending time with Greg, and that was a step in the right direction.

'And I'm sure he will,'Hester replied, determined to make as many opportunities as possible for them to be together. It was partly for their own sakes, because they seemed so ideally suited in strength of personality; partly because of the romantic link with the past and her own stupidity over losing James Darby's love; and partly to thwart her domineering husband's ambition to marry Greg off to the beautiful Louise Judd. 'But first you must become acquainted with your new home, Roslyn. We will do a tour of the manor, but I'm afraid you will see it has a rather faded glory these days. When your father lived here, it was far grander.'

Roslyn saw just what she meant when they
181

toured the rooms of the manor. It was a large, sprawling house, but the carpets were a little thin, and there was a slight air of neglect over everything. Nothing, however, could detract from the joy Roslyn felt at being in the place her father had loved so well, even though it made her own home in Ceylon seem like a palace in comparison.

At least it was warm indoors, with great fires leaping in every room, and the icy chill she'd felt on seeing the snow faded somewhat. Hester's welcome more than made up for Thomas' rebuffs.

By the time the men appeared at the house for dinner that evening, Roslyn's natural high spirits were fast returning. She still wore the russet dress on Hester's advice, needing its warmth after her illness, but she pinned back the neckline to reveal her golden throat and the ruby pendant in its glowing setting. Her dark hair was brushed to a gleaming sheen, curling in little tendrils around her face. She looked forward eagerly to seeing Greg again, and to see by his eyes that he appreciated the fact that she was no little scruff as he had first thought.

But he would know all about her womanly shape, she thought suddenly, as she sat near the fire in the drawing-room sipping a pre-dinner sherry with her aunt. Her cheeks warmed still more as she remembered the intimate moments they had already shared. She had lain in his arms in his bed, albeit in bewilderment and grief at Nadja's death...she had sat, numb and trembling in the bathtub, and let his hands caress her with a washing-cloth...they had been more intimate than two unwed people should ever be, and the shameful truth of it all was that she had enjoyed it. Despite the circumstances in which the intimacies had happened, there had been a need in her that cried out to Greg. A longing for his arms and his touch...and more, much more. She wanted all of him...

A sudden searing memory of the fumbling agony of her ravishing at Bahu's house swept into her mind, making her hand jerk a little as she held the sherry glass to her lips. But it would not always be like that, she thought desperately. Nadja had assured her that when a woman's body was surrendered in love, it was the most beautiful thing on earth. To possess and be possessed...Greg would never be so brutal. Her breathing quickened as the immodest thoughts came and went with sweet savage longing. When he came into the room she could hardly bear to look at him, for fear he would read everything in her face.

She missed the little shock that ran over his rugged features as he took in this changed young woman with glowing eyes and cheeks, every lithe line of her perfectly curved body silhouetted against the firelight. At that moment she was the most exquisite thing Greg had seen in his life, and desire ran through him like a flame. The ruby glowed at her throat, above those glorious breasts that had hardened beneath his hands in such delightful response. The proud Darby head sat above those elegant shoulders, framed by her silky dark hair. Greg remembered how that dark hair had looked, fanned out across the whiteness of her pillows when she had thrashed about in her delirium, calling his name...wanting only him, it had seemed. He felt a raging need to lie with her, to see that lovely face gazing up at him knowingly, not just in the fever of delirium. He wanted her so badly that it stunned him. Lust had driven men wild, but he had never expected to be driven by desire here in his own house, by the daughter of his father's old adversary.

CHAPTER 9

Greg masked his emotions by resorting to his previous coldness towards her. Roslyn was bewildered at his apparent change of attitude. He was acting the way he had when he first met her—suspicious and arrogant. It angered and humiliated her. She turned instead to Francis at the dinner table, who seemed only too eager to hear about her life in Ceylon. His mother sat back and let the two of them prattle on, her own interest conveniently satisfied, while Thomas glowered through the meal and said little.

'And you had servants waiting on you, I suppose?' His fresh face smiled across the candlelit table at his lovely young cousin. Roslyn laughed. She was beginning to sparkle at this young man's obvious admiration, despite her chagrin over Greg.

'Of course! I didn't have to do a thing for myself—'

'You'll find it very different here, my lass,' Thomas grunted. 'We don't go in for fancy maids and stuff in Yorkshire.'

'I expected to find it different, Uncle,' she said coolly. 'I hardly expected to be able to bask in the sunshine every day, nor to be entertained by lavish spectacles of bejewelled elephants parading in the streets, nor to find the colour and the beauty of lush plantations and soaring mountains in the wilds of Yorkshire!'

Thomas Radcliffe's face went a dull puce colour.

'I'm beginning to wonder what the blazes you came here for at all, if it's so unattractive,' he roared out. 'Why didn't you stay with your blasted elephants and all t'heathen nonsense if it meant so much to you?'

Roslyn felt her temper rising, but before she could snap back, Hester spoke quickly.

'Thomas, you know very well why Roslyn left Ceylon. I did not think even you could be so heartless as to ask her such a thing!'

'Oh aye, her father snuffed it,' he retorted. Roslyn flinched at the crudity of the man, but she refused to let him bait her further. She ignored him and, eyes alight, she continued her conversation with Francis. '...Everything glitters and glows. On the back of the leading elephant there is a golden casket containing the replica of the right eye-tooth of Buddha...'

'No more of this!' Thomas hollered from the head of the table. His fist thumped down on the table, rocking the wine glasses. 'By God I'll hear no more of this heathen idolatry here. This is a God-fearing house, young woman, and I'll thank you to remember it while you remain under my roof.'

He gulped his wine noisily. Roslyn's lips compressed. For a few moments she had let her thoughts roam delightfully into the past, revelling in scenes that had once been so dear and familiar. She wouldn't give this oaf the satisfaction of letting him see he could upset her.

'Naturally my father and I respected the culture of the people in whose land we lived,' she spoke witheringly, as if someone of Thomas Radcliffe's boorishness could not be expected to understand. 'But we both remained as Christian as anyone here, I have no doubt.'

And a sight more charitable, she thought, if her uncle was anything to judge by. Aunt Hester, she allowed, was the gentlest of persons...

'Leave it, Father,' Greg said tetchily. 'You'll bring on an attack of apoplexy, and we'll end up with another invalid in the house.'

Thomas turned his glaring attentions to his elder son.

'I'll give you a run for your money any day, lad. I'm beginning to wonder what kind of son I've spawned in you lately. The sooner you wed the Judd lass and prove your manhood the better. A string of grandsons to carry on the Radcliffe name would be more in keeping than namby-pambying to James Darby's daughter.'

Roslyn's heart jolted. This was the first time she had heard any reference to another girl in Greg's life. She had never even considered it, though she should have done. It was impossible that a passionate man like Greg should not have had women in his life...but to hear Thomas refer to a wedding made the colour blanch from her face. It flooded back as she heard Greg's angry reply. Whatever his father thought, there was nothing of the dandy about him.

'I'll wed when I choose, and whom I choose,' he said grimly. 'And the more you push me towards it, the more I'll resist. The farm can fall down round our ears before I'll marry just to please you—'

'And so it will if some money's not forthcoming from somewhere,' Thomas roared. 'I'd send Francis a'courting the lass if I didn't know from her own father's lips she's only too willing to tie the knot with you. I don't know what's wrong with you. When I was a lad I'd have been only too eager to bed a comely beauty like yon Louise. Are you lacking in lust?'

'I'm not lacking in table manners,' Greg said

coldly. His face was tight with fury at his father's verbal attack, but he held himself in check. It was appalling and humiliating that Roslyn should witness his father's coarseness so soon. It was all the more infuriating that Francis should sit silently gloating that the attack was not directed at him...

Thomas scraped his chair away from the table as soon as he had finished eating without waiting for the rest of them. He stumped off to his study, saying he had work to do, and the atmosphere in the dining-room relaxed considerably with his departure.

'You must forgive him, Roslyn dear,' Hester began at once. 'He has many problems on his mind—'

'You forgive too much, Mother,' Greg interrupted. 'He's a brute and a boor, and as for bringing a bride into this house—one hour in his company and she'd be put off for life!'

'It hasn't put off the lovely Louise, by all accounts,' Francis said mildly. 'Why don't you put Father out of his misery and get on with it, Greg? Her father's money would put the farm soundly back on its feet again, and we'd have less of his tantrums to endure.'

Roslyn became more wretched by the minute at being an unwilling listener to this family talk. And more and more jealous of the unknown Louise Judd, who was apparently not only a great beauty, but one whose dowry would restore Radcliffe Manor to its former grandeur. A formidable rival, she thought, for all that Greg seemed so opposed to the idea. That fact was the one small consolation in an otherwise uneasy mealtime. Though how much of Greg's opposition was due to his father's insistence, she dared not imagine. When they had all finished, they retired to the drawing-room to drink coffee and pretend Thomas' unpleasantness had never happened.

'And is that really a prince's ruby, Roslyn?' Francis' words startled her as he sat down beside her on the sofa. His eyes seemed to be mesmerized by the gem, as they had been during the meal, she now realized. Involuntarily her hands went to it, and she glanced towards Greg. Surely he had not told them...?

'I'm afraid your delirium made you reveal many things you never intended,' he stated. 'No one could doubt the truth of your grim experiences in fleeing from Ceylon when it was told with such frenzy, and the tale of the ruby was just one thing that seemed to prey on your mind.'

And the others...? Oh, surely she had not babbled on about the rape...her heart thudded painfully in her chest, and her skin prickled as if all her nerves were suddenly awakened. Surely she could not have betrayed her secret horror...she realized Francis was still waiting for her reply, his hand reaching out for her permission to hold the jewel for a moment. She held it away from her throat for his perusal.

'It's perfect,' he breathed. 'But no more perfect than the setting of your throat, Roslyn. You complement each other.'

The unexpected compliment surprised and pleased her. She thanked Francis with an unconsciously coquettish prettiness.

His gentleness soothed her ruffled feelings, and as he urged her to tell him more coherently about the circumstances surrounding her father's possession of the ruby, she warmed towards him still more. His eyes were bright with interest and excitement as he listened. Clearly the distant world of India and Ceylon was as fascinating to Francis as it had once been to her father, Roslyn saw with amusement, and a certain affection. How James would have loved to see this spark in his kinsman's eyes!

'And you truly believe it has magical powers?' Francis persisted. 'It is hard for a Yorkshireman to credit.'

'My father believed it, and so do I,' she said simply. 'And you could not live in the East as

191

long as we did without knowing all things are possible. Even beneath your snow that seemingly kills the earth, new life will grow again with the coming of spring. If you believe this and know it to be true, why doubt the power of the stones of the earth?'

The quiet dignity of the little speech obviously impressed Francis and his mother. Greg spoke brusquely.

'There's more need to be thinking of the vagaries of the weather in the north of England than to be bothering with mysteries. If crops fail and sheep die, it's hard work and a supply of brass that's needed to put things right again, not magic!'

Roslyn flushed. Somehow she always managed to upset him without meaning to.

'I don't know what you mean by brass,' she told him.

Francis gave a hoot of laughter that his brother's barb had been wasted.

'He means money, Roslyn! The stuff he'd be bringing into the house if he were to do as Father wishes and make Louise Judd his bride! Though I think Miss Judd must look to her laurels now we've a lovely new cousin around the place.'

If she had any money she would gladly pour it into Greg's lap, Roslyn thought passionately

...she glanced up at his dark, angry face.

'You talk as much rubbish as Father sometimes, Francis,' he snapped. 'And I'd advise *you* not to talk so patronizingly when he's around, Roslyn. He won't take kindly to such behaviour from someone living on his charity.'

'It wasn't meant to sound like that at all,' she said hotly. 'As for living on charity' her pride stung at his words. But it was perfectly true. She was beholden to this famiy now, and she would have to bite her tongue when she was provoked, no matter how much it galled her. She suddenly felt very tired.

She turned to Hester. 'Would you mind if I retire early, Aunt Hester? I'm beginning to feel the effects of my first day up.'

'Of course, my love,' she said at once. 'It's been a long day for you. Can you find your way to your room?'

'I'll show her,' Francis said at once, and she had no choice but to allow him to open the door for her, though she would much rather it had been Greg. As it was, the elder brother bade her a rather distant goodnight and remained in the drawing-room with his mother. She could easily have found her room by herself, Roslyn thought, but if Francis wanted to act the gallant she could hardly object. And as he opened her door with a flourish, she smiled her thanks. To her surprise he caught hold of her hands. 'You cannot dazzle me with a smile like that without my claiming a cousinly kiss, sweet Roslyn!' he said lightly, and then swiftly clasped her in his arms and pressed his mouth to hers. It was an exuberant rather than passionate kiss, and he released her almost at once, his face flushed as if with triumph. The pressure of his embrace had pressed the ruby against her skin, the gold setting like little needlepoints against her soft flesh, but she smiled good-humouredly, knowing he had meant no offence.

'Goodnight, Francis!' she said deliberately, and closed her bedroom door behind her, the smile still on her face.

He reminded her so much of the young officers she and her father had known. Lightweight and frothy, compared with the Greg Radcliffes of this world...had she seen the smile on the face of Greg's brother as he stood motionless outside her closed door for a moment longer, she might have questioned her assessment of him. Greg had always had so much, to Francis' eyes. The elder son, inheriting the manor, always the respected one, no matter how the family fortunes declined.

He, Francis, would always come off second best. The frivolous manner he had adopted over the years was no more than a facade and now a chance to score unbelievably over his brother had presented itself in the delicious shape of Miss Roslyn Darby. A luscious beauty comparable to all the Louise Judds in the country, and one with a fortune around her neck...

There was a clean nightgown on Roslyn's bed, for which she was grateful to Hester. She accepted now that there would be no one to help her undress, no lady's maid. She paused in her unfastening of her dress to consider Greg's words. *Did* she think herself superior to them? Did she speak patronizingly? Surely not! She was as unable to change her own background as he was, and having servants around to attend to her every wish had been perfectly normal to her. He had no right to make her feel so guilty.

She slid between the cold sheets. The remnants of the fire burned low in the hearth now, and she blew out her lamp. How many nights and days had she lain in this bed, she wondered, tossing and turning, burning up with fever and clinging to the hand of whoever was sitting at her bedside? Clinging to Greg's hand and babbling out her innermost secrets...

Had she told him of her ravishment? The agony that she had done so gnawed away at her.

She couldn't bear him to know of it. It degraded her still more to think she may have described it in horrifying detail to him of all people. What would he have thought of her? The shame was hers, no matter how helpless she had been.

She drifted into a dream-filled sleep. A golden fantasy world where she was surrounded by loving attention as she had been in Ceylon. Where days were blue-hazed and shimmering with heat, and the sensuous scents of exotic flowers and trees hung heavy on the air. Where dusky-skinned dancing girls teased and tantalized with their sinuous grace as their bodies writhed invitingly.

The fantasy shifted. Roslyn was no longer watching from the outside. She was part of the dancing, her golden body sheathed in gossamer blue silk, jewels in her nose and in her navel, glittering gold braid outlining the silken sari in which she danced enticingly and erotically. The gilt bangles on her wrists and ankles shone in the leaping firelight almost as brightly as the desire in Greg Radcliffe's eyes as he watched.

Roslyn's hair was a tumbled cloud about her shoulders. She could feel its softness caressing them as she moved about the carpeted room on bare feet, performing movements intended to arouse the senses, movements she was unaware she knew. Her belly rotated erotically toward's Greg's receptive gaze, the jewel in her navel gleaming and retreating into its delicious hiding-place as she moved. She performed a dance of love solely for his eyes, with all the abandonment of the harem, twisting and sway-ing, unconsciously mimicking the voluptuous breast-shaking of the Kandy whore who had enticed her father.

The dream held her in a fever of desire. She was no longer Miss Roslyn Darby, the lovely virginal heiress to the Darby tea estate. She was a wanton, enacting out the rites of love in the dance, discovering an excitement that was tak-ing her to the point of ecstasy with the promise of what was to come in Greg's responsive eyes. His sensual mouth was parted, watching her every movmement as if he could not have enough of her. His eyes hungered for her, and she gloried in the knowledge. She teased him with her fingertips as she passed, running them through his unruly dark hair. She teased him with her breasts, thrusting them close to his face and moving slowly from side to side with an inviting smile on her shining lips. She teased him with her golden limbs, stroking her fingers lightly, one bare foot resting on his knee for a moment, stroking all the way up to where the gossamer silk caressed the dark triangle of downy hair guarding her well of delight. Nadja's phrase was so perfect, her thoughts whirled rapturously as she touched Greg's mouth with her lips in a soft kiss...and the moment was almost here...she could see the impatience in his eyes, and with a little laugh of delight she placed the end of the sari in his hand and twirled away from him...

The silk garment unwrapped itself from her lovely body and fell in a shimmering heap on the carpet. Roslyn stood naked in front of him, her golden skin glistening with the exertion of the dance, her breasts heaving. Desire ran through her like a flame as Greg discarded his clothes with feverish eagerness. Her breath caught in her throat as she looked at his beautiful muscular body. She had never seen a man's body before...the oaf who had ravished her had been mercifully cloaked in darkness, so that she looked at the shape of her lover with fascinated eyes; at the broad shoulders and the matted dark hair covering his wide chest; the dipping waist and firm belly...her gaze ran downwards, and a pulse beat rapidly in her perfumed throat. He moved with excrutiating slowness towards her, as if to tantalize her the way she had tantalized him with her dancing. It seemed as if he would never reach her. The short distance between them seemed to be an endless void he could not cross.

Roslyn's arms stretched out towards Greg, welcoming him with the promise of a night of passion. Their fingertips were almost touching ...the heat of the leaping flames in the hearth matched the fire of her longing, but still Greg did not touch her. It was becoming more than she could bear. She was consumed with a frustrated anguish. There was a throbbing in her temples like the insistent beating of distant drums...the flames were leaping higher as she twisted her head back and forth in mute entreaty. She could not speak...the flames were enveloping her. She could feel their tingling caresses burning her soft skin, and smell the acrid stench of the tea bushes...

Suddenly Roslyn was convulsively awake. She lay shivering in her bed at Radcliffe Manor, bathed in sweat as the dream became a nightmare, with only the continuing moan of the wind across the Yorkshire moors to break the silence. There was no soft-lit carpeted room in which she danced like a concubine for a man's pleasure; no gossamer garments and glittering enticements that paled beside the sight of her own naked body; there was no Greg...

Her face was suffused with colour as the wantonness of the remembered dream filled her mind. That it had ended with the sharp pain of her last memories of her beloved home was smothered in the memory of Greg and his love-making. She tried in vain to push away the memory of her dream-Greg, his arms reaching out to take her in exquisite consummation; and of herself, yearningly ready for the fulfilment his magnificent body would give her...and denied it.

The next time she awoke it was morning. She had been left in peace to sleep, for there were sounds of activity outside and in the house. Someone had been to her room with a jug of water which was now lukewarm, and she assumed it to be Ellen, the kitchen-maid whose job was not to wait on t'likes o' *her*. She reached beneath her pillow where she placed the ruby pendant in a little leather bag each night and once she had attended to her toilet, she fastened it round her neck. She was feeling stronger, and eager to see this new countryside that was now her home, although she felt sure she would be unable to enjoy its winter cold.

Dressed in another of the garments Aunt Hester had provided so generously, a blue woollen dress with flattering looped hipline, she found her way downstairs and to the dining-room where her aunt still lingered over her breakfast. She smiled at Roslyn at once and welcomed her to the table. There was a choice of mushrooms and bacon, or porridge oats, followed by thick farmhouse toast and home-made preserves. Roslyn was now quite raven-ous, and she decided on the mushrooms and bacon.

'May I take a walk this morning, Aunt Hester?'

'Of course, my love. You're to do just as you like. You'll need some strong boots on your feet and a cloak though. You can use my things, as I think our feet are about the same size. If not, we must stuff the toes of the boots with scrim-cloth until we can get you some suitable ones.'

When Roslyn tried to express her gratitude, Hester patted her hand.

'You deserve everything I choose to give, dear,' she said quietly. 'And since I read your father's letter, it pleases me more than ever to know I can care for his daughter. We both made stupid mistakes, Roslyn, even though in James' case the outcome was a life as exciting as he would have wished. But now that you and I are together, you must let me indulge myself in caring for you as if you were my daughter too.'

Roslyn knew that the love Hester had once

felt for her father still burned brightly. She was touched by it, but smiled ruefully.

'I'm afraid Uncle Thomas was not so pleased to read his letter from Father!'

Aunt Hester gave a low chuckle. 'He was not! They were always rivals, and I don't think Thomas ever forgave James for being everything he was not. Handsome, tall, full of ambition and not afraid to go out and seek his fortune...although I'm not disclaiming any of the blame for marrying Thomas. He could be quite persuasive when he chose to be, for all his boorishness. I suppose it struck a chord of vanity in me.' She gave an elaborate sigh.

'You must have been very unhappy at times,' Roslyn said in swift sympathy.

'Yes.' There was no denial. 'And your presence has stirred up a lot of memories, my dear. And for Thomas to learn that James had been a wealthy man, was a bitter pill for him to swallow. But that won't harm him!' She looked deep into Roslyn's blue eyes. 'If there is any advice I would give you as a mother, Roslyn, it is to be very sure you do not marry the wrong man...Goodness me, how solemn we are at such an hour! Finish your breakfast, dear, and I'll ring for some fresh tea.'

Later, suitably dressed in a warm plaid cloak and Hester's boots, Roslyn strode outside into the thin December sunlight for her first taste of Yorkshire winds. They bit into her cheeks and whipped up a glowing colour. Her feet crunched on the unfamiliar substance beneath them, and she was intrigued to look back at the house and see the trail of footprints in the snow behind her.

The house was lit by the morning sunlight now, and Roslyn saw that it had a gaunt grey beauty with the whiteness of the moors and hills surrounding its weathered stone, the smoke spiralling from its chimneys, the tiny panes of glass in the windows fired to red and gold by the sun's rays. It would never compare with the white splendour of the Darby mansion in its lush green setting, with the brightly-coloured tea-pickers like brilliant birds of paradise among the tiered tea bushes. But it had a strength about it that was strangely comforting...

'You're the bonniest sight I've seen on this wintry day,' a voice suddenly startled her. She had walked around the house to the out-buildings spread around the rear. Francis lounged against the doorway of a barn, his eyes smiling at her. In his arms he held a tiny lamb. Roslyn gave a little cry of pleasure at seeing the fluffy animal, and slithered to him across the snowy ground.

'Oh, he's so sweet,' she breathed as she put out one finger to touch the woolly creature.

'I'd exchange his paltry life for mine any day if it touched such a spark in you, Cousin!'

Roslyn blushed at his teasing. And yet she couldn't deny that it was flattering to know he was flirting with her. She knew she made a pretty sight against the snowy background, in the warm plaid cloak, her dark hair untamed and loose. She looked at Francis provocatively beneath the fringe of her dark lashes.

'Why is his life paltry?' she queried. 'He looks cosy enough there.'

Francis' smile widened. In the dimness of the barn door he looked startlingly like Greg, Roslyn thought, with a catch in her throat.

'I'd like to think you were referring to the fact that he's held in my arms! Do you dare to change places with him?'

Roslyn laughed. 'You talk such nonsense, Francis,' she echoed Greg's comment to his brother, but her voice was teasing. 'Tell me now, what's wrong with this baby?' She stroked the lamb's muzzle, unaware how the sight of her gentle movements stirred the young man.

'He's born out o'season,' he told her, 'and can't stand up to the cold. Father and Greg would have left him to die on the hillside, but it's doing no harm to bring him in here and let it happen in comfort.'

Roslyn gaped at him in horror. She hadn't thought Greg capable of such cruelty as to leave this tiny creature to die in the snow. Francis realized his own advantage, in her protest.

'They'll tell you it's the way of things on a farm,' he said carelessly. 'And they're no doubt right. If an animal can't survive on its own, its expendible. Do you want to come in and see how I feed it?'

Roslyn slipped inside the comparative warmth of the barn. It smelled musty with winter hay and animal scents. She watched as Francis picked up a bottle with a teat on the end and forced it into the lamb's mouth. It seemed too weak to suck, and the milk dribbled over Francis' hand.

'Can I try?' Roslyn asked. She sat down in the soft hay while he placed the lamb in her lap and handed her the bottle. But she didn't have the heart to force the teat into the unwilling mouth, and Francis knelt beside her to guide it.

'Come on, baby,' she crooned softly. 'You'll never grow big and strong if you don't take your milk!'

As if it understood what she said, the lamb gave a feeble pull at the teat for a few seconds, and Roslyn glanced at Francis in triumph. Her eyes and cheeks glowed with pleasure as she felt the nestling warmth of the scrawny lamb against her. Francis' desire heightened. He touched a tendril of the tousled dark hair as it fell over Roslyn's face.

'You're like a woman with a bairn,' he breathed close to her cheek. 'But I think you'd have no need for feeding bottles if it was your own bairn, my bonny Roslyn.'

His gaze roamed leisurely over her shape, concealed behind the plaid cloak, but imprinted sharply in his mind. He had felt the warmth of those luscious curves pressed against him as he pulled her laughingly into his arms last night, and the lust to know them more intimately was quickening his blood. But he realized he had gone too fast when he saw the look of shock in her eyes. She'd have been even more shocked had she but known how his mind was stripping away the winter garments she wore; picturing her with an infant of her own pressed rapturously to her breasts...

'I'm known for my appalling taste in compliments at times, Roslyn,' he said lightly by way of apology. 'Mother calls it the hazards of living too closely to animals, but I do assure you it was not intended to be disrespectful. On the contrary! Now, I think we'd best lay this little charmer down to sleep.'

'Have you been initiated into the delights of snowballing yet?'

As he had intended, his quick tongue and change of subject covered up the brief affrontery she had felt.

'I have not—'

'Then it's time you were.' He had put the lamb down on the hay and was pulling her to her feet, careful not to let the moment seem more than friendly. Once outside the barn in the crisp air, he began scooping up light handfuls of snow and tossing them at her cloak. She ducked involuntarily, and then the exuberance of the game touched her, and she bent to pick up some of the powder herself.

'It has such an odd texture!'

'If you hold it too long it will start to melt,' Francis laughed. 'Throw it! Come on!'

She flung the handful of snow straight at him, catching him on the side of the head. He laughed again, and scooped up some more. Suddenly Roslyn felt light-hearted, remembering her father's tales of his young days. This was how it must have been for him and Thomas, before the ugliness of rivalry had driven them apart. She felt the joy of childhood as a ball of snow exploded with a little sting against her cheek, and seconds later she was hurling the snow as recklessly as Francis, laughing and skidding as it clung to her tumbled hair and glistened on her skin. She was exhilarated for the first time in what seemed a nightmarish period of her life, and when she slid ungracefully to the ground with a little squeal as her feet lost their grip, Francis hauled her up laughingly, holding her close in his arms. Before she could stop him he'd pressed a second kiss on her lips, and this time she could not mistake his passion. She was unable to push him away for minutes that seemed like an eternity. The strength of him pressing the pendant deeper into her skin, hurting her as she struggled.

'Don't tell me you begrudge me my prize for being the winner in our little game?' he said at last when he held her away from him. His eyes sparkled, and Roslyn felt a shiver of unease run through her. Francis was light and charming, but he could be passionate and demanding when he chose, and she had a suspicion that this had been more than a little game to him. She suspected it had been designed for this purpose...to end with her held captive in his arms as his so-called 'prize'...

'You're not paid to indulge in games,' Greg's cold voice spoke sharply from the corner of the barn. Francis whirled angrily, his face a dull red at being caught dallying. Roslyn too felt her face go brilliant. Did Greg think she was a party to this? It would seem so, by the look on his face as his gaze took in her dishevelled appearance, with the scattering of snow clinging to her. 'And you'd do better to get inside by the fire, Roslyn, unless you want to be back in bed for another week. We've enough to do here without pampering to such foolishness. You've made a remarkable recovery from your illness, it would seem.'

He spoke as if he thought she had wanted to languish her time in bed in a delirium, Roslyn thought furiously. As if it had been a ruse to acquire the attention she was used to. He had absolutely no sensitivity. She had dreamed of him all these years, and he turned out to be as boorish as his father. She flounced away from him with as much dignity as was possible with her feet sliding away from her in the snow that was beginning a slow thaw. But if she had looked back, she'd have seen that Greg was more interested in lecturing his brother on the senselessness of trying to keep a sickly lamb alive when there was more need to keep a weather-eye open for the strong ones in danger from the sheep-rustlers plaguing the area.

'And I'll thank you to keep your mind on the farm and away from Roslyn,' Greg snapped as an afterthought. Francis leaned against the frame of the barn and spoke tauntingly.

'Don't tell me you've aspirations there yourself, Greg! I'd have thought the lovely Louise would have kept you busy enough. Anyway, what's it to you if I do take a fancy to our delectable little cousin? I might even marry her, make an honest woman of her if you and Father consider it so necessary,' he sneered. 'Though the game beneath the bedsheets is all the same whether there's a ring on the girl's finger or not, and a shade more exciting without it!'

'It's a pity the young ladies you fawn up to can't listen to some of your gutter talk,' Greg said icily. 'You disgust me with your foppish charm in public and your crudity at heart...'

'However nobody knows that but you, do they, dear Greg?' Francis scoffed. 'And don't try dropping hints. Nobody would believe you. I haven't met the young lady yet whose head I can't turn, and well you know it. God knows what Louise sees in *you*, with your dull ways and your mind always thinking about business. You should try a few more frivolous diversions occasionally, as I do!'

Greg looked for a minute as if he would hit him, but he knew from past experience that was why Fracis goaded him this way. And he wasn't worth the effort...they had moved inside the barn to conduct this interview in privacy, and Greg looked down instead at the still little body lying in the hay.

'Divert yourself by burying your pet,' he said coldly. 'As I predicted, it's dead.'

CHAPTER 10

The brief snowfall vanished as quickly as it had come, but to Roslyn the Yorkshire countryside continued bleak and cold. Indoors, she sat as close to the fires as possible, and Hester insisted on heaping more logs on them to ensure that Roslyn was warm enough...

'Do you think we're made of brass, woman?' Thomas would roar time and again.

'Roslyn needs the warmth...'

'Roslyn! Roslyn! The whole house seems to revolve round the chit! This is my house, and I say what's to do in it...'

'Not for much longer,' Hester said mildly as he stamped out, complaining viciously that the heat and woodsmoke were choking him in his own parlour. She gave Roslyn a half-smile at her questioning look. 'The manor and farm and all the estate becomes Greg's on his twenty-fifth birthday, dear, and there's not a thing Thomas can do about it. As the day draws nearer, he becomes even more irascible, but it's as inevitable as breathing. At the turn of the year when Greg attains his birthday, Thomas may as well shout to the moon for all the authority he'll hold around here.'

'He's not the kind of man to hand over the reins as easily as that, is he?' Roslyn had come to know her uncle well in the weeks she had been at Radcliffe Manor, and Aunt Hester gave a rueful laugh.

'He'll fight tooth and nail to remain the master here,' she agreed. 'But the inheritance goes back generations, and the eldest son always assumes the responsibilities of the manor on his twenty-fifth birthday, and everyone knows it, the farm labourers, the manager, stable-lads.'

She could not hide the satisfaction in her voice, and Roslyn guessed there had been many times when Thomas Radcliffe had made himself objectionable to his workers. The fact that Greg was the new owner would make no difference to the way his father spoke to his family though. But it meant that Greg would be even more determined to restore the manor to its former glory, Roslyn thought uneasily, and that maybe the idea of making a rich marriage would not be so abhorrent to him if he went into it on his own account and not because his father was pushing him towards it.

'Why the frown, my dear? I assure you that Greg being the master will make no difference whatsoever to your being here...'

'It's not that,' Roslyn said quickly. Her lovely face was flushed, she knew, and she hoped her aunt would think it the heat from the fire. She should really protect her skin with a hand-cream as did her aunt at times, but the warmth of it was so delicious on her cheeks.

'I was wondering about the young lady Uncle Thomas has mentioned several times, Aunt Hester.' She tried to sound casual even though her heart was thumping. It would not do to show too much interest. She had been somewhat heartened that the young lady had not come calling since she had been in Yorkshire, and neither had Greg made any journeys to York to visit her. Surely he would have done so if he had really been enamoured of her? Roslyn could not imagine a bold young man of Greg's disposition being content to stay away so long from a young lady he courted...

'Louise and her family always winter abroad,' Aunt Hester dashed any such fond hopes instantly. 'They left for the South of France shortly before you arrived, Roslyn, and will return in the middle of February.'

Roslyn knew a small feeling of relief that the young lady Thomas wanted for a daughter-in-law was out of the country for another two months. She had no wish to see the rich sophisticate gazing up into Greg's eyes. She felt a stab of jealousy run through her at the thought of the unknown Louise Judd. She knew it was ridiculous, but it was undeniable. She had thought of Greg as hers for so long it was still a shock to think there was someone else who could claim his attentions...someone who had known him far longer than had Roslyn herself.

And the love that had been a dream in her heart for so long was proving to be as deep in reality as in her fantasies...Greg Radcliffe was even more dynamic than she had dreamed, more aggressively masculine and capable of making her forgot all the decorum of being a genteel young lady. She wondered if he ever guessed how her heart sang when he came near, but she thought not. She kept herself too rigidly in check to betray the wild feelings, surging through her at his touch or his glance.

She gave a small start as the object of her thoughts came stomping into the room, kicking off the clods of mud sticking to his leather boots and ignoring his mother's grumbling admonitions as she rang for a servant to clean up the mess.

'I've no time for fussing over a bit of mud, Mother,' he brushed aside her words. 'I've called for a glass of hot punch before I make the rounds of the cottages and hear the complaints, since Father chooses not to do it. It'll be my responsibility soon enough, so I may as well hear the worst of it first-hand. I'll not have much comfort for them, though I fancy they'll get more sympathy from me than they would from him.'

Aunt Hester decided she and Roslyn would have some hot punch as well. She looked thoughtfully at her son, his handsome face rugged with the glow from the biting wind outside, his dark hair ruffled appealingly on his collar. Why couldn't he see what was so plain to Hester herself, she wondered? These two were made for each other.

'Why not take Roslyn with you this morning, Greg? She's seen the grounds and the house, but she has no idea of the extent of the farm and the estate yet. It'll not be too cold for her if she wraps up warmly and you take the trap—'

'I'm too busy to spend the day showing visitors around,' he said shortly. 'I can get

215

round quicker on horseback—"

'I've no wish to be a nuisance to you, Greg,' Roslyn said stiffly. 'If it interests you, I'm quite able to ride. But I assure you, I'm quite content to sit by the fire with your mother.'

He seemed unsure whether it was meant to be a rebuff or not. It merely irritated him, as she had the knack of doing. Perversely, he downed the hot punch in one great swallow and got to his feet.

'Never let it be said that the Radcliffes fell short of what the Darbys are used to,' he snapped. 'Be ready in five minutes and I'll have the trap brought to the front of the house. If Mother thinks you should see the cottages then by thunder, you had better see them!'

He banged the door behind him, and Roslyn heard her aunt give a low chuckle. She dared not stop to ask what was so amusing, but ran upstairs to pull on her long leather boots and the thick cloak her aunt had given her, tying a woollen scarf round her head and neck.

Those two were so predictable, Hester was thinking gleefully to herself. She had seen the signs from the beginning, and prayed that she had been right. They were both passionate, impulsive, quick to take offence and quick to rise to any bait that was offered them. They would have the most glorious fights...and the most rapturous reconciliations...but she was letting her hopes and her imagination run away with her. Suffice it to say that she was well satisfied by the fact that neither Greg nor Roslyn seemed unaware of the other. That at least was a beginning.

Roslyn sat beside Greg in the narrow trap, a rug tucked firmly round her waist and legs to keep out the cold winds. She sat stiffly, as if completely oblivious to the fact that his thigh was pressed necessarily close to hers, and that she could feel the warmth of his body at every point of contact between them. That he considered this afternoon's excursion an intrusion on his working time made her frequent apologies to him more exaggeratedly formal, and his acceptance of them ever more frigid. She must have apologized five times in as many minutes, Roslyn thought, with a surge of something like hysterical amusement as Greg flicked at the horse's reins and snapped out his commands like a general mustering his troops. It was so ludicrous that she gave a nervous laugh as the trap lurched forward over a rut in the ground and she was forced to clutch at Greg's arm to stop herself hurtling out.

'My goodness, but the Yorkshire roadways are as uneven as they were in Ceylon,' she said lightly. Greg looked at her darkly from beneath his bushy brows.

'Don't tell me you've found something here that doesn't compare unfavourably with Ceylon!' His voice was heavy with sarcasm, the accent more pronounced as always when he was being particularly caustic. Roslyn flushed.

'Why must you always take everything I say to be critical?' she cried out in frustration. 'I hate it when you're so unkind to me!'

Greg looked at her derisively.

'I'm so sorry, my lady. I was forgetting you're used to servants wiping your feet. I apologize for the state of the roads and the mist on the moors, and the fact that you had a rude awakening when you saw the poor state of Radcliffe Manor, when no doubt you'd been expecting the proverbial fatted calf to be waiting for you after your father's romantic tales! If he thought so damn much of the place, why did he go off and leave it!'

'You should know that!' Roslyn whipped back at him, high spots of colour rising in her cheeks. 'I'm sure your father has been unable to resist crowing over the years how he stole your mother away from mine—'

Greg's laugh was grating.

'Stole her indeed! Are you implying that my mother has no will of her own? That's a fine way to refer to the lady who defends you so prettily, and spends her own money on seeing you clothed and fed. Is that the woman you choose to scoff at, Roslyn Darby?'

She was overcome with embarrassment.

'You're twisting my words,' she said angrily. 'I love your mother as if she were my own. It's not her I scoff at.' She stopped. Because *he* was constantly ill-mannered, was no reason for her to mouth insults against Thomas Radcliffe. She realized Greg assumed her words were directed at himself when he jerked the horse's reins and brought the trap to a halt, so quickly she felt herself lurch forward. And then both his hands were gripping her arms as he glared into her eyes, his own dark and glittering with cold fury.

'And why should you scoff at me, may I ask? I did not have to travel all the way to London to collect you, Miss Darby. I did not have to agree to your coming here—' as her mouth opened to speak, he rushed on. 'Oh aye, to all intents and purposes Radcliffe Manor still belongs to my father, but not for much longer. And no doubt my mother's soft memories of her one-time lover would have made her beseech me to let you come. But in the end it all came down to me, since we can discount Francis' opinion. *I* chose to collect the unkempt-looking baggage who had landed on our shores uninvited and unwanted, and *I* choose whether she stays or goes. I hope I make myself clear, and I ask again—why should *you* scoff at *me*?'

Roslyn felt the breath tightening in her chest as she glowered back at him. Her breasts heaved with the effort not to wrench her arms away from his imprisoning grip and beat at his body like an enraged animal. It would be useless to try, because he held her in a grip of iron, and she knew there would be bruises on her soft golden flesh where his fingers pressed her so tightly. Since she could not attack him physically, she did so verbally.

'You are without doubt the most arrogant, egotistical man I have ever met.' She almost spat the words at him. 'How dare you speak to me that way? My father was worth ten of yours, and how your poor mother has put up with him all these years is a mystery to me. And to have a son as unbearably self-opinionated as you, into the bargain! She must have been truly thankful for a second son who did not think a Yorkshire farmer was almost as divine a being as the Almighty! Do you treat every young lady of your acquaintance to this arrogance? Is that the way Yorkshire ladies like to be addressed? Miss Louise Judd, for instance? She has my devout pity if your courting methods include suppressing her will to yours. You may be master of Radcliffe Manor, but you would never master *me*!'

Greg gave an expressive oath. Roslyn remained unblinking as she stared into his face. She felt a strange excitement now she had spilled out exactly what she felt about him, and she wasn't finished yet. Her voice was becoming high-pitched in a way Nadja would have told her was most unladylike, but there was no one around to hear on the top of this windswept moor that was a cold bleak wilderness to her, no one but Greg Radcliffe.

'What kind of society lady is she, this Miss Louise Judd, if she can contemplate marrying such a country oaf? I think her standards must be very low,' she said witheringly. 'Back in Ceylon, my father would not have considered entertaining the like of country farmers to one of our sumptuous dinners. We were used to princes and officers at our table—'

Suddenly Greg's hands were shaking her so hard her teeth chattered and the world spun round for an instant. She gasped for breath as his voice grated harshly in her ears.

'I'll hear no more of this! Why did you not stay in Ceylon instead of coming here to stick like a thorn under my skin? Surely one of your fine princes or army officer would have taken you in when your father died? Anything would have been preferable to having to lower yourself to live in the house of a Yorkshire farmer, wouldn't it?' He was being heavily sarcastic now. His eyes flickered over her heated face, where her blue eyes flashed like deep-hued sapphires and her mouth was parted with anger at his tone. His gaze went lower, to where the swell of her breasts still heaved tautly against the woollen cloth of her cloak. 'I'm sure one of the dark gentlemen of Ceylon would have been delighted to add you to his harem or whatever it is they put their concubines in out there. You have all the necessary attributes, as I seem to remember.'

His dark eyes flickered again in sudden recollection of the sight of her in the lukewarm bathtub at the inn in London, and of his own clumsy attempts to bathe her. Her blue eyes vacant with pain and shock at her situation ...her glorious golden body sparkling with droplets of water, the globes of her breasts lifted by the water so that they rested tantalizingly on its surface like rosy-tipped orbs...the sudden heat in his loins at the warmth of that soft firm flesh beneath his hands...the same heat that was stirring inside Greg now at the keen memory. She had been unkempt when he first saw her, but there had been nothing unkempt about her then, and nor was there now, dressed in more ladylike attire with his mother's aid, her lovely dark hair glossy with nightly brushing...he pulled her towards him by the back of her hair with an impulsive movement. To Roslyn it was an added insult after his reference to the harem.

'How dare you!' she gasped. 'I trust you do not fully understand the ways of the harem, or you would not insult me in that way. I *hope* it is so, Mr Radcliffe! I cannot think that even you would be so insulting as to compare me with a concubine—'

Whatever else she would have said was crushed into silence as his mouth fastened on hers in a savage kiss. His arms still held her imprisoned so tightly she could hardly breathe. His knees pressed into hers in a tiny trap, and her nipples stood out taut against his chest. They seemed to dig into him like spear-points, and Greg felt a rough earthy excitement sweep over him as she began to struggle, against him. She drove him mad with her seemingly lofty superiority. She drove him wild with her sensuality, and the smooth-hipped way she appeared to glide rather than walk across a room. She excited him and irritated him beyond any woman he had ever known before, and he felt a basic need to possess her, to feel her soft and submissive beneath him...and yet not so, he realized swiftly. It was her very spirit, so different from the simpering white-skinned English beauties with their coy coquetry, that made Roslyn Darby such a very exciting and desirable young woman. Even Louise, to whom he had half-heartedly made some overtures on the occasions when the wine had overtaken reason, had fought off his fumbling advances with such pretty mincing ways, all desire had instantly left him. He could not imagine this girl failing to respond to a man's desires...

As thoughts of Louise slid into Greg's mind, he felt some of the fever leave him. His grasp on Roslyn slackened slightly, until he suddenly realized her arms had found their way around him and that she was returning his kiss with an urgency that confirmed his belief. He felt a momentary stab of delight run through him, and then Roslyn pushed him away from her.

'Can we please move on from here?' Her voice was icy with only the barest tremor in it, as she tried to convey that his kiss had not meant the slightest thing to her, though that could not be farther from the truth. Her hands were clenched tightly together on her lap. 'I'm cold and if I catch pneumonia from this damp awful moor, there will be more complaints if I have to have the doctor called in again and spend more time in bed!'

She stared straight ahead so that only her profile was presented to Greg. She had a smooth elegant forehead and a delightfully tip-tilted nose. He had forgotten just how pretty it was. And her mouth, above that firmly jutting jawline...her moist red mouth was soft and trembling, despite her coldness, the full bottom lip still glistened with his kiss. Her elegant high cheekbone was tinged with high colour complementing the golden hue of her complexion. Greg's instinctive anger at her tone was smothered in the echo of her last few words. Time in bed was exactly the way he'd choose to spend his days and nights, if he had the delectable Roslyn Darby beside him...

Greg urged the horse into action and they continued the trek across the moor that encompassed the Radcliffe estate. It was a very widespread area of land, with sparse hillsides dotted with sheep, on which an occasional shepherd would raise a hand to touch his cap to Greg, and the yapping dogs would scamper at the wayward animals in their care. The cottages belonging to the farm workers were spread about too, like little stone-built oases in a bleak landscape, a curl of grey smoke rising from every one into a grey sky. Roslyn shivered, remembering the vision she'd had

225

on board ship about this very landscape, everything cold and bleak and grey, with the faces of people unclear to her, yet spelling out danger in some inexplicable way.

That one of the faces belonged to Greg Radcliffe would seem to be certain, but she could not really believe he represented danger to her, unless it was to her peace of mind. Certainly, they clashed with each other, and he disturbed her...but she was undeniably drawn to him by a force stronger than herself. No matter how much he insulted and angered her, she could never lose the feeling that here was her destiny. She had crossed oceans to find him, and so many things could have prevented their meeting; she might have perished in the fire that killed her father; she could have fled to one of the officers on the island and married him; she could have been lost at sea or landed in the hands of white slavers.

In one way she was fulfilling her father's destiny, Roslyn thought. If she married Greg ...she would be enacting out the law of karma, the Buddhist belief that said that a man's actions controlled his destiny even after death. And hadn't her father's death been the sole spur that drove her to England—and to Greg? And if her spirit was inherited from James

Darby, and Greg's spirit inherited from Hester, then if the two of them were ever made one flesh, it would be as it was written. James and Hester reborn in their children...

'You're very silent,' Greg's voice made her jump. She admitted to herself that she had been held in a trance-like state while her thoughts and will infused together, as if there was no escape from the destiny planned out for her. Her skin tingled beneath the pendant as if to remind her that the mysticism of the East had not done with her yet, reminding her of Nadja's intonation of the *four noble truths* of Buddha, and in particular at this time of the seventh step of the *noble eightfold path*, which seemed to echo the capabilities of the ruby's magic—*the right awareness of the past, the present and the future*—for a second Roslyn felt herself sway towards Greg, and the landscape blurred in front of her as his arms closed round her once more, more tenderly than the last time.

'I'm sorry,' she murmured. 'I'm afraid I am feeling the cold more than I expected. It's sitting still for so long in the trap, I expect.'

'We'll soon put that right then.' He let her go and set the horse on a path leading down the slope of the hillside. 'A hot drink is what you need. The cottage ahead is the farthest from the manor. I start there and work my way back, ending at the farm manager's house which is only a stone's-throw from the manor. The wife here is a bonny lass, who'll make us welcome.'

Roslyn felt a stupid burst of jealousy for the 'bonny lass' who could put the trace of a smile on Greg's stern face at that moment. He rarely smiled at *her*, she realized, though when he did it was usually when the physical, awareness between them made itself evident. Maybe they were destined never to be friends, she thought at once. Maybe they were only to be lovers—or enemies...

The cottage wife was a rosy-cheeked country girl with a broad accent and work-roughened hands. She was obviously ill-at-ease with Roslyn in the cottage and unsure how to address her, since Greg introduced her merely as his cousin. With Greg she was far more at home, and Roslyn didn't miss the way he patted her bottom as the girl, Betsy, went to the tiny kitchen to make them some hot tea. Roslyn glanced round the meagre cottage as she sat stiffly on the high-backed settle with its uncomfortable wooden seat. The cottage was dark and dingy, with little in the way of comfort except the sparking fire in the hearth, and the curtained-off kitchen area behind which Betsy was clattering about with cups and spoons.

Suddenly Roslyn became aware of a clamminess in her hands. The two homes could not be in more contrasting parts of the world, but she was reminded instantly of Bahu's hovel on the edge of the forest on the way to Colombo in Ceylon. There was the same aura of poverty, of simple living, of the only cheerful thing, apart from the occupant here, being the fire in the hearth. There was no appalling smell of dung-fire, nor the spicy curry smells clinging to everything, nor at this hour of the day the pungent, smoking candles burning. But the whole place evoked a memory so sharp she was unable to speak. In any case these people spoke in a tongue she could hardly follow when they talked so quickly together. She sat silently while Betsy handed her the tea and a brittle home-made biscuit that had no sweetness or flavour.

Betsy showed Greg where the window-frame was rotting for lack of new timber and where the roof leaked. In the absence of her husband, who was out with the sheep, it was left to her to pass on the complaints; though Roslyn suspected the man of the home would have done it with more aggression than this simple country girl. She seemed more conscious of Greg Radcliffe's charms than the bad state of repair of the dwelling, and when they disappeared upstairs to inspect the damp patch in the bedroom, Roslyn could hear the girl's silly giggling. It shouldn't bother her, she told herself, but it did. It was nothing to her if Greg chose to amuse himself in this way, but it was...she was thankful when Greg became more business-like and told Betsy he'd do what he could as soon as possible, and they were able to leave the cottage.

She sensed that Greg was annoyed with her cool reaction. He acted the lord of the manor, she realized, and part of his role was to make the tenants feel easier. He didn't say as much, but she could feel the tension growing between them as they visited a dozen more cottages on the route back to the manor, and in each one she became more withdrawn and silent.

He assumed she was looking down on these people, she thought miserably. But it wasn't that at all. How could she tell him it was past associations with such meagre dwellings that were tightening her insides like clutching hands? She ached with the tension of it, and she could do no more in each cottage than sit rigidly until Greg had finished his inspection and taken note of the work that needed to be done. With every visit he became more angry with her, and more appalled at the bad state of the cottages, which seemed to be deteriorating rapidly and needed more money than the estate could spare to make them properly habitable. The tenants were his responsibility, and the weight of them hung heavily round Greg's neck at that moment. He could well do without Miss Roslyn Darby's superior disapproval. He'd noticed it when her lips compressed in a tight line as he'd teased young Betsy...hell and damnation, Greg thought, he'd known Betsy Langham since she was a tiny child running barefoot on the moors, and no young woman from across the sea was going to make him feel guilty at his methods of relaxing the anxious tenants! If anything, Roslyn's reaction made him exaggerate his teasing attentions to the rest of the tenants' wives, just for the hell of it. But by the time she'd refused tea in three cottages and sat coldly remote while he drained yet another cup himself, he was beyond pandering to her.

'Is it too much to pretend to accept their hospitality, Cousin?' he snapped. 'I'm awash with tea, but a few sips in each cottage won't put too much of a flush in your cheeks, will it?'

'I'm not bothered about my complexion,' she snapped back. 'I'm tired, that's all.'

They had paused in the trap on the last stretch of moorland before descending to the

231

manager's house and the sprawling buildings of Radcliffe Manor, gaunt and grey in the misty surroundings. Roslyn gave an involuntary shiver and her eyes were tearful as she glanced up at this man she both loved and hated. He leaned back against the trap, his face cold and dark and unfriendly, even at the sight of the tears in her lovely blue eyes which took him a little by surprise. He had a heart of stone, Roslyn thought passionately. How could anyone ever hope to make him understand what a completely different life this was to her?

'You don't know—you just don't know how different it was for me in Ceylon,' she said in a choked voice. 'I know what you think of me—that I'm spoilt and expect everything to be done for me. I wish I could make you understand about my father. He was like a king of the whole plantation. He didn't have to lift a finger to do anything. Neither did I, and I had never known anything different. To my father it may still have been something of a novelty, and to some extent he delighted in it. Who wouldn't, when he'd achieved everything by sheer hard work and determination? He was proud of his tea plantation, and I was proud of him. We were so happy—' she swallowed back the tears. 'Yes, I was pampered, if by that you mean I had a loving father who gave me everything I desired! Wouldn't you do the same for your children if you could? If things had not gone so terribly wrong, I'd still be there, at home in Ceylon, with everything dear and familiar around me, instead of here in this cold and barren place where nobody cares if I live or die. Perhaps it would have been better if I'd perished in the flames with my father!' she finished bitterly.

Greg was moved by the sincerity of her words. Spoken with a low passion that barely concealed the tears, he realized for the first time what a traumatic experience Roslyn had gone through to reach Yorkshire. She had all her father's determination, he thought grudgingly. All she wanted was to reach Yorkshire and be with her kinfolk, expecting a welcome as her right.

His mother had certainly welcomed her, because of who she was...but he knew it was more than that. Hester would have loved Roslyn because of herself. Francis...well, Francis was never averse to the sight of a pretty girl...it had been left to the rest of them to show all the animosity Roslyn had experienced, himself and Thomas Radcliffe. Thomas had every right to feel antagonism towards the daughter of the man his wife had once loved—and perhaps still loved. But Greg himself...for the first time he tried to discover the reason he had been so against Roslyn's arrival here, and the answer eluded him. There was no reason...other than the inborn one of mistrust he had felt on receiving her prettily-worded letter, and the knowledge that her presence was going to cause upheaval in the family. That was reason enough in his mind! But perhaps it had been hasty of him to judge her before they had even met. He had judged and condemned without even seeing her. He looked at her now, her delicately-lovely face clouded with a misery that tore at his heart. Small and defenceless, she looked totally alone. He felt a wild urge to gather her up in his arms and wipe that look of unhappiness from her face. She did not see the conflicting emotions on his face, for she was still too wrapped up in her thoughts. She had so wanted to come to England, and suddenly it all seemed so futile. Her slender shoulders drooped.

'I don't belong here.' The words were forced out of her in a long sigh. 'I don't belong anywhere!'

She moved back a step as if to avoid his touch. The small movement filled Greg with compassion and irritation too. Of course she belonged here. She was James Darby's daughter, and if things had gone differently, she might have been his sister...though the last thing he wanted of her was a sisterly affection, he realized with certainty. His acute awareness of her made him brusque.

'My dear girl, there is no point in looking backwards. What's gone is gone, and to say you don't belong here is nonsense. All right, you don't have the kind of home you're used to, but this is your home now, and I'm afraid it's the best we can offer. It's a pity James Darby did so well if it's left you so discontented with his roots!' He meant to be flippant, but it was not the right time.

Roslyn flushed deeply, hurt beyond measure at his seemingly brutal words. The hot tears sprang to her eyes again, and her mouth trembled.

'How can you be so callous? I expected you to be so different, Greg. I expected...oh, it doesn't matter what I expected. They were all foolish dreams!' He didn't know what she was babbling about, but for the moment he let her ramble on. 'You don't know the meaning of love! You see me as the pampered daughter of a rich tea planter, but I have nothing in the world except the ruby I wear at my throat! It's not until you are entirely without love in the world that you know the real meaning of loneliness. I'd give everything I owned for someone of my own, and not have to be beholden to someone's charity!'

She was almost sobbing now, and Greg pulled her roughly into his arms. She stood there, hardly realizing where she was, as the sadness of the past weeks swept over her again. She was like a child lost in the desert, whirling in a vortex from which there seemed no escape, and the world only stopped spinning when she heard Greg's blunt, rough voice speaking close to her cheek.

'You have someone of your own, if you want him. I've a proposition to put to you, and I'll make no bones about it. The farm is in a bad way, and I need money to put it right. You know by now that my father's pushing hard to make me wed Louise Judd, but I've no stomach for that, however attractive her dowry.'

Roslyn felt her heart begin to pound. She was pressed very close to Greg as he held her. She could feel the pressure of the ruby pendant between them as the hardness of his body pushed it against her skin. She could feel its prickling as he spoke...

'It would be advantageous to us both to marry, Roslyn. I'm not pretending a wild love for you, but neither do I pretend to be undisturbed by you, as well you know. You'd have security, and be mistress of Radcliffe Manor, and as for me—'

Roslyn looked up into his eyes, her own glistening and wide. As for him—what? She felt a shiver of excitement run through her. She could hardly believe she was hearing aright, and she was stunned into silence until he finished. But he *had* proposed marriage.

'I'm referring to the ruby pendant,' Greg went on baldly. Roslyn blinked. 'As my wife, I would require you to let me use it as surety with the bank to obtain credit until the farm gets back on its feet. We need fresh animal stock and seed, and repairs for the cottages before the tenants seek employment elsewhere in better surroundings. There is much that could be done with the ruby as a guarantee, and I would see that it was all done legally. The ruby would always belong to you, but I would make good use of it and we would both benefit. Well? Do we strike a bargain?'

CHAPTER 11

Roslyn could hardly breathe. Against her throat the ruby's sting was sharp as Greg held her firmly in his grasp. Was it a warning to her not to accept this startling, unbelievable proposal? How could she tell? Her senses were numbed momentarily, and as she leaned heavily against the man who had occupied her thoughts for so long, she suddenly realized her eyes were open wide, but that she no longer saw the drab greyness of the moors stretching away from her. Instead, there was that strange cloudiness around the edges of her vision, and in its centre her father in his loose white clothing, master of his domain, starkly poised against the glittering white Darby mansion with its brilliant flowers and foliage and all that was represented by Ceylon and home. Was James smiling? Was he telling her to agree to this insulting proposal and that all would be well? Or was he warning her? She could not tell. James' face was obscured by the dazzle of her own tears, and it was impossible to gauge the ruby's message. She blinked, and the vision was gone, and she realized Greg was gently holding her away from him now, his eyes looking challengingly into hers.

'Well, Roslyn? Have I shocked you with my Yorkshire bluntness? I must admit the idea has only just occurred to me, and that I might have handled it with more finesse. I might even have pretended that I was fired with a great passion for you, and not mentioned the ruby until we were safely wed. Would you rather I had been that devious? Somehow I think not. Far better that there is honesty between the two of us if our marriage is to stand any chance of survival, for rest assured that once wed, it will be for life. Is the idea completely abhorrent to you?'

The proposal was so unexpected, so different from the romantic one she had dreamed of hearing from his lips, that Roslyn was unable to say anything at all. His words stung her as he said quite casually that he had no great passion for her. That he would make use of the ruby was as nothing to her, she realized. What was important was the feeling between them, and if she believed the blunt words Greg said, then there was none on his part.

Oh, but there *was*! Roslyn knew well he was not unaffected by her. And there was more than that. Nadja's teachings in the ways of love had told her what to expect when a man was aroused by a woman. She had experienced the quickening of his breath against her cheek...the rapid beating of his heart against hers...Oh yes, Greg Radcliffe was not immune to her as a woman, but that wasn't love. And she had loved him for so long. How could she go into a marriage of convenience when her soul cried out to Greg to love her.

'I—I have never thought of marriage as being a business proposition,' she stammered at last. In answer his arms tightened round her. She felt his hands roam slowly down the curve of her back. His voice softened a little, deepening to the seductive tones she remembered so well.

'I do not propose it will be all business, Roslyn! It will be a marriage in every sense of the word. You will have my name, and if God wills, my children.'

Wild colour rushed to Roslyn's face. She looked up into Greg's dark, sensual eyes, seeing the desire in them. A thrill raced through her body. She had dreamed of Greg possessing her. Wanted nothing more than to be with this man for the rest of her days for as long as she could remember. And now that he was offering her her heart's desire, she was standing here a hesitant child. His eyes mesmerized her.

His mouth touched hers seductively, as his voice murmured against her lips, vibrating softly on her skin.

'You and I were destined to be together, Roslyn. You must feel it as much as I do. Some things are meant to be, and nothing we do will change them.'

He chose the right words, whether knowingly or not. Roslyn was dizzy with the nearness of him, and the glorious, exquisite feelings rushing over her. He wanted her, and all else could be ignored. That there was great physical attraction between them was evident. Even now, she could feel the passion rising in him as he pressed her close, and this time she let the dizzy excitement it evoked have its way, feeling her breath begin to pant and her throat become dry. There was abundant love on her side, and surely in time, Greg would love her too. Perhaps he already did, but his dour Yorkshire background would not let him admit to such a headstrong feeling so soon. Love would surely follow if she married him...

'Yes, yes, yes...'The words seemed to be torn out of her. 'I will marry you, Greg...'

She said no more, for his mouth crushed hers into silence. She felt the triumphant strength of him, but she was still too bemused by him and all that had transpired in the last minutes to think logically of all that her marriage to Greg would mean. For now, it was enough that he held her and wanted her, and must love her a little already...the pendant touched both their skins as his lips moved down to her throat where the neckline of her dress opened. It burned slightly, and Roslyn gave a small shiver. She kept her eyes firmly closed, delighting in the delicious sensations Greg's lips awoke and willing all else away. But she could not will away the sudden memory of Nadja's sing-song voice, so close and vibrant in her ears that the old nurse might have been standing right beside her.

'A man will pretend much to obtain his desires, my sweet one. Even to a whore he will pretend love. Perhaps it eases his conscience a little, but the sweetness soon becomes bitter and he turns away from her, despising that which he once lusted after. There is no subsitute in the world for love that is true. Always remember that, little Missy.'

The shivers of delight turned cold for Roslyn, and sensing her change of mood Greg's caresses became less passionate.

'We have stayed here too long, and your face is pinched, Roslyn. Come, back into the trap, and we'll finish our rounds and then we will go and tell the family our news.'

Roslyn's heart gave a great lurch. How would the family react? She had no need to worry about Aunt Hester, but the others...she sat beside Greg in the trap, feeling the coldness settle in the pit of her stomach, unable to stop the unease that was rapidly replacing the elation. She knew she had reacted impulsively to Greg's proposal. She had not given herself time to think properly. How could she, when he was offering what she most wanted in all the world?

But under what terms...? Was she being un-utterably foolish in allowing her heart to rule her head? Greg had said it would be a marriage in every sense of the word, but if he did not really love her, how would she feel, knowing he saw the consummation as part of the bargain—as little more than duty...?

Greg had no idea of the doubts thrashing about in her mind as they stopped at the last call of the day, the farm manager's home. He helped her down from the trap with a new tenderness, and there was a moistness in her eyes because of it. Even if she had doubts, she could not change her mind now. How could she, when he looked at her with eyes that were warm, and a smile on that so-sensual mouth? She was weak, and always would be where he was concerned, she thought tremulously. She prayed that the future would not be filled with misery. His own mother had made a disastrous mistake in her marriage, and time had not put it right. Roslyn swallowed hard as she felt his hand firm beneath her elbow as he rapped on the door of the small house.

This time they were offered a glass of home-made wine, and Roslyn did not refuse. If she was to be Greg's wife, she must do as he wished, and act the role of lady of the manor...he raised his glass to her as he sipped the wine, and she did the same in silent acknowledgment. As yet, no one knew of their engagement, for the family had a right to hear first, no matter how unpleasant it might turn out to be. Roslyn shivered, thinking it was not the happiest way to view the telling of a betrothal. But nor was this the most normal of betrothals.

By the time they were on the last stretch of road leading back to Radcliffe Manor, Roslyn's thoughts were in a whirl. She had expected to be wooed and courted...but if all Greg had been interested in was the surety of the ruby for the sake of the farm, then such wooing would have been dishonest, and he'd already said he wanted there to be honesty between them...Roslyn didn't want to admit that in her heart she might have preferred just a little deception, and that Greg might just have pretended that he *was* fired with a great

244

passion for her after all...

The big old house and farm buildings came into sight, gaunt and grey in the fading light of the afternoon, with the insidious white mist swirling about its foundations so that it looked as if it floated on a grey-white sea. Did Greg expect her to be thrilled because all this would be hers as well as his when she became his wife? Perhaps a lady born and bred in Yorkshire may have been, finding the old manor a splendid place in which to live, and the prestige of being Mrs Greg Radcliffe, wife of a well-known gentleman farmer a privilege indeed. But Roslyn was not a Yorkshirewoman, and as yet she could not compare such wintry surroundings with the vivid colour of Ceylon, where the sun kissed her face every day of the year and the sky was blue and the air warm and balmy...

'Not regretting it already, I hope?' Greg's voice penetrated her thoughts. She shook her head quickly.

She said with a small smile, 'Greg—if we are to be married—can it be soon?'

He looked at her quizzically. '*If?* That sounds as if there are doubts in your mind, Roslyn. I have tried to be honest with you, but if there's anything that disturbs you, now is the time to say it—'

She shook her head. Illogical though it may be, the idea that her hesitation might make *him* change his mind was enough to throw her into a panic. And there was something else worrying her.

'It's just—Greg, I'm sorry, but I keep thinking about Louise Judd—'

'I've told you,' he said tersely. 'She means nothing to me, and I won't be manipulated into a marriage I don't want.'

Then that surely meant he wanted this one. The thought heartened her a little. She rushed on.

'Then I'm sorry I mentioned it, but your mother tells me she will be back in Yorkshire in February. Greg—I don't wish to appear forward in any way—but I would like us to be married before that time.'

She had said it, and her heart was pounding because of it. It was most unladylike to suggest the date of a wedding to a gentleman, but in this case Roslyn felt the need for urgency. She would feel safe once she had Greg's ring on her finger—though precisely why she could not explain. Safe against the guiles of Miss Louise Judd perhaps, because once wed, Greg said it would be for life—he gave a short laugh, and placed his large hand over hers.

'My sweet one, we will be married as soon

246

as you like. The fact is, I see no reason to wait myself, and the sooner you belong to me the better I shall like it. We will arrange it in the first few days of the new year and we will take a few days' honeymoon at the coast. You'll like Scarborough. It has an old castle on a hill and a magnificent bay. Does that please you?'

Roslyn nodded. Her throat had tightened as he called her his sweet one even in that bantering way. The very endearment her nurse had used. And the mention of a honeymoon had conjured up other images, and of course, if they were to give the appearance of a normal young couple, then a honeymoon at the outset of their marriage would be expected. A few days at the coast, presumably in a hotel alone with Greg...It would be difficult not to let him know her true feelings for him in such a situation, and she was not sure yet how much of a loving wife he wanted or expected her to be.

They arrived at the front of the house and Greg was alighting. A stable-lad came running up to take the horse and rub him down, and to put the trap away. Greg gripped her fingers tightly.

'Whatever the reaction to our news, Roslyn, you have me by your side now. James Darby's daughter is no longer the poor relation dependent on charity, but my future wife.'

He was giving her a new status, she realized. And whatever she had been at home, until today she had been solely dependent on the Radcliffes' charity. Things would have been very different if Greg had chosen to marry Louise Judd, and that young lady had moved in to Radcliffe Manor. There was as much to be gained from this marriage for her as for Greg, and Roslyn pushed down the feeling of unease that was still with her. Perhaps her swift acceptance of his proposal was the best reaction after all. If she had stopped to think too long about it, the doubts might have overcome the acceptance of her destiny. Strange that Greg should have put into words her very own feelings at that time. And strange, too, to remember that they had started out that afternoon so antagonistic towards each other, and now they were bound together in a betrothal of marriage, and Greg's attitude was softer towards her than at any time since she had known him. There was a sudden surge of bubbling elation inside her, singing through her veins. Whatever the reason for marrying her, the fact was he wanted her to be his wife, and on a sudden impulse she hugged his arm to her as they mounted the steps to the house, her eyes shining with happiness as she looked up at him.

Greg was startled to see the sudden glow on

her face. The vague feeling that he had handled the situation badly and insulted her by indicating that it was the ruby that had instigated his proposal had never quite left him. Looking down at her lovely face now, her eyes shining, lips parted and moist, he could very easily forget there was a precious gem involved in their transaction at all, he thought. She was soon to be his wife, and the thought of holding her in his arms every night was indeed a pleasurable one. He had had a taste of those delicious charms already, and determined that this marriage was by no means to be in name only. He smiled back, his fingers touching her cheek in a moment of tenderness at the thought of the delights to come. It was a moment of closeness of spirit that was akin to love.

'We'll tell them at dinner,' he whispered as they entered the house, and she nodded in agreement as his mother appeared to claim her company and bid her join her by the drawing-room fire, for she must be perished. Strangely she was not. As Greg went striding off, Roslyn knew there was a fire burning inside her that warmed her more than any glowing logs in the hearth...

Roslyn dressed carefully for dinner that evening. For the first time since arriving in England she felt a whole person again. Greg had given her that, she thought, with a glow still surrounding her. She was a woman who was desired and wanted. Perhaps not loved yet but the love would follow. She made herself believe that. She closed her mind to all else. She wore a low-necked gown for dinner, even though the family did not usually dress too formally, but tonight was something of an occasion. The ruby pendant gleamed at her perfect throat, the rose-coloured silk of her gown complemented it superbly. Thomas Radcliffe would raise his eyebrows at such ostentatiousness, but she cared nothing about his opinion. All she wanted was to see the approval and admiration in Greg's eyes.

She was not disappointed. She saw that he too had dressed more formally than usual, and that the other three looked at them both in some surprise when they all took their places at the dining table. Roslyn heard Aunt Hester draw in her breath, and knew she had guessed as she looked from one to the other in turn. But she said nothing, and it was not until the meal was nearly over and his father was flushed with wine, that Greg cleared his throat. He reached across the table for Roslyn's hand, and Thomas Radcliffe's brows drew together in a bushy line as he saw the action.

'What's this?' he growled. 'I'll have no canoodling at my table—'

Roslyn saw Greg's mouth tighten. But he looked steadily at his father.

'Roslyn and I have news for you all,' he said firmly. 'I have asked her to be my wife and she has consented. We will be married right after my birthday in the new year—'

Thomas Radcliffe leapt to his feet. His fists thundered on the table. His face was puce, his voice spluttering with rage as he glared at Greg. The veins stood out on his forehead and neck like knotted cords.

'You've done what?' he roared. 'Of all the women in the world, do you mean to tell me you've picked on James Darby's daughter to wed? Over my dead body! I forbid it, do you hear? I'll have nowt to do with it—'

'Nobody's asking you to have owt to do with it!' Greg's face was as enraged as his father's as he too leapt to his feet. They stood glowering at each other down the length of the dinner table. 'It's my choice, and I have chosen Roslyn. You can't forbid it, and I'd remind you that in three weeks' time, Radcliffe Manor will belong to me, and I have the right to say who lives here and who doesn't. If you're so opposed to my marriage, then perhaps it would be

251

best if you lived elsewhere!'

Hester gasped at this outburst. She touched Thomas' arm nervously, but he shook her off as if she was an insect. Francis sat without speaking, a frozen look on his face. And then Aunt Hester jumped to her feet and came to hug Roslyn.

'It's wonderful news, dear, and I for one couldn't be more pleased,' she cried.

After a moment's hesitation, Francis forced a smile to his handsome face. 'My congratulations, brother,' he drawled. 'You've taken us all by surprise. May I add my good wishes to you too, Roslyn?'

He rose and gave a little bow, then pressed a light kiss on her lips. She had the uncanny feeling he was not as pleased as he pretended to be, and told herself not to be foolish. It was nothing to Francis whether Greg married her or Louise Judd...unless Francis too had been relying on the Judd fortunes to put the farm on its feet and bring back luxury to Radcliffe Manor...

'And what of the Judd lass?' Thomas had not done with them yet, and his strident voice rang round the wood-panelled room. 'What am I to say to her father when he's as good as told me his brass will be at my disposal as soon as you wed his lass? It will be like throwing a bucket of cold water in his face as thanks for his generosity.'

'I never intended marrying Louise,' Greg said coldly. 'Not for you or anyone.'

Thomas' small eyes glittered furiously into Roslyn's face, his glance sweeping her from head to foot.

'And what has this chit got that's so damned attractive then? She's the colour of a half-breed and she's got Darby's blood in her veins and too much of his damned spirit for a decent wench. Or is there another reason for such haste?' he roared out suddenly as the thought struck him. 'You've not planted a child in her belly, have you? Is that what you were up to when you were away in London? I can see no other reason for wanting to tie yourself to a penniless foreigner!'

Roslyn felt the fury take hold of her at his insulting words. She shook all over as she pushed aside Aunt Hester's restraining hands and tore round the dining table to stand before Thomas Radcliffe. Her eyes flashed their anger; her cheeks were fiery red; her breasts heaved as her hand came up to strike her uncle on the side of the cheek. The action was so spontaneous no one spoke for a moment. Thomas merely gaped at the small figure daring to attack him at his own table, and then Greg knocked over his chair as he strode towards Roslyn and made to pull her away.

'*No!*' she gasped. 'I've put up with his insults for too long, but this time he's gone too far. How *dare* you suggest such a thing! If you think so little of me, at least give your own son some credit for decent behaviour.'

'You...you little...'he spluttered.

'And as for the precious dowry your Louise Judd would have brought to Radcliffe Manor,' Roslyn rushed on scornfully, too incensed now to care what she was saying. She gripped the ruby pendant tightly, thrusting it beneath Thomas Radcliffe's gaze. 'Do you see this ruby? And do you not think it is worth more than Radcliffe Manor itself and more land than you can envisage? It's worth a prince's fortune, and that's what *I* bring to my husband as a dowry! Greg can use it as surety to restore this crumbling place to the home my father knew, and at this moment that means more to me than anything else!'

There was complete silence as she finished speaking, and she was suddenly aware of Greg's fingers digging into her arms. They were cruelly sharp, and glancing at his face, she saw that it was dark red with rage. Too late, Roslyn realized her mistake: she had betrayed the reason for Greg's proposal. She realized instantly what a fool she had been to blurt out the truth, for she was as good as admitting that Greg did not want her for herself alone. And she had thrown back any pretence at love for him saying her father's old home meant more to her than he did...she heard Francis' mocking laugh at the other end of the table.

'Well, well, Greg. I underestimated you! So this is to be a business arrangement, is it? What a waste of a lovely young lady to be wed on those terms. And no tiny feet to go pattering through these draughty rooms—'

'Don't excite yourself, brother,' Greg said coldly. 'I assure you my wife will be kept well satisfied, and not be wanting in any respect.' He continued grimly. 'Best watch your tongue in future, for I'll have no parasites at Radcliffe Manor when it belongs to me. A man who won't pull his weight, or attempts to take what's mine, will be shown no mercy.'

Roslyn felt a thrill run through her at his words. Greg was more ruthless than she had imagined, yet she could not but admire him. She might rail at his arrogance and his determination to make Radcliffe Manor beautiful and prosperous again, no matter how, but he was a man such as James Darby had been. A man in every sense of the word, and he'd left no one here in any doubt that theirs would be a true marriage. The hot colour stained her cheeks even more as she remembered the clinical way he'd said it. As if to tell them all that he'd gone into this farce of a marriage expressly to save the farm and the manor, but that he was fully prepared to do his duty by his wife. His *duty*...how could the loving physical act between a man and a woman be termed a duty...?

'If you wish to change your mind about the marriage, now is the time,' she said stiffly to Greg. 'If I had thought it would cause such a holocaust of feeling, I might have thought twice—'

'No one's changing their minds,' Greg snapped. 'You and I struck a bargain. A Radcliffe doesn't go back on his word, and I fancy a Darby is of the same inclination.'

He made it impossible for her to scream at him that she wouldn't marry him if he was the last man on earth...besides, she knew that despite everything, he was the only man she had ever wanted to marry. But she would never become enslaved to him. If he expected a servile little wife with no will of her own, he was in for a shock. In Roslyn's mind a marriage should be a partnership between two people who cared deeply for one another. She chose not to think that the liaison between her and

Greg could hardly be called that…but she still clung to the hope that love would grow out of the physical attraction that was undeniable.

Looking at the man of her dreams now, his hard eyes challenged her to suggest a Darby was less honourable than a Radcliffe.

'I never go back on my word,' she spoke just as coldly. 'I want the wedding to be as soon as possible.'

Thomas Radcliffe pushed past the two of them.

'Then don't expect me to be there to wish you well,' he shouted. 'I'll not give my blessing to any union with the whelp of James Darby.'

He stormed out of the room slamming the door behind him. Greg told his brother he wished to speak with him privately, and the two of them followed their father without another glance at Roslyn or Hester. Roslyn wilted once they had gone and sank down on a chair with trembling legs, wondering what on earth she was letting herself in for in marrying Greg. Wondering yet again if she was launching herself into a life of unhappiness. Marriage with a man who did not love her might be far worse than no marriage at all…

She felt Aunt Hester squeeze her hand, and looked into her sympathetic face with eyes that were softly brimming. If it weren't for Aunt Hester, she thought fervently...

'My poor love, it's hardly the reception you expected to receive at your news, is it? But if it's any comfort to you, Roslyn, it gives me more pleasure than I've had in years to know that you and Greg are to be wed. I know it will turn out to be a happy union, for all that there are practical reasons as well as other ones for the wedding,' she said delicately. 'I refuse to be gloomy, and neither should you be! We have a wedding to arrange, and much to do. You will want new clothes to take on your honeymoon and to delight your husband, and I'll hear no arguments about my providing your trousseau for you. We will go to York and this time we'll visit all the best establishments. Greg will have a bride to do him proud!'

Roslyn was touched. Hester obviously was determined to see it as the love-match that should have been hers and James Darby's. And her optimism was infectious. Yes, there was a wedding to arrange, and she would want to look her best, to be as beautiful as possible for Greg. So that he would never give a second's thought to the girl he might have married if Thomas Radcliffe had had his way. When his head lay beside Roslyn's on the pillow, his thoughts must be only of *her*, and a shudder of delight ran through her.

Greg had spoken with a flat finality out there on the moors. Once wed, it would be for life... he'd said it almost as a warning, that if she couldn't face the prospect, her answer had better be no. But at the moment, Roslyn could imagine nothing more ecstatic than to spend the rest of her life loving Greg.

CHAPTER 12

The euphoria lingered long after Roslyn retired early to bed. She and Hester had become animated over the coming wedding, and the trauma of telling Thomas had receded. He could do nothing to stop it, and since he chose to stay away from them for the rest of the evening, Roslyn gradually relaxed. She had seen nothing of Greg or Francis either, and was relieved to indulge in women's talk with her aunt. And now she lay sleepless in her bed, her dark hair brushed out to form a gleaming frame on the white pillow, the soft glow of the lamplight left burning awhile, and only the low moan of the wind outside to disturb her.

She was going to marry Greg. The thought

burned like a flame of pure elation inside her. To have and to hold for ever and always...no other thought was going to spoil the realization of all her dreams...she closed her eyes tightly, trying to picture the fulfilment of all her childhood fantasies...

The click of her door made her eyes fly open. She had not heard the handle turn, but now she saw Greg's dark shape etched against the doorway. He had removed his jacket, and wore only a white shirt and the tightly-fitting trousers that moulded his strong legs. Roslyn felt her heart begin to thud as he stood there unsmilingly. She forgot all her delight in the coming wedding. All she remembered was that she had displeased him in her blundering revelation downstairs, and that clearly he had not forgiven her. The knowledge made her forget the impropriety of his being here.

'Greg,' she said nervously, 'I did not mean to tell them about our—arrangement! Your father made me so angry. He treats me like dirt—'

'You should not have let him bait you.' He was distant. 'You could hardly have expected a welcome into the family from him, knowing who you are. I thought you might have held your tongue a little, but I was forgetting that fierce pride of yours. I had not realized either how much Radcliffe Manor meant to you. It saves us too much pretence now that I know it's the house you love, because of its associations with your father.'

'Did you expect me to profess undying love for you after the kind of proposal you made me?' Roslyn said passionately. She sat up in bed now, and the covers fell away from her. She wore a cambric nightgown, but it hid little from his eyes since she had left the neck—ties unfastened in the warmth from her fire. He came slowly towards the bed with all the stalking litheness of a tiger. Roslyn felt her breathing quicken as he sat on the bed beside her, leaning towards her, his hand reaching out to tip her face up to his. She was mesmerized by his dark intensity, and unable to move away. Neither did she want to.

'Would that be such an impossible thing to imagine?' his voice changed to seductive coaxing that never failed to stir her. 'I shall expect a very loving wife, Roslyn, make no mistake about that. Marriages have begun on far less than we have. Do you deny that there's a fire in you that matches mine, sweet Roslyn?'

His free hand was reaching for her breasts, unconfined now with only the thin cambric covering them. He cupped them gently, feeling their instant response, and a low laugh started deep in his throat. Roslyn felt a heavy spreading ache of desire through all the most secret parts of her body, and as his lips claimed hers, she kissed him back, passionately, and new shooting sensations enveloped her as Greg tossed the bedcovers aside and covered her body with his own. He was still fully clothed, but she could feel his hard strength through the cloth that separated them. His tongue parted her lips, pushing into her mouth and exploring every crevice of it, as if symbolizing a more complete union...

'I could take you here and now,' he murmured against her lips, the arrogant triumph in his voice. 'Your nature betrays you, Roslyn, and I defy you to cry out or struggle.'

She felt him heavy on her as he reached out to turn out the lamp so that the room was only dimly lit by the dying embers of firelight. The oil-lamp smoked a little. Roslyn's head twisted from side to side as his hands slid downwards on her body, pushing the nightgown away from her golden flesh.

The pungency of the lamp reached Roslyn's nostrils. In the dimness she was only aware of the dark shape above her, pressing into her, and the searching fingers...suddenly the hands were not Greg's, but the native who had found such an unexpected prize at Bahu's house on the night of the monsoon. This was not Greg, but a fiend who tried to rape her...Greg swore angrily as she twisted herself from under him and pushed against him with all her strength.

'Are you so uncouth that you cannot wait a few more weeks to ravish me?' She whipped the words at him, praying he couldn't tell how she was shaking with fear and taking refuge in scorn. 'When I am your wife, you can do as you will with me, but until that time I'd ask you not to treat me as a whore!'

For a minute she thought he would strike her, and then he gave a harsh laugh and stood up to look down at her, dark and massive at the side of the bed.

'You win this time,' he spoke in a hoarse voice. 'But remember the words you just said, Roslyn, for make no mistake *I'll* remember them. When you're my wife, I'll treat you how I will, and if that demands the responses of a whore, so be it!'

She gasped, but he was quickly gaining control of himself, and she heard the familiar coldness in his voice now.

'What I came here for was not to ravish you, as you so eloquently phrase it, but to tell you that we will go to York tomorrow. We will go to a reputable jeweller and have a valuation on the ruby to present to the bank, and take it from there. We will also buy an engagement ring if you desire it, and then see about arranging the wedding date.'

He spoke as if he was purchasing a new flock of sheep. She bristled at his words, but he did not wait for argument. He suddenly turned on his heel and left her without another word, and she was left shivering in the darkness alone. She pulled the nightgown down as far as it would go and tied the strings at its neck, curling herself into a ball. He was not at all as she had imagined him to be, she raged inside.

The sketches from his mother had not told of his ruthlessness. Francis had said that if necessary his brother would leave a lamb to die on the moors, sacrificing the puny for the strong. For a brief moment she pitied Louise Judd, the puny one, tossed aside as if Greg had never cared a jot for her now that Roslyn's fortune was the greater enticement.

She felt uneasy at the thought. Could she tell if Greg really had cared for Louise? She had only his word for it...that should be enough, but the doubts still remained. And just how strong was *she* anyway, she thought bitterly? If she was really strong, she would refuse to marry Greg at all, and if she was thrown out of Radcliffe Manor, she would make her own way in this alien land.

But she was not that strong, and she knew it. She kept her eyes tightly shut and tried to sleep.

The next few weeks rushed by in a series of vivid impressions in Roslyn's mind. She saw little of Thomas except at meal times, and then he rarely spoke to her. It was a relief more than an affront as far as she was concerned. Francis seemed to have recovered his good temper and his teasing manner towards her, and was usually charming whenever they were together. Aunt Hester openly twittered about the wedding, as if it was the greatest love match of all time, and Greg...he was as business-like as if he had never lain with her and stirred her emotions to fever pitch.

His mother accompanied them to York the following day, and Roslyn became better acquainted with the tiny twisting streets with their quaint names and overhanging shop-fronts, the ancient walls with their medieval gates called bars; the vast imposing structure of the Minster, towering over the city; the site on the Knavesmire where the Tyburn gallows once stood and where the outlaw Dick Turpin was hanged.

Roslyn would dearly have liked to ask where the Judds lived in the city, but could not bring herself to do so. There was no need, for Aunt Hester pointed out the large town house quite naturally. She went off to visit a friend while Roslyn and Greg conducted their business with the jeweller, and arranged to meet them later at a tea-room near the river.

Roslyn felt like an exhibit at a slave market as the portly jeweller ushered them into a room at the back of the establishment. She could almost see him rubbing his hands as Greg explained their visit. The pendant was round her neck as always, and she unbuttoned the woollen cloak to reveal it to the man. She saw him visibly step back, and then Greg was unfastening the pendant's clasp for her to hand the gem to the expert.

She felt a tremor as it passed out of her hand to his, but he seemed aware of nothing but the magnificence of the ruby. The devil's kiss only exuded its magic on its rightful owner, Roslyn remembered...unless it was stolen, in which case only bad luck would follow the thief...

'My dear sir, what you ask is impossible,' the jeweller said after some minutes.

'What do you mean by impossible?' Greg demanded impatiently. 'It's a perfectly simple request, surely. I want a written valuation on the ruby to present to my bank. If you are

266

incapable of calculating it—'

'Please, Mr Radcliffe, you misunderstand me,' he wheezed. 'Though in one respect you are quite right. I am incapable of calculating its worth. I defy anyone to do so. The ruby is the most perfect I have ever seen, and in my opinion is priceless. I urge you most strongly to entrust its safe keeping to a bank's vault. It is most unwise for the young lady to wear it so conspicuously. May I ask how you came by such a gem, sir? It is from the East, is it not?'

His two listeners were silenced by the hush-ed reverence in his voice. *Priceless*...Roslyn swallowed. She had loved the devil's kiss from the moment she saw it on its nest of white silk at the Darby mansion, but she had never dreamed her father's legacy was as precious. Greg cleared his throat.

'It is from the East,' he said non-commitally. 'It was given as a gift to my—fiancée. But I must have a written valuation, Mr Jessop. Please do your best to accommodate me.'

The jeweller saw he would get no more in-formation. He sighed, knowing what Greg ask-ed was impossible, but complying with his wishes. The figure he wrote was ludicrously large and, had it not come from a reputable and trustworthy man, the bank might have laughed in Greg's face. As it was, Mr Jessop insisted on writing a short letter to accompany the valuation, assuring the reader of the gem's authenticity. Greg did not correct him in his assumption that the ruby was to be kept in the bank's vault. Finally he showed them out, bowing and gushing as if they were royalty. Greg let out a long breath when they were outside on the road again.

'Well, Roslyn.' He tucked her arm in the crook of his own. 'It seems I've found myself a prize! I thought Jessop's eyes were going to pop out of his head when he saw the ruby!' His voice was uneven, and his words less tactful that he would have wished. The truth was, Greg himself was somewhat shaken at the immensity of the ruby's value, and only now realized what he had done in his blunt, crudely-worded proposal of marriage. He had scorned Roslyn's imperious ways and sneered at her pampered background, not really believing any of it. Now, he began to understand a little of what it may have been like to rub shoulders with princes, and never to lift a finger in the mansion where her father was king. Instead of making him feel humbled, however, it had the opposite effect. As Roslyn's husband, he would still be master, no matter from whose purse-strings the brass flowed.

'I'll leave you at the tea-room with my mother,' he said abruptly. 'I've no wish to listen to women's talk, so I'll see to the business at the bank and meet you later. I gather you've some fripperies to see to?'

Roslyn's face flushed. 'If by fripperies you mean the clothes I wish to purchase for my wedding, then yes!' She spoke in a tight voice. 'I had thought there was mention of an engagement ring as well, but I see it's been overlooked in the importance of the surety for your sheep!'

Greg stopped walking, his face still. He had truly forgotten.

'We'll make another visit for that, and the wedding ring as well,' he announced. 'When we've more time to browse, for I know you ladies will want the rest of the afternoon at the dressmaking establishment. We must see to the banns as well—'

'Please don't put yourself out on my account. And since I have no friends in this part of the world, I do not wish a large wedding. I would like it to be as quiet and informal as possible.

Greg stared at her set face. How dare she put conditions on the wedding arrangements! But he shrugged. It would suit him just as well. They'd be just as surely wed, and it would save the embarrassment of his father making a big scene and letting the whole county know his feelings about the marriage. He nodded.

'As you wish. I will arrange it at the village church near to Radcliffe Manor for the first Saturday in the new year.'

They parted company at the tea-room by the river. She watched him stride away along the cobbled waterfront. Her betrothed, Roslyn found herself thinking, who showed her as much tenderness as if she were a stray dog, unless it suited his purposes to do otherwise. She pushed open the door of the tea-room and joined his mother. She had achieved her heart's desire, but in a manner such as she had never imagined.

The rest of the day was spent joyfully in Aunt Hester's company, visiting the dressmakers, and Roslyn's spirits lifted. Orders were given for her requirements, and her aunt was over-generous, brooking no arguments. She would be required for final fittings in two weeks' time, and all would be ready by Christmas. It would be a trousseau fit for a princess, the starched and corseted proprietor told them flamboyant-ly. Including two delicious nightgowns of a soft silk fabric which, Roslyn was assured, were the latest in bridal accessories.

The weeks passed quickly. Greg had made all the arrangements and chose not to play the part of the ardent lover, since the family knew very well his reasons for marrying Roslyn. Occasionally he did so, but in mockery, which angered and upset Roslyn.

He had informed them that his visit to the bank had been entirely successful. Money had been advanced for repairs to the farm cottages and the manor itself, and new livestock would replace those that had been lost through disease in the previous year. There would be money for additional seed. If he was pleased at the outcome, he didn't show it, Roslyn thought, never realizing how the notion that he was so beholden to her for his change of fortune was turning sour in Greg's stomach.

Christmas festivities were a novelty for Roslyn. At home, her father had made a token gesture to the kind of Christmas he remembered from his boyhood, but it had never seemed the same to him, under sunny blue skies and in scorching heat. In the Yorkshire home of his early days now, there were roaring fires to keep out the cold damp winter, a fir tree brought indoors and decorated with cones and mistletoe, and roasted mutton for the table, with sweetmeats and hot mead to drink. Small gifts were exchanged by the family, and even Thomas Radcliffe unbent enough to wish Roslyn a merry yuletide and cracked his face into a grimace of a smile. On her finger she wore the ring Greg had bought her, three small rubies in a heavy gold setting. Nothing like as grandiose as the pendant, but in keeping with it.

At the turn of the year it was Greg's birthday, a momentous one, because it meant Radcliffe Manor now officially became his. It was a bitterly cold day, and there were no big celebrations, since the wedding was near, and Thomas was suffering a bad bout of influenza and could not be doing with too much noise. His bellicose attitude seemed largely to have dwindled in the past days, perhaps because he was powerless to prevent the events ahead. He was no longer master of Radcliffe Manor, and James Darby's daughter was to be its mistress. They were two bitter pills to swallow.

Francis continued to fawn and flatter whenever he felt so inclined towards Roslyn, partly because he saw how it irritated his brother. It often soothed Roslyn's ruffled feelings, and she saw no reason to discourage him. He was the only person to whom she could talk at length about her old life, since he seemed ever-eager to hear about such a different world.

On the eve of the new year, they were gathered around the blazing fire without Thomas' disquieting presence, since he had stumped off to bed to nurse his influenza.

'Did you celebrate the new year in Ceylon?' Francis handed Roslyn the dish of nuts he had cracked for her.

'Oh yes, there were toasts drunk and small parties among friends,' she nodded. 'Father often said we should go to the coast to see the festivities there, but we never did. In some parts, the young men and young girls dress themselves all in white and take basketfuls of white flowers to throw into the sea as a gift for the gods, to ensure a good sea-harvest in the following year. They take candles to the beaches and work them into the sand, so that the whole beach is a blaze of tiny lights. It must be quite a sight with the white figures and the flowers on the sea—'

'It's a good thing my father's not here to listen to such talk,' Greg said shortly. 'He'd be calling it more heathen rubbish.'

Francis smiled into Roslyn's defiant face.

'Take no notice, Roslyn. My brother has no imagination. I sometimes wonder how you ever came to accept his proposal! You'd have done far better to be marrying me.' He spoke with a teasing laugh in his voice, not meaning to be taken seriously. But Greg's face was dark with anger.

'I'll hear no more of this, Francis. Remember Roslyn is my future wife—'

'You don't need to defend me—' she began.

'I'm not. I'm just making sure Francis keeps his place,' he said grimly. Roslyn heard his mother sigh. Greg's temper had certainly not improved in the weeks since he had proposed, and she hoped fervently it was only due to a natural impatience to claim his bride.

'I think I shall go to bed,' Roslyn was stopped by Greg's hand clamping over hers.

'Not before midnight. It's bad luck,' he said. 'And we must start our marriage with good omens, my dear!'

There was still half an hour to go and Francis seemed to be enjoying the uncomfortable atmosphere between the supposed lovers. At midnight, Greg took her in his arms in front of them and pressed a kiss on her mouth as an exchange of good wishes for the year ahead. Hester kissed her next, and then Francis laughingly said it was his turn. He'd had too much to drink and kissed her more enthusiastically than was necessary, as intimately as had Greg. As soon as she could, she bade them all goodnight and went to her room. The old year was over, and somewhere in the distance she could hear the chimes of church bells ringing in the new. The year that would bind her to Greg for the rest of her life. For some reason a little chill ran through her, and involuntarily she clutched the ruby pendant at her throat as if to assure herself of its protection.

Though Hester had protested at the quietness of the wedding, Roslyn had been adamant. She would have no curious eyes watching and wondering, and no nobility of the district trying to put two and two together and making five. The insulting suggestion that the newly-weds had been lovers in London and that the marriage was necessarily hasty seethed inside Roslyn's memory. But, true to his word, Thomas Radcliffe did not attend the wedding in the small country church, and it was left to Hester and Francis and a few estate workers to make up the congregation and witnesses.

It was the wedding of her dreams...and yet it could not be farther from the fantasy in which she had floated towards Greg to see the love glowing in his eyes as she reached him. This Greg was set-faced and barely smiling as he placed the gold band on her finger, and the joy Roslyn should have felt had vanished like the early morning mist.

Once the brief ceremony was over the carriage took them back to Radcliffe Manor for the wedding breakfast and in no time at all it seemed, they were being taken to the railway station at York for the journey to Scarborough. Roslyn had begged for the journey to be taken by train, since she had never ridden on one, and to please her, Greg had agreed. If only for the fact that it might be a fraction safer in the wintry weather and the cracked frosty ground over which the journey by road would have taken them.

Both Hester and Francis waved them off at York, and then at last they were alone, speeding towards their honeymoon destination. Roslyn felt bewildered and angered at his lack of solicitude towards her. This marriage had been his idea, and in no way had she engineered it. He had been quite open about his reasons for it, and she had agreed to them. He had said it was to be a marriage in every sense of the word, so why was he acting to coldly? Was he regretting it already? The thought that Greg might be yearning towards another lady sent a stab of ice to her heart.

If it was so, did he really expect her to consummate the marriage? Roslyn's pride vied with all her doubts. Had she been very foolish after all, in agreeing to marry Greg? They were bound together now, but Roslyn's unease would not be stilled. No matter how often she told herself it was pointless to be jealous of an unknown rival, the other girl was far from unknown to Greg, and that was what mattered. How long had he known Louise Judd? All his life, perhaps. In any case, much, much longer than he'd known Roslyn. She had entrusted her life to a stranger that morning, a stranger who had wanted her for the fortune she wore round her neck.

She gave a gasp as Greg's hand suddenly took hold of hers. Her thoughts had been taking her almost to the point of hysteria, and she had seen nothing of the hoar-white countryside through which the train was taking them.

'Are you well, Roslyn?' At least his voice was concerned now, and she nodded dumbly.

He changed his seat to sit beside her and to start rubbing her hand in his.

'You're so cold!' he exclaimed. 'This damn train is like ice. Once we reach Scarborough you'll be able to have a hot bath. The hotel is a fine one near the sea with fires in every room. and I shall be there to warm you!'

It was too late. If he'd spoken the words earlier in that husky tone, it might have made all the difference. Now, with all her senses alive to every nuance in his voice, Roslyn could only think bitterly that he was probably reminding himself of his 'duty' towards her. She looked away through the blurring scenes outside as the train rattled on its way to the coast.

'Greg, if you do not wish to-to fulfil all the obligations of marriage...' Her cheeks burned a brilliant red as she strove to find the words, and she heard him give a short laugh as he pulled her into his arms.

'You need have no fears on that score, my sweet Roslyn. Our mutual fulfilment is as important as the other rewards we bring to each other. Perhaps I have not made that clear to you, though I think you have some idea that I am a normal healthy man in all respects.'

His voice was teasing now. She forced herself to smile back. She was Greg's wife. Not his slave or his mistress, but his *wife*... a little of the coldness left her.

'I will not refuse you,' she murmured.

He remained with his arm round her shoulders until the journey ended and they alighted at the station at Scarborough. Outside, a hire-carriage took them through the winding streets that descended towards the coast, and Roslyn had her first glimpse of the wide sandy bay, lashed by a grey sea that pounded and spumed against the rocky cliffs. The contrast between her first sight of the North Sea and the turquoise splendour of the seas around Ceylon couldn't be more total, and she gave a shiver.

She realized she hadn't felt warm all day, and the thought of a hot bath at the hotel was very welcoming.

She was relieved to discover the hotel was as fine as Greg had promised. The rooms were large and well-fitted with velvet furnishings and wide beds and plush armchairs. The floors were thickly-carpeted, the dining-room spotless with uniformed attendants. They were given a short tour of the hotel before being shown to their suite of rooms. Greg had spared no expense in the honeymoon retreat, she thought fleetingly. As well as the bedroom, there was a small dressing-room and a bathroom, a new innovation. No tub to be brought to the bedroom, but a fitted bath with an ornate floral design imprinted inside and out.

'I'll personally attend you with that later.' Greg's voice held more than a hint of laughter now. 'Since you are so unused to bathing yourself—'

'I have managed quite well since coming to England,' she reminded him, her face flaming.

He laughed out loud, his dark eyes raking her contours as she removed her outer coat and moved back to the bedroom, where a welcoming fire burned brightly in the hearth.

'Nevertheless, it will be my pleasure,' he said softly. 'And I hope yours too.'

The management had sent up a jug of hot punch on their arrival, and feeling warmed, Roslyn wandered over to the velvet-curtained windows. There was a magnificent view of the bay, and the sea looked less tempestuous from this distance.

She felt a sense of claustrophobia at being in this room with Greg. It was still only late afternoon, and the sight of him sprawled out on the large four-poster bed was making her nervous.

'Can we take a walk along the beach?' she said quickly. 'I've never walked along the sand before.'

'If you wish, though it will be cold—'

'We have all night to get warm.' The words were out before she realized the connotation he would put on them, and he smiled with obvious enjoyment at the thought.

'So we have, my sweet one, and it will be all the more delightful for the anticipation. Wrap up warmly then, and we will take a brisk walk along the seashore before dinner. But I do not think it wise to stay out over long.'

It was only a short walk to the seashore. The wind was bitingly cold, yet bracing. The smell of the salt air was not unpleasant, and the feel of the yielding sand beneath her boots a novelty to Roslyn. She did not like the way the flurries of sand whipped up into her face, stinging her eyes and half-blinding her, and she was glad of Greg's hand holding tightly on to hers. The light began to fade as a sea-mist started rolling in towards them, and she made no objections when Greg said they should go back to the hotel.

As soon as they returned, invigorated and with eyes and cheeks glowing, Greg ordered the bath water to be brought up for Mrs Radcliffe. Roslyn's heart jumped at hearing him speak her new name. But it *was* her name now. Mrs Radcliffe. Mrs Greg Radcliffe. She tasted its newness on her tongue and the ripples of excitement would not be denied.

She discovered that Greg had every intention of attending her with her bath as he had said. He let her go into the bathroom alone at first, and when he appeared, she was already immersed in the soothingly hot water, into which handfuls of sweet-smelling herbal essence had been dissolved. Roslyn's heart started to pound at the look in her husband's eyes as she lay back against the luxury of the full-length bath. He rolled up his sleeves very slowly, never taking his eyes from her, and then he picked up the wash-cloth and began soaping her body. Never by a word did he betray the way he was aroused by her, as if some instinct told him to go gently now. She was his, but he sensed that

281

she was brittle as glass, and he acted as impersonally as he could.

He did not linger over the ritual. He suggested she should dry herself in the bedroom by the fire, and when she was half-dressed in her chemise and petticoats, she turned suddenly to see him standing in the doorway of the dressing-room, completely naked. Roslyn's face flooded with colour. She tried to avert her eyes, but the image of his magnificent torso; wide dark-matted chest and tapering waist; firm flat belly and long muscular limbs crowned by a tangled dark mass... the image of his body stayed fixed in her mind as she heard Greg's soft laugh.

'Do I embarrass you, Roslyn? A wife should not be ashamed to see her husband!'

'Our absence will be noticed from the dining-room if we stay too long up here,' she stammered, but she found she was mistaken in his intentions.

'We will stay just long enough for you to aid me in my bath,' he said smoothly.

'I—' she began hotly. He walked purposefully towards her, taking hold of her wrist. The sweet scent of the herbs drifted up between them, and Greg could not explain to himself why he felt the compulsion to humble her. If she would only stop gazing at him with that hostility in her eyes, and the dazzling red gleam of the ruby pendant like an accusation at her throat. She only removed it for bathing, as if to remind him constantly that he was beholden to her for his change of fortune.

'This morning you promised before God to obey me,' he said in a rasping voice. 'Have you forgotten your vows so soon?'

Roslyn bit her lips together. A wife's duty was to please a man in all respects. It was an honour...she held her head high and went to the bathroom, standing with the wash-cloth in her hand until he approached to slide into the same water. She added the waiting pail of hot water to it, resisting the temptation to fling it in his face. She soaped him silently, running her small hands over his skin, and feeling her throat tighten as she did so. He watched her without comment as she performed the intimacies that were necessary. The pendant hung away from her as she leaned forward, the deep golden valley of her breasts alluringly near to him.

Greg felt a burning need to wrench the pendant away from her and throw it as far as he could. To end the falseness of this marriage, and start their union in the rapture of love... Yes, he wanted to hold her in his arms and possess her, more than anything in the world...

he wanted to know every detail of that superb golden body as intimately as he knew his own...he wanted to hear her panting beneath him in the ecstasy of love...he was trapped in his own net, Greg realized with appalling clarity. He loved her, and could not bear to have her touch him in this servile way a moment longer. Her pointed nails scratched his skin slightly, and he jerked away from them.

'A serving-girl would do the job less clumsily,' he growled at her. 'Finish dressing, and I'll attend to it myself.'

Roslyn threw the wash-cloth into the water and fled out of the bathroom. Her chest was heaving with a tightness that was making her ache inside, and she was close to tears. She had failed in her first attempt at pleasing her husband. For some reason she had only succeeded in making him angry. That he had sought to humiliate her she had no doubt, but she had been clumsy and nervous, hating the feeling that he was testing her in some way.

Well, now he knew that she had no intention of being treated as a servant, she thought bitterly. Scratching his flesh with her nails had been an accident, but next time it would be deliberate. He could force her to do his will, but there were subtle ways of letting Greg know she still had a spirit of her own and intended to keep it. She slid the dress she had chosen for this night over her head, a cream silk with a watery sheen to it. On her finger the wide wedding band and Greg's ruby ring—at her throat the gleaming ruby pendant. In the hotel mirror she knew she looked lovely and desirable—the dewy-eyed bride. How different things might have been...Roslyn caught her breath, imagining their marriage starting out without the bargaining that demeaned it so. That demeaned *her*, Roslyn added bitterly.

She had been weak to agree to his terms. Grasping at the thought of marriage to Greg as if it were a lifeline thrown to her in a boiling sea. He had tossed the words at her almost callously. She was glad now that she had made that remark about wanting Radcliffe Manor so badly on account of her father's love for it. At least it gave her some dignity. She closed her eyes briefly, willing away the memory of his mouth kissing hers and the hot promise in his eyes.

His was the devil's kiss, Roslyn thought abruptly. His treacherous kiss had done the final persuading, and she hated him for it.

CHAPTER THIRTEEN

It was her wedding-night. Roslyn stood at the window of the hotel room and looked out at the wide expanse of sand and rippling sea, silvered by moonlight. She wore one of the new nightgowns bought specially for her trousseau, soft and clinging and moulding her shape. It was a crisply beautiful evening and it should have been the happiest night of her life, but she was chilled with nervousness despite the roaring fire in the bedroom. Excitement at the culmination of all her dreams couldn't yet quell the apprehension she felt.

All the old nightmare was back with her. She could only think of the monsoon and the lustful fumblings of the dark-skinned man who had raped her so gleefully. Loving was not like that. Loving was the merging of footprints in the desert sand...

She gave a little start as Greg's arms went round her, his hands covering her breasts. She could feel the lean hardness of him against her back, and she swallowed dryly, praying briefly that she would know the right way to please him, her beloved Greg who was now her husband. He twisted her into his arms and she saw he wore no night garments. Her hands touched the firm shoulders and moved round his back, feeling the different texture of a man's skin. His mouth bent to kiss hers, and she could feel the surging desire rising to match his. No matter what the circumstances of their marriage, he kindled a flame in her that became a raging fire of wanting. Roslyn was as yet unaware of her own sensuality, but under Greg's gently persuasive hands and lips she arched towards him involuntarily.

'My sweet, sweet Roslyn.' His voice was softly urgent against her mouth. 'We've waited too long for this and I'm impatient to know every part of you more intimately.'

Still kissing her and holding her, he led her to the bed. Deftly, he lifted the hem of the nightgown as he lay her gently between the covers and edged it over her head. Roslyn's breath came sharply in her throat as his eyes gazed down at the golden contours below him. The air was slightly cool on her skin despite the fire, but it was a sensual feeling, tingling through her from her head to her toes. She saw Greg's dark head move downwards, and then she felt his lips on her feet, kissing each toe separately in whisper-soft caresses. It inflamed her senses.

He moved upwards, his hands and lips following the same trail, and she realized the sharp breathing had quickened even more. He touched her gently, then more surely, alternating the love-play so that she was never quite certain which sensation was the most exquisite before he was on to the next...

'I can wait no longer,' Greg said with sudden urgency. His hand reached out to turn down the lamp, and at once Roslyn gave a small cry.

'No—don't put us in darkness, Greg, please. I—I wish the light to be left burning...'

He gave a low laugh of pure delight.

'My little love! Nothing pleasures me more. I think we will remove the one remaining object between us though.'

He reached behind her neck and unfastened the ruby pendant before Roslyn realized what he meant. She had forgotten she still wore it, but the sight of it gleaming brilliantly in the lamplight was a sudden reminder to Greg of the reason for this marriage, and he had no wish to think of that now. He eased the length of his body over the golden girl who was now his wife, and without the accusing pendant between them a new recklessness swept through Greg's already heightened desires.

She was his, and she would know it this

night, he thought. He inched into her welcoming softness, too inflamed to register that the passage was easier than he might have expected. Too full of love and desire for this glorious creature who seemed to know instinctively how to match his movements to care about anything but the ecstatic consummation of their union. She had the responses of a wanton when he demanded it, and the soft subtle reactions of a lady when he chose to slow the pace of his love making. She was perfection. She was all woman. When his capacity for loving was temporarily over, he still held her in his arms, stunned by the magic that had transported them to such heights.

Finally he rolled away to the far side of the bed, telling her sleepily that he would awaken her later when he was rested, for the taste of her was pure honey and he was eager for more ...Roslyn's eyes were damp as he turned out the lamp now. Damp with sheer exhaustion and happiness, for her Greg had been truly hers and she his, and all her life had been leading up to this, she thought humbly. Greg Radcliffe had been her destiny, as she had always known it.

Let the more prosaic Englishmen scoff at the ways and omens of the East, Roslyn's thoughts ran on. It was destined for them to be together, and it had happened, and more wonderfully than any dream that had ever passed like a mirage before her on hot airless nights in Ceylon. She gave a small shiver. The night here was certainly not hot. The fire had dulled to a glimmer now, and Roslyn reached to the floor for her nightgown and slid it over her head once more. Her hand touched the ruby pendant on the side table. She smiled softly in the darkness and fastened it back round her neck. Her talisman had not failed her, bringing her love and protection, and the promise of greater happiness than she had ever known...she turned on her side, pressing luxuriously against Greg's relaxed body, exulting in the fact that it was her right to do so for always now...

It was pitch dark when she awoke, startled, to hear the sound of Greg's voice beside her. He had woken with the gnawing feeling that something needed to be questioned. She felt his hand on the curve of her cheek, and his fingers tracing the soft fullness of her mouth. Roslyn began to tremble. She was cold, and as she moved slightly, she could feel the pendant like ice against her skin. And yet she was aware of another sensation, akin to burning...she gave a little gasping cry.

Greg's breath was warm on her cheek as he leaned over her. She could not see him, and a wild panic, was taking hold of her.

'I have a suspicion that that was not the first time you have lain with a man, my sweet wife. The experience was a very delightful one, but I'm thinking you were not as virginal as a man expects from his bride. It was gratifying that you did not scream out and tell the world of our joining, but you did not even try to fake a little pain, and that disturbs me. How many have been there before me, Roslyn? Am I wed to a concubine after all?'

His voice harshened as he felt her heart thudding beneath him. He had lain awake for an hour now, telling himself that she belonged to him now, and he'd see no other man had the chance to take what was his. But he was torn by the thought of her lovely body writhing beneath some other man—or men. He could not rid himself of the image of it, and though it might torment him still more, Greg had to know the truth of it. He felt his hand twisting her small chin. At some time she had retrieved the nightgown that was so provocative, and a sixth sense told him she would be wearing the ruby as well. Its presence was like a great wall between them, though he could not begin to explain why he should feel so bitterly about it when it was the means to restoring Radcliffe Manor to its former grandeur. He heard Roslyn give a low moan of pain as his fingers gripped her cruelly and he relaxed his hold on her chin.

'How can you be so cruel?' She still trembled, the words a whisper in the darkness. 'And how dare you accuse me! You shame me, and our love...'

'Our love!' He spoke the words contemptuously where such a short time ago he too had been engulfed by its perfection. Now, he felt only a great insult to the right of every man, to find the woman he had married was no longer a virgin. He put his mouth close to her face again. 'How many, Roslyn? I demand to know the truth. You belong to me now, and I'll be obeyed in this!'

She was sobbing now, the hot tears running down her face and on to his hand. Tears came easily to women of easy virtue, Greg thought remorselessly, as did the art of feigning pleasure when needed. And though he had been so enraptured by her responses earlier, now that he had had time to think, he wondered how she had learned all these things. In his world, young ladies were not instructed in the art of loving a man so beautifully. They had no Nadja to teach them, patiently and intimately, and he knew nothing of such instruction. A bride should learn the ways of loving from her husband, no matter how painfully, and Roslyn's very perfection damned her in his eyes.

Her refusal to answer only incensed him more, and with a sudden oath he wrenched up her nightgown and spread her wide. If she protested he would ignore her cries, he thought ruthlessly. She deserved to be treated like a whore, and he mounted her swiftly, with none of the finesse he had shown earlier, thrusting into her with cruel, stabbing movements, his hands gripping her shoulders, the crude words of lust on his lips as he took her.

Roslyn lay as if numbed as he speared into her. The darkness was thick with his rasping breathing, and the smell of his body sweat strong in her nostrils. Earlier it had excited her rather than repelled. It had been part of the rapture that joined them. Now, it was Bahu's rank hovel, and the steamy stench of the native who had raped her, and the horror of that night suddenly made her beat against Greg's back with her fists, and twist her head from side to side on the pillow with remembered terror.

'Is that the way your lovers like you to behave?' he grated. 'They must have been like animals—'

Roslyn found her voice at last, almost screaming at him in the darkness. 'I did not have lovers! I did not know any man until the night I fled from my burning home. And then I was

293

raped—*raped*—do you hear? By a dark-skinned native in the darkness who gloated because he'd won such an unexpected prize!'

He could not doubt her sobbing words. He paused in his thrustings, feeling his passion die. He slid away from her, though his hands still dug into her flesh.

'Is this the truth?'

Roslyn nodded. She felt bruised and sore, not only in body but in spirit. How could Greg have used her so? Was their happiness to be so brief...?

'But someone taught you what a man expects from a woman. Did this native spend so much time with you that you learned to enjoy it?' He clung on to his dignity, though he was angered at himself at what he had done, and Roslyn's silent weeping tore at his heart.

'A woman is taught the ways of pleasing a man by her nurse.' Roslyn spoke numbly, as if repeating a well-learned lesson. 'It is the way of things in the East. Nadja prepared me well for the union with my husband. I had not realized until now that one could be prepared too well. The lesson would have been better left unspoken.'

By the time she finished speaking, her voice was filled with bitterness. He reached for her with more gentleness, but she flinched away from him as if she feared more rough treatment. He was not the kind of man to beg for favours, and he turned his back on her abruptly. They were together in the four-poster bed, yet they might have been oceans apart, and neither spoke again for the rest of the night.

Somehow they got through the days and nights together at Scarborough. Nothing would ever be the same again, Roslyn thought with a choking pain. It would have been better if she'd never known the sweetness of Greg's love than to have it snatched so cruelly away by his own suspicions of her virtue. A woman raped would always be condemned, even though it was no fault of her own, she realized bitterly.

But their close physical proximity could not stop the unbidden arousal that each felt so keenly. There were times when Greg took her roughly, as if determined to force his will on her, daring her to disobey. But there were other times, when the chilly nights sent them unconsciously seeking the warmth of each other's arms in their sleep, and then they would awaken langorously, still only half-aware that the needs of their bodies were overcoming all else. Then it was almost like the first time they had known the sweet pleasures of love...ecstatic and fulfilling...Greg was unable to deny that his desire for her had strengthened, not lessened, but since his terrible accusations he had been unable to voice the words of love he felt for her lest she should scorn him.

She had changed towards him. He sensed it as sharply as if she drove little knives into his heart. He could not blame her, but neither could he bring himself to blame himself. She was his wife, and he was the master of his home and of her. She would obey his wishes in all things, including his physical needs. Greg had known other women, but never one who had the power to stir him to desire as Roslyn.

As for her—she still felt she was being used. The nights when Greg reached for her in half-sleepy unawareness were the best times, when the love that flowed between them was almost as unmarred as if his rough assault on her had never happened. She could push it to the back of her mind then—but at other times, when it was merely a man's need that made him pull her silently into his arms, there were empty tears of bitterness inside her. It was plain that he intended asserting his marital rights over her whenever he desired, and that he expected her alway to fulfill her obligations to him. It was not the way she had anticipated marriage with her fantasy prince.

They were both relieved to leave Scarborough and return to Radcliffe Manor. The day they arrived home it was stormy, and rain lashed the carriage as Francis and Hester hurried them into it outside York Station. The sky was overcast, and Roslyn thought gloomily that it echoed the feelings inside her. She tried to act the part of the happy bride, but since the family knew very well the circumstances of the wedding, it hardly seemed worth the effort. And though Aunt Hester chatted with determined brightness for most of the journey, Roslyn was fairly sure Francis' keen sardonic eyes missed nothing of her wan face and Greg's tight jawline. They were hardly the traditional newly-weds—she blushing, he proud— and neither made any attempt to appear so.

'There have been even more complaints about leaking cottages since you've been away, Greg,' Francis drawled. 'This weather is revealing more rotten timbers daily. Father took it on himself to make a resumé of all that's needed to present to you on your return. Not the happiest way to start married life, but I've no doubt you'll be anxious to set about the repairs now.'

Now that there was money available in the bank, was what his words implied. Roslyn kept her gaze steadily fixed on the drizzle and mist ahead of them, wondering why on earth she had left the hot sunny climes of Ceylon for this place and these brooding people. As Greg gave her hand a small squeeze to temper his brother's taunt, she felt a sudden rush of love for him. She knew the reason only too well.

'I'll go to York tomorrow to order all that's necessary and arrange for delivery,' he said tersely. 'I may decide to stop overnight and see to other business, such as buying new stock. It may even take two nights away if I have to go further afield.'

'What—leaving your new bride so soon?' Francis said in a mocking voice. 'I would not be so willing if she were mine!'

'Just remember that she is not,' Greg remarked smartly.

Francis gave a coarse laugh. 'Dear brother, Roslyn may start to wonder what kind of "business" you have in mind if you stay away from her arms too long!'

'Francis, please!' His mother spoke severely to him from the front seat of the carriage. 'I won't have you upsetting Roslyn.'

Roslyn felt a renewed jealousy take hold of her as she listened.

'I'm sure Greg and I can withstand a night or two apart,' she said lightly. 'It will make the reunion happier for being parted!'

She knew she was being bold, but the astonishment in Francis' eyes and the low chuckle of approval from Greg made it worthwhile. Let them think what they liked, she thought defiantly, but preferably let them think that the honeymoon had been wildly successful! It was a matter of pride, and she let her hand remain in Greg's for the rest of the journey for all to see.

'Roslyn dear,' Aunt Hester leaned forward, anxious to cover the small silence. 'There have been some reports of house burglaries in the district. I don't want to worry you, but I was thinking about the ruby pendant, and if it would be best to put it in the bank for safekeeping until the scare is over...'

'No, I can't do that,' Roslyn answered at once. 'It is safer with me, Aunt Hester. It must remain with me.'

She was reluctant to elaborate and have Greg scoffing at her for her beliefs in magic. But she might have known Francis' imagination would have been alerted. He lost his mocking look and smiled into her eyes in the old friendly way.

'Is that one of the conditions of the ruby working its protective powers, Roslyn?' he teased. 'They have some powerful magic in the East!'

She found herself smiling back. The ruby

nestled safely against her skin, and she felt the comfort of its presence, as she so often did, and the strong belief that nothing could harm her while it remained around her neck. The devil's kiss...from the moment she had heard its name she had been enchanted with it, and she suddenly remembered blushingly how she had likened the phrase to the effect Greg had on her when his mouth demanded hers.

They were almost home. *Home*, Roslyn thought with a little glow. The home her father had known so well, and of which she was now mistress. A smile curved her soft lips at the sheer pleasure of knowing how happy he would be if he knew. Francis saw the smile and caught his breath. By heavens, but he envied Greg this one. His lovely bride, with all the ripeness of a sun-kissed peach...and the precious ruby too. It was a damnable thing to be the second son, Francis thought sourly. Second son, and always second best. There was a chance that Louise would look on him favourably now that Greg was married...provided the Judd family didn't cut them dead altogether. But even the luscious Louise could not compare with his brother's wife. He turned his eyes away from her before she could begin to guess at his lustful thoughts.

Greg helped her down from the carriage, his hands firm around the small waist he knew so intimately now. For a second he smiled into her eyes, as if to remind her of the sweeter moments they had shared. Roslyn didn't need reminding. They were etched deeply in her memory.

They arrived home to find Thomas Radcliffe had lost much of his bluster. Now he was no longer master at Radcliffe Manor, he was surly rather than aggressive, petulant in the way of some old folk approaching senility. Since his influenza he had adopted a more stooping posture and the pettiness too of old age. He picked at his food and slopped his drink and found fault with everyone. Roslyn thought Aunt Hester had a saint's patience to put up with him.

Since they had been away, Aunt Hester had moved all Roslyn's possessions into Greg's bedroom in readiness for their return. Her father's leather bag and its contents was now at the foot of what was to be Roslyn's wall closet, and her dresses hung above. A tall chest contained her underclothes and other belongings. She looked through it all when they retired for the night. Her hands touched the blue silken sheen of the sari with its gilt trimming, and she let the sensuous feel of the fabric run through her fingers for a moment.

'What's that?' Greg spoke behind her. She hadn't heard him approach, and she made to push the garment inside the drawer quickly.

'It's nothing—only an Indian garment,' she said. 'I was merely looking through my things—'

'Show it to me,' he commanded. Roslyn felt a slow tingling run through her at the arrogant look in his dark eyes. She held out the sari silently, and he took it from her curiously. He had never seen such a garment before, but the rustling silk was pleasant to the touch, and a smile warmed his mouth.

'Do Eastern women actually wear such things?' he said incredulously.

'Of course,' Roslyn shrugged. 'In our climate the thinner the garments, the better.' She saw Greg's eyebrows rise a little as she referred to 'our' climate. 'This sari may not be worn in the streets, except for special occasions, as it's particularly fine silk. It would certainly be used at weddings or festive occasions, and the dancing-girls in the harem would wear such things.'

He held it out to her. 'Put it on and dance for me,' he said softly. Roslyn felt her face go hot. She made no move to take the sari from him. He stared steadily at her. 'I want my wife to dance for me,' he repeated in a tone that said he had every right to ask and to be obeyed.

Roslyn looked at him with a burning anger inside. All right, she would dance for him! She would show how an Eastern girl enticed a man to her bed, seductively and wantonly. She would show Greg the difference between his prissy English girls and the sensuous people who were so practised in the art of pleasing a man...she took the sari from his hands and moved behind a draught-screen. Her fingers shook as she removed the heavier English clothes and the constricting undergarments, feeling the cool softness of the blue silk as she fastened it round her body. The very texture of it made her a different woman. She was not cold in the fine gossamer silk, for there was a kind of feverishness burning inside her now. She shook out the long dark tresses of her hair so that it fell about her shoulders and caresseed her own skin. Her feet were bare as she finally stepped out from behind the screen to stand in front of Greg, lying full-length across the bed they would share.

His eyes widened. Was this really his wife, this ravishing vision in blue silk, gold trimming glittering in the firelight and the ruby sparkling like fire at her throat? This stunning sight that transformed her from the spirited

Roslyn he knew to a pleasure-giving concubine all but took his breath away. He sat up slowly, feeling urgent desire gripping him as her little bare feet began to move. Her body arched and dipped slowly and gracefully as one foot pointed sideways, tracing a delicate circle on the carpet, rising and falling as the gleaming blue silk followed her undulating movments.

Her whole body became supple and lissom as the remembered movements of the dance rushed back into her mind. She danced provocatively, throwing back her head so that her long hair touched her waist and swung around her face. She wrapped her own arms around her body, her fingers caressing it, passing lightly over her breasts and the lines of her legs beneath the sari, in the way she had seen dancing-girls perform in Ceylon.

There was no music, but Roslyn needed none. The music was all in her head...the beat of jungle drums, the rhythm of quickening heartbeats, the harsh breathing and the thin wail of Eastern instruments. She was mesmerized by the music of her mind. She was no longer here in this shared bedroom at Radcliffe Manor. She was back home in her own lovely room on the Darby plantation, practising for her own pleasure in front of the long mirror after a day out at Kandy or a ball where the entertainment had been sensual and abandoned for the Darby-wallah and the other English ladies and gentlemen.

Greg watched, his eyes smouldering, as she seemed to forget he was in the room. She appeared not to be dancing for him, but for herself, as if she was away in some secret world of her own that excluded him. Her brilliant blue eyes were almost glazed, her cheeks flushed, mouth parted and glistening as if in readiness for a lover. The voluptuous breasts were caressed by the silken garment, their tips pointed against it as if to tantalize him still more.

He needed her to be aware of him, he thought aggressively. She was his woman...*his* concubine if she was anyone's, and he would have her. He *must* have her, here and now...

She danced on, not even noticing that he was shedding his own clothes. The cloudiness was around the edges of her vision as the glorious happy past claimed her in sweet memories. The five months that had changed her from a pampered child to a bewildered woman might never have been. She was Roslyn Darby again, darling daughter, adored by all, and she dreamed of a man she would never meet.

She was suddenly aware that she was moving forward, and that the end of the silken sari was caught by strong hands. A joyous laugh bubbled up in Roslyn's throat, for it was still the dream, and she spun towards Greg as he unwound the garment from her luscious body, until she was caught in his arms. She was still dreaming...the ruby's magic was still weaving its potent spell. The firelight was caressing her nakedness as she sank to the carpeted floor before it with Greg's body swiftly covering hers. Giving her no time to cry out or protest...but there was no thought of rejection in her head. Only the fulfilment that came from loving and being loved.

It was a night such as Roslyn had never known before. Yet the feeling that she was still held in some hallucinatory power never quite left her. This couldn't be real, her mind insisted. Greg couldn't be saying the sweet words of love in her ear. It was still an extension of the dream...the mirage of the mind she spasmodically experienced...

By the time Greg lifted her on to the bed, she was exhausted. The exotic dance had sent her into some kind of trance from which she hadn't yet recovered, and she did not want to. She had dreamed that Greg loved her and wanted her for herself...and it was a dream from which Roslyn never wanted to waken.

CHAPTER 14

Roslyn awoke to find herself alone. It was morning and she discovered she had a stabbing headache. She was cold, and then she realized-why. She was unclothed beneath the bedcovers. The memory of the previous night surged into her mind, but she was too unwell to feel anything but the sharp humiliation of having danced for Greg in such an abandoned way. She remembered he had made love to her in an almost frenzied fashion, but this morning the thought didn't give her any pleasure. She felt heavy and dull-witted with the pains in her head, almost as if she had been drugged. She must have been drugged in her mind to behave in the way she had last night, Roslyn thought. She struggled into her nightgown, fastening it as high in the neck as possible, as if to shut out the shameful memory of Greg's hands caressing her body so urgently.

She was glad she had done so a few minutes later, when there was a tap on her bedroom door and Aunt Hester stepped inside. Roslyn struggled to sit up, but the effort was too much.

Someone had opened the curtains, and the daylight seemed to glare into her eyes.

'Are you well, my love?' Aunt Hester said anxiously. No matter how Roslyn tried, she could not bring herself to call Greg's mother anything but Aunt, after so many years of thinking of her that way, but the lady was quite unperturbed. And she would never in her life be able to call Uncle Thomas 'Father'.

'I have a terrible headache, and the light hurts my eyes,' she murmured.

'Then you must stay where you are, and I'll have some food sent up to you,' Hester said at once. 'Greg has already gone off on his business, and sends you his regrets that he did not say goodbye. He said you were sleeping so soundly it would have been a pity to disturb you.'

It was silly to feel the awful sense of letdown, Roslyn told herself, but now she wouldn't see Greg for several days, or however long he stayed in York or elsewhere. She was piqued, and the stabbing headache only made her feel more aggrieved. He could have made the pretence at regretting having to leave his bride so soon, the thoughts raged round her brain when Hester had left her. Sending a message through his mother was hardly the same as waking her with gentle kisses and telling her in private

308

how much he would miss her.

But why should he, if it wasn't the case, Roslyn thought in sudden misery? And his rapid changes of mood from tender ardent lover to a remote stranger she hardly knew, didn't make her feel any the warmer towards him. She wanted his attention, and not the unwilling dumping of a tray in her room by a sullen-faced serving-girl. Roslyn sent her packing with a few sharp words and forced some of the food down with an effort.

Eventually she must get up. Lying down was only making her head worse, and she needed the keen fresh air of the moors to clear it. She dressed warmly and made her way out of doors, ignoring Hester's protestations that it was too cold a day for walking. Away in the distance she could see Francis' tall figure mending some broken fencing. He called out to her and she made her way towards him, catching her breath as it rolled away from her in little white clouds with the exertion of the climb.

Up here the air was pure and sweet. It was like being on top of the world, with rolling moorland stretching away for miles in undulating contours, dotted with grey-white sheep forever chewing dumbly, the low stone walls criss-crossing the bare terrain at intervals. The occasional shepherd's hut broke up the monotony of the landscape. It was almost beautiful in its starkness, Roslyn surprised herself by thinking.

To Francis' eyes she was by far the most beautiful sight to come his way on this raw January morning. Her cheeks glowed almost as brightly as the ruby he knew she'd be wearing beneath her dress. Her bosom heaved with the effort of reaching the top of the moors, and she stumbled a little on the rough ground. He laughingly caught her in his arms to steady her. He had already made up his mind to act the trusted friend. He knew his brother well enough to guess that this marriage would be a stormy one. Greg would hate the feeling of being beholden to his wife, no matter how convenient and necessary to him.

'Your kingdom, madame,' Francis said softly, one arm sweeping to embrace the whole of the visible countryside. The other arm was loosely around her shoulders. 'Have you climbed to the top of the mountain to survey it?'

Roslyn laughed, her blue eyes sparkling in such a way that Francis felt a sharp envy of Greg at knowing all the charms of this lovely woman.

'It's hardly a mountain! But Radcliffe Manor does look lovely, doesn't it? I wonder how many times my father climbed up here to stand

and look on it like this!'

It was an emotive thought, and she tried to put herself in James' shoes for a moment. James had loved the house, and yet he'd wanted to leave it...

'He'd have been proud of you,' Francis said suddenly. 'It must have taken a lot of courage to leave Ceylon and throw yourself on a family who didn't even know of your existence.'

'I don't know about courage.' Roslyn was unusually humble for a moment, and touched by his words. 'Sometimes I think it was just foolhardy, and my reception was no more than I deserved. Oh—I don't mean you, Francis. You and your mother were very sweet to me, and I suppose I could understand your father's anger, though I hadn't expected it to be quite so vicious. But Greg—'

'It wasn't as my father hinted then? Greg didn't attempt to compromise you at the inn in London?' If his voice hadn't been so bland and innocent, she would have turned on him angrily. As it was, she answered him just as frankly.

'He did not. In fact, I think Greg truly hated me the first time he saw me. I wore a shabby dress that was filthy, and my hair was dull and unkempt. It was little wonder he thought I had come to sponge on him and his family. Thankfully, I finally managed to convince him otherwise.'

Francis' arm tightened about her shoulders.

'I cannot imagine you looking dowdy and unkempt in the way you described it, Roslyn. You're the loveliest woman I've ever seen, and Greg is the luckiest devil alive to have you for his wife.'

Roslyn felt a chill run through her. Why did he have to use that particular word to describe Greg? It was nothing more than a brotherly burst of envy, but it reminded her too sharply of their marriage pact. Greg had wooed her with his devil's kiss, and she had loved him too long to resist.

When had Greg realized the potential of James Darby's daughter, she thought bitterly? Was it when he'd found her, numb and chilled in a bathtub of lukewarm water after Nadja's death, with the ruby gleaming on her golden breasts? Did the idea of it nudge into his mind even then? She wondered why he had bothered to put it all so bluntly to her, when he could see by her responses that she was besotted by him. Or was this his way of telling her that once he had what he desired and the honeymoon was over, the marriage would be no more than a sham? The thoughts spilled over in her head, as she realized she was clenching her hands so tightly together her fingernails were digging into her palms.

'Roslyn, why did you agree to this preposterous marriage?' Francis' voice was warm in her ear. 'You and I could have been happy together. And now the Judds are back...'

Roslyn jerked away from his tightening hold on her. The distaste she felt at the way he was behaving towards his brother's wife was completely overshadowed by his last words.

'Your mother said they always wintered abroad and wouldn't return until the beginning of February.' Her voice betrayed her own feeling of panic.

'So they intended, but I gather Louise's father was unwell and they decided to come home early. He's a fanatical patriot, and always said if he was going to die anywhere it would be in his own bed on English soil. It doesn't stop him enjoying the Swiss resorts every winter though—'

The rest of his words were lost on Roslyn. All she could think of was that Louise Judd was back in York, and Greg had gone there the minute he returned, leaving his new bride without even a word of goodbye. Her eyes blurred for a moment.

'How do you know all this, Francis?' she said numbly.

'There was a note to the effect from Law-rence Judd, and a brief message of congratulations on Greg's marriage. Apparently they saw the item about the wedding in an English newspaper Lawrence had sent out to him regularly. I told you he was a patriot. Oh —and his illness wasn't serious. They're giving a ball in a few weeks' time, and we're all invited. I daresay Louise wants to look you over, Roslyn.' He couldn't hide the smirk in his voice, but Roslyn could ignore that. She shook with vying emotions as she listened to him.

Horror at the thought of attending the Judds' ball and being the only stranger there...and the thought that if Lawrence Judd was so much a patriot he'd be even less enchanted to meet Greg's wife, who was the daughter of an English emigrant instead of his own daughter. Dismay that she was unable to put off the meeting with Louise much longer...and cold furious anger at Greg, for leaving her to find out all the information from his brother. There was also a sick jealousy that he had gone running to see her so quickly, and no doubt in her mind now that it was the case. And on seeing her again, would he realize his mistake in marrying Roslyn, she wondered despairingly? However much he protested that he would not

314

be pushed into marriage because Thomas Radcliffe had wanted it—left alone, would they not have wished it for themselves? Roslyn was tormented by doubts, and she would have been even more disturbed had she noticed the satisfaction in Francis' eyes as he saw the reactions flitting across her face.

Superficially light-hearted, Francis had every bit as much ruthlessness in his nature as his brother, though few suspected it. And he could still hold a trump card. One member of the family had run off to foreign parts. Why not another...why not himself, accompanied by Roslyn and the precious ruby—back to the land she loved...? It was a momentous idea, and one which would give him total triumph at last over his elder brother. His fortune and his wife... and the lure of Ceylon which was as attractive to him since Roslyn's vivid descriptions of it as it had ever been to James Darby. He had complete confidence in the plan, but he must go cautiously...

'I'm so sorry, Roslyn. I've upset you. But even if Greg calls on Louise today, they are old friends. It will mean no more than that, I assure you.' He managed to convey to her mind the exact opposite. He touched her cheek with his lips very lightly. 'You know I would never do anything to harm you or upset you. I think too highly of you for that.'

She forced a smile on lips that suddenly felt so wooden. Francis was being very sweet, his handsome face filled with contrition, and involuntarily she kissed him back, full on the mouth.

'Thank you for telling me,' she said huskily. 'And now I think I had better go back to the house before I am chilled right through.'

But it was a chill of the soul rather than of the body she felt. Francis caught hold of her hand once more.

'If you ever need a friend, Roslyn, turn to me. If I can be no more than that to you, be sure I will always be your most steadfast friend, and one who loves you.'

She was not ready to take in the full meaning of his words, but it didn't matter. He wanted her to remember them later when the time was ripe. When the poison he dropped into her ears had done its work, she would be ready to come to him. As he watched her walk away from him with that strange sinuous grace, the thought of possessing that luscious body was almost as intoxicating as the triumph over Greg and possession of the ruby would be.

Roslyn walked back to Radcliffe Manor feeling betrayed. Greg should have told her the

Judds were back in England. Why hadn't his mother mentioned it this morning? Or had Greg instructed her not to do so? Her heart thudded jealously at the thought of Greg's reunion with Louise. Would there have been tears and recriminations at first...and then a glorious forgiving and reconciliation? Louise could never be Greg's wife now, but she could still be his mistress, and the thought brought renewed pain.

She wouldn't let herself think of them together. The headache that had receded earlier was now back again, throbbing at her temples with the insistence of native drums inside her head. She stood still a moment as the dizzy sickness washed over her, but though she briefly closed her eyes, the images were still there... Greg, masterful and demanding and persuasive as she knew only too well he could be...his arms round a young woman with silvery-blonde hair falling about her shoulders...Greg, who belonged to *her*...

Roslyn was cold all over, save for the burning sensation at her throat where the ruby touched her skin. Her mouth was suddenly dry as dust. There was danger threatening. She sensed it as surely as if it was written in letters in the sky. There was a sudden helplessness about her, as if she had set out on a course from which there was no turning back, and which could only end in disaster. The ruby was telling her to beware...she clutched at its comforting smoothness inside her dress. It would protect her. There was all the wisdom of the East in its power.

Thomas and Aunt Hester were together in the drawing-room when Roslyn returned to the house. Thomas had recovered enough to be downstairs, but he was tetchy and abrasive to anyone who spoke to him. Roslyn was in no mood to watch her words. She discarded her outdoor cloak and sat beside Hester on the sofa, warming her cold hands in front of the fire.

'Francis tells me the Judds have returned from abroad,' she said at once. 'And that we've been invited to a ball in York. Why didn't Greg tell me before he left, Aunt Hester?'

She heard Thomas give a rasping chortle in his throat, but Hester spoke quickly, a tinge of colour in her cheeks.

'The note from Lawrence Judd and the invitation only arrived yesterday, my love. Greg wanted to tell you himself, but he said he would choose the time. Since you've heard something of Louise, he felt it was his place to inform you, and I'm annoyed that Francis should have done so.'

Yesterday! So Greg had known of Louise's

return before he ordered Roslyn to dance for him in the sheer blue gold-trimmed sari...he'd as good as proved his mastery over her by revelling in the abandonment of her dance and then sating his lust in the feverish desire that had overtaken them both. Roslyn's face burned at the memory of it.

'So the thought of meeting this lass bothers you, does it?' Thomas Radcliffe's voice growled with venomous amusement.

'You forget he chose me as his wife,' Roslyn answered coldly. She stared at him defiantly. She had no love for this man who had been hateful to her ever since her arrival. 'Greg told me he had no wish to marry Miss Judd. It was you who kept goading him towards it, because of her money—'

Her voice dwindled away. She anticipated Thomas' words before they came.

'And why do you think he married you? Out of *love?* My son has been a disappointment to me in many ways, but I have to hand it to him this time. He went for the bigger prize and won it, but forbidden fruit can be all the sweeter—'

'Thomas, don't say such things to Roslyn!' Hester leapt to her feet, visibly upset at his coarseness. But Roslyn could stay and listen no more. She snatched up her cloak and stalked out of the drawing-room with his raucous laughter still ringing in her ears.

In her own room Roslyn sat heavily on the bed. She shouldn't let him upset her so, but she couldn't help it. How on earth Hester could have allowed him to woo her she couldn't imagine. On an impulse Roslyn searched in her drawer until she found the pencil sketch Hester had given her of James. She looked into his face and felt a wild surge of nostalgia for her old life. To exhange all that for this...the warm spicy air and wide blue skies; the tiered grey-green slopes of their own plantation; the colour and glitter...Kandy and the bejewelled elephants trumpeting long into the starlit night..

Nothing on earth could compare with that, and of her own choice she had come here in search of a dream. She was in this alien land, trapped in a hollow sham of a marriage with a man who, by all accounts, loved someone else. All because of the ruby. The devil's kiss.

For the first time Roslyn wished she had never set eyes on the Siamese ruby, nor heard the romantic tale of how her father had come by it. Its value was undisputed, but it had not brought her love, only disillusion, and she could never be rid of it, for old superstition was too well instilled in her. In hung like a great millstone around her neck. Roslyn rarely cried, but now she wept bitter tears. If only things were different. If only Greg loved her. He sometimes spoke the words of love to her, but only when his body claimed hers. It was easy at such moments to speak of love. The memory of it now was all the more humiliating when Roslyn remembered how quickly he had found the need to go to York when he discovered Louise Judd had returned from abroad.

Greg came home to Radcliffe Manor three days later. In that time Roslyn had steeled herself for his return. She now totally ignored Thomas unless he spoke to her directly, but at least from Hester and Francis she really felt the affection for which she yearned. She was becoming fond of Francis. He was the brother she never had, and she had not realized what a delight that could be. Greg found them laughing together in the drawing-room when he arrived late in the evening, his parents already having retired for the night. Roslyn's face flooded with colour at his sudden appearance. The urgent desire she felt to fling herself into his arms was tempered by rememering where he'd been, and the sardonic look in his eyes at seeing his wife and his brother so enjoying each other's company.

'I see you've managed to keep yourself amused in my absence, Roslyn,' were his first words to her. She bristled at once.

'No more than you have, I suspect,' she shot back at him. 'Is Miss Judd well after her holiday abroad?'

Greg started. So she had been told, and it didn't take too much imagination to guess who had told her. He looked coldly at Francis, but he had had a long journey back, not wanting to stay away another night. He had no wish at that moment to harangue Francis.

'Perfectly well,' he said instead to Roslyn. 'And looking forward to meeting you at the ball in York, of which I'm sure you've also heard.'

'Is she?' Roslyn let her eyes widen. 'I cannot imagine why she should. I'd have thought we two were the least likely of acquaintances.'

In the firelight she looked more beautiful than Greg remembered. There was a glow about her, and her lovely blue eyes were the colour of cornflowers tonight, matching the dress she wore. He longed to see her generous smile instead of the sudden tight-lipped look she was giving him. The way she'd been smiling into Francis' eyes moments before. If Francis had been poaching on his preserves he'd kill him, Greg thought explosively. But Roslyn's words reminded him of the uneasy meeting

322

he'd had with Louise, and he made an effort to lighten his reply.

'I assure you Louise is eager to meet you, Roslyn. But more of that tomorrow. I suggest we go to bed now. I am tired—'

'But I am not,' Roslyn said defiantly.

She trembled as Greg strode across the room and pulled her to her feet. She was outraged at his treatment, but Francis said nothing, knowing better than to interfere when Greg was in this mood. He would sympathize with Roslyn to better effect at some other time.

'When I want my wife, I expect her to obey me,' Greg said sharply. He spoke to his brother without looking at him, his eyes boring into Roslyn's. 'We'll have words tomorrow, Francis. My business in York and elsewhere was entirely satisfactory.'

Roslyn had no choice but to follow Greg to their bedroom. Was she to obey this monster who came to her straight from his mistress's arms? But she found that it was not to be. Greg was unutterably tired from the journey and the various transactions he'd made in the past few days, and the visit to the Judd home, which he'd felt morally obliged to make.

He kissed Roslyn's cold lips goodnight, and told her mockingly that contrary to what she might imagine, a man's body was not capable of the impossible, and that he'd do right by her when he was rested. He fell asleep almost immediately. To Roslyn, with her scant knowledge, he could mean only one thing. He was fully satisfied by the charms of Louise, and had no need of his wife for the present. Her outrage that he would come straight home demanding his marital rights from her was replaced now by indignation that he could be so blatantly callous about it, and a huff that he did not want her...

She looked down on his sleeping face, more vulnerable when it was relaxed. The anger in her dissolved. Gentled in sleep, he was totally hers, Roslyn thought. No one else saw him like this, his strong features softened, his unruly dark hair on the pillow next to hers. She unfastened the ruby from round her neck and placed it beneath the pillow with trembling hands. No matter what he did, she loved Greg and would love him until she died. *It was written*...she reached and turned out the lamp at the side of the bed.

She could hear Greg's rhythmic breathing. Softly she traced her fingers around his mouth as she had done so many times before. Only then it had been a pencil sketch of the living breathing man she never dreamt to see. This man whose skin she touched was real, and she loved him so hopelessly she found it impossible to resist leaning over him to touch her lips to his, feeling the beat of his heart beneath her breasts.

Oh Greg, her heart cried out silently to him. Only love me a little...in the glow from the firelight she was suddenly aware that his eyes were open. Before she could stir his arms had moved to hold her, and she felt the arousal in him. He turned her on her back and entered her swiftly, his mouth still on hers. It was a gentle joining, for he was truly fatigued, but when they slept, they slept in each other's arms.

The next day started out brightly. The past was over, Roslyn told herself, and that included her yearnings for a life she would never know again. She must think of the present and accept Yorkshire as her home, and with a thin January sun turning the morning mist to a sea of diamonds across the long moorland vistas, it wasn't quite so difficult. Today there was timber arriving for the repairs to the tenants' cottages, and Greg was at his most amiable, knowing he could set off and give them good news.

'Do you want to come with me, Roslyn?' he smiled at her, and she knew he was remembering the last time they had toured the cottages, culminating in his proposal. And whatever the reason for their marriage, there had been glorious moments, as well as stormy ones. She nodded eagerly.

'We'll take some time off from the farm afterwards, and I'll show you some of our spectacular ruins,' he went on. 'You won't have heard of Fountains Abbey, I suppose?'

She hadn't, but she was more pleased than he could have guessed to know she was to spend the day in his company, and away from Radcliffe Manor. Sometimes it began to feel claustrophobic to Roslyn, with Thomas' scowling face and Hester trying to placate him and constantly apologizing for his bad manners. It was only when Francis was around that she felt able to relax. And when Greg was there too, she thought, and then reconsidered. Relaxing did not fit with her image of Greg.

The business at the cottages was conducted quickly, leaving the tenants in a cheerful frame of mind. They hadn't started out until after lunch, and Greg had suggested they go on horseback, as later they would traverse rough country. It was pleasant to feel the wind in her hair and the scent of bracken and gorse was earthy in her nostrils. It was good to be alive, Roslyn thought as they rode across the moors, and Greg told her something of Fountains Abbey before they reached the medieval ruins.

'It goes back to the twelfth century, when Benedictine monks came here from York. By the sixteenth century the monks were very prosperous through their dealings with the wool trade. We'll have to go carefully when we approach it, as the lane is steep, but I think you'll find it worthwhile, Roslyn.'

'My father would have come here,' she commented, finding pleasure in retracing his footsteps.

'He'd have found it interesting enough before he went in search of wider pastures,' Greg said. 'I defy anyone to find it lacking in beauty and grandeur. I cannot offer you temples and elephants, Roslyn, but Fountains Abbey has a mysterious quality all its own.'

She hadn't thought to compare it with anything in Ceylon, and she wished Greg hadn't assumed that she would. She rode behind Greg's straight back, faintly resentful that he'd dispelled some of the euphoria she'd been feeling. But as they neared the gaunt ruins, magnificent in the dwindling sunlight and with a hint of mist creeping round their foundations, she caught her breath. The thick stone walls refused to crumble with time; the piles of rubble where some had surrendered only emphasizing the splendour of a powerful past. Surrounded by woodlands and a winding river meandering through the grounds, it gave out an aura of great peace.

'Can we explore it?' she asked eagerly.

'Of course.' Greg slid off his horse at once and helped her dismount, his hands easily spanning her small waist. For a moment she thought he was going to kiss her, but he let her go and tied the horses to a stake. The ground was rough and uneven, but as they neared the ruins, Roslyn began to feel dwarfed by them. They lingered a long while, but although Roslyn found it fascinating, she was never quite at ease inside the cavernous stonework with its high arches and precarious pillars. She was glad when Greg finally said they must start making their way home.

Outside, Roslyn was alarmed to see the mist had crept over the entire landscape now. It was still late afternoon, but the day had darkened and the sun had disappeared. She felt as if they walked through a grey-white swirling sea of cloud as they reached the point where the horses were tethered. Roslyn shivered, suddenly aware of the coldness seeping into her body. Except for the touch of the devil's kiss that dug like thorns against her flesh as Greg hoisted her into the saddle. She felt a great unease for no explicable reason crawling over her. When she looked back at the ruins they seemed to soar and grow out of the swirling greyness that moved all around them. It was still daylight, yet she felt as if she was plunging into a sea of darkness. She felt Greg grasp at her reins, and she gripped them tightly.

'We've left it a bit late, but if we make speed we'll get home before dark,' he assured her. 'And once away from the valley, the mist won't be so thick across the moors, Roslyn. I'll keep hold of your reins, but the horses are sure-footed, never fear.'

But she *did* fear. Fear seemed to envelop her as the horses picked their careful way up the steep lane and back on to the moorland track. She could hear the thud of her own heartbeats. And contrary to what Greg had said, the mist was every bit as thick on the moors as in the valley. Somehow Roslyn had expected it to be so. She saw it with a sick inevitability. She wondered if Greg had deliberately kept her out to frighten her so that she would turn to him in grateful relief for getting her safely home. *If* she got safely home. They still had a good distance to go.

About halfway back to Radcliffe Manor Roslyn felt a sudden jerk on her reins. The horse broke into a gallop and she realized he had broken away from Greg's hands. Her own grip on the reins tightened, but she was unable to control the runaway horse. She heard herself screaming Greg's name as it stumbled over the slippery uneven moorland, and then she was thrown off, landing heavily and striking her head against a rocky outcrop. The mist changed into blackness.

She must be dreaming. Greg was holding her in his arms and caressing her, calling her his darling and his sweet one...but her head hurt and she was too lethargic to open her eyes. She was so cold, and misty images kept floating round in her consciousness, dark faces and greed-filled eyes...grasping hands...she realized Greg's hands were around her throat, and suddenly her mind was crystal-clear even though her head still throbbed unbearably. Greg was taking the ruby from her...perhaps he thought she was dead, and he would report that the ruby had been lost or stolen...she found new strength in her limbs and voice and beat her hands against him in the gloomy daylight. Above her in the shadows, he appeared like some dark demon...she felt total panic.

'You shan't have it,' she shrieked, her hands

clawing at her throat to confirm that the pendant was still there. 'Get away from me, you devil—'

Greg's hands were shaking her. 'Stop it, Roslyn,' he was shouting angrily against her ear. 'Stop it, do you hear me?'

His hand struck her a stinging blow on her cheek, and she gasped with shock. Did he mean to kill her here and now she wondered numbly? Kill her and take the ruby and go back to his mistress...was that the reason for this ride out to the old abbey? She heard herself sobbing quietly against his chest as he held her now. Presumably, she thought bitterly, she had spoiled his plans by rousing too soon from her fall.

'Did you really think I was trying to remove the ruby?' he demanded. 'Do you think so little of me, Roslyn?'

'Your hands were at my throat,' she said shrilly. 'It was either my life or my fortune you were after. Deny it if you can!'

He inched away from her, his face still close to hers. Her head swam and she couldn't focus clearly. But his voice was as cold as ice when he spoke to her.

'I had no intention of taking either, my precious wife,' he said with cold sarcasm. 'I was making sure the pendant was still fastened securely after your fall and lifting your head from the rocks. As soon as you're able you'd better ride in front of me. I'll send for the doctor as soon as we get home, for I think your mind has been affected as much as your body!'

He pulled her none too gently to her feet and whistled for his own horse. Roslyn's was grazing nearby, and he tethered the reins together. He helped her to mount and climbed up behind her, urging the horse to a steady trot. She was so dizzy the motion made her feel abominably sick. She might have thrilled to feel the close proximity of Greg's strong body pressing against hers, and the grip of his arms around her, but not this time.

Now she was only aware of the cruel destiny that had sent her across oceans to find this one man in all the world. A man who did not love her and had trapped her into a farcical marriage. A man who meant her harm. Perhaps he had already plotted for this day while he had been in York, but the power of the ruby had protected her, this time at least. Roslyn felt a great shudder of fear that perhaps she would not be so fortunate next time. She could not rid herself of the certainty that Greg spelled danger to her—it was the shattering of all her dreams...

CHAPTER 15

The doctor pronounced that Roslyn was suffering from concussion and should remain in bed for a week. He intimated delicately that it might be best for her to sleep alone, and to her great relief Greg temporarily moved out of their bedroom into another one. Her dire suspicions had lessened a little with the coming of daylight, but they still lingered deep down, and she was not yet ready to trust him completely.

She tried to believe Greg's explanation out there on the moors, and to acknowledge his fury at her accusation. But in her worst moments she actually made herself believe he had been trying to strangle her, and the gulf between them widened further every day. He could not forgive her for her suspicions, and she could not retract her words.

Hester came and sat with her many times while Roslyn stayed in bed. She wished she could confide in the older woman, but it was impossible. How did one confide that she thought Hester's son meant her harm? It sounded preposterous in the daylight hours, with Hester chatting away or working at her embroidery and so lovingly keeping her company. Roslyn stayed silent.

Strangely, it was Francis who encouraged her to talk about Fountains Abbey, and as always, he was eager to hear about Ceylon.

'You should go and see it for yourself,' Roslyn smiled at him. He was a dear to take the time to sit with her. She hardly saw Greg, except on what was clearly a duty visit.

'Perhaps I will one day,' Francis told her. 'It's a shame your day had to end so unhappily, and for your lovely skin to be marred by bruises. Let's hope they'll all be gone by the time we go to the Judds' ball.'

Roslyn wished privately the concussion had happened the day before the ball, then she'd have had a genuine excuse not to attend. Francis' sympathetic eyes lingered on the bruises on her cheek and throat. Suddenly she had to tell someone. His eyes widened in disbelief as she spoke of Greg's forceful fingers.

'Oh, you're mistaken, Roslyn! Greg is devoted to you, no matter how—well, we all know he has an eye for the ladies, but I'm sure he's more than happy with his bride! Who wouldn't be? And why should he take the ruby, you goose? He already has access to its value, so why steal it? Forgive me for being so frank,

Roslyn, but we're all aware of the circumstances, and I'm sure if Greg had wanted to marry anyone else, he'd have done so.'

'I know,' she said miserably. As for the circumstances he mentioned—she'd been the one foolish enough to blurt them out, but he needn't have reminded her. Francis had the unfortunate knack of making things slightly worse, Roslyn thought. Of making her remember things she'd rather not, like Greg's former association with Louise, and that this marriage was merely one of convenience. While the ruby existed, Roslyn thought dully, how could she ever be sure whether Greg's feelings towards her were real or pretended?

'Cheer up, love! I'm supposed to be putting a smile back on your face,' Francis said. 'It's high time you saw some different company though, and I promise you'll enjoy the Judds' ball. And if you get tired of seeing Greg dance attendance on Louise, I'll stick close and partner you all evening,' he added with teasing gallantry.

Roslyn thanked him dryly, not altogether happy at the picture he was painting.

A few days before the ball, the doctor pronounced her fit again. And Greg proceeded to move his belongings back into their bedroom. Roslyn was a bundle of nerves at the prospect of sleeping beside him, all her old assurance deserting her at the memory of his hands at her throat. But surely he would not try to harm her in the privacy of their own room? Francis had obviously thought she was imagining things. Roslyn would not have expected him to be so staunch in his defence of Greg...in a way, it only made her more suspicious, as if Francis was hiding something from her.

When she retired that night, she pretended to be asleep when Greg came into the room. She could hear him undressing while her eyes remained tightly shut. The bed dipped as he slid in beside her and his arms reached out for her. She seemed to freeze in his arms, unable to make any response as he sought her embrace.

'What's this then?' Greg said softly. 'Rejecting your husband's advances?' His tone said it was unthinkable, and hearing it Roslyn's spirit was restored. She lay rigidly against him.

'That is exactly what I am doing,' she said in a low voice. 'And if you make any attempt to force me, I will scream my loudest and all the whole household will know!'

His anger was almost tangible. She half-expected him to force her, but he flung himself away from her at once, leaving her on the far side of the bed. She knew his pride well enough to realize he would pursue her no farther that night.

'I have no wish to force you, Roslyn,' he said harshly. 'If I get too hungry for a woman's arms I'll find my pleasures elsewhere if they're not available at home. You have my word on it.'

The slow tears ran down Roslyn's smooth cheeks. What had she accomplished, except to push Greg into another's arms? And she might as well have been on the other side of the world in the Darby mansion, for all the distance between them now.

The carriage took them on the road to York in a flurry of rain. Thomas had decided to stay at home with an attack of gout, so there were four of them attending the Judds' ball.

Hester was clearly happy at the prospect of a ball, and Francis at his most charming. Greg was distantly polite, and only Roslyn was beset by nerves. To be presented as Greg Radcliffe's new bride was one thing—in different circumstances it would have been the happiest of occasions. But in the present mood between them, and on their way to meet Louise, whom Roslyn could only see as her rival—she felt as if a hundred butterflies danced up and down in her stomach.

And when they finally met, Roslyn knew she was right to be alarmed. The occasion reminded her instantly of similar evenings in Ceylon, when she had been the glittering star and everyone had fawned around her. Tonight was Louise's night, and she was a formidable rival indeed. Tall and willowy with glorious gold-blonde hair and honey-coloured eyes, and a pouting smile that would always draw a clutch of male admirers. Her gaze swept over Roslyn's silk-clad figure and rested briefly on the dazzling ruby pendant. Just long enough for Roslyn to be fully aware that Louise knew exactly why Greg had married her. She fought to stop herself from trembling in front of this white-skinned beauty.

'So this is Roslyn.' Her accent was similar to Greg's, which matched the two of them still more in Roslyn's mind. 'My best wishes on your marriage. I have already congratulated Greg, of course, and told him what a fortunate man he is.'

'Thank you,' Roslyn said stiffly. They were joined by the Judd parents, and Lawrence Judd looked her over more openly.

'You've not done so bad, lad,' he admitted broadly. 'Though I'd hoped you'd wed my lass and well you know it! But I can see the attraction that tipped the scales here all right.' As

Roslyn's eyes flashed, he chuckled down at her from his brawny height. 'Aye, you've a look of James Darby about you, lass,' he said, as Thomas Radcliffe had done. 'It'll take a vigorous man to tame that spirit.'

'I'm not a mare, sir,' Roslyn said icily, and Lawrence Judd slapped his thick sides with laughter.

'That you're not, my dear. And I like the look of you. As your host I shall claim your first dance, so let's leave these old friends to get re-acquainted and join the fun, eh?'

Roslyn had no option, since he was holding her firmly by the arm. She suffered agonies at leaving Greg with Louise and seeing the triumphant smile on the other girl's face. She glimpsed them a little later, spinning among the brightly-coloured gowns, in the exhilaration of the waltz. For a man who had spurned the chance to marry Louise, he looked completely happy to be in her company, Roslyn thought with stabbing jealousy. And even when the music ended, Greg made no move to leave Louise's side, but paid court to her quite openly. At one point during the evening, he turned and looked at Roslyn mockingly, and she remembered his words...'I'll find my pleasures elsewhere if they're not available at home...'

'My dance, I think, Roslyn.' She found Francis at her elbow. She did not lack partners all evening, for everyone was eager to look at this lovely exotic bride Greg Radcliffe had found for himself, and she was often in Francis' arms and listening to his flattering remarks. Hester and Mrs Judd spent most of the evening with the older ladies, surveying the brilliant scene in the sparkling ballroom.

'You should not let it show so much, Roslyn,' Francis said softly in her ear as he put his arm round her for the dance.

She knew what he meant and didn't bother to pretend otherwise.

'How can he humiliate me like this?' She spoke in a tense low voice so that only Francis could hear. 'He has only danced with me once all evening—'

And that had been sweet torment, feeling Greg's arms around her, and seeing his smiling face looking into hers as if he really cared...knowing she could weaken instantly to his desires if he made them evident again...but he did not. Once their dance ended he gave a little bow, and she had to watch his tall arrogant figure, devastatingly handsome in dark evening clothes, making its way back to Louise.

She was aware of Francis' arms tightening round her more than was proper in such a public place, and of the smell of wine on his breath. His voice was not quite steady as he breathed soft words to her, his eyes clearly troubled at her unhappiness.

'If you were mine, Roslyn, I would never leave you for a moment. Dearest Roslyn, hasn't it dawned on you yet that you married the wrong brother? He treats a woman as a slave, but I would make you my queen. I would love you—'

She swallowed at the sudden intensity in his voice. It was wrong of Francis to speak to her this way, and even worse for her to listen to him. She had not wanted to come here and be humiliated by her husband, who was making no secret of the fact that he still admired Louise. Roslyn too, had been plied with wine all evening, and the persistent flattery of this handsome young man, who was so frankly adoring, was sweet music in her ears. She was suffused with a sudden warmth...

'It's very hot in here, Francis. May we sit down a while?' she said faintly. He took her hand at once and led her through the twirling dancers. The room was so crowded no one took any notice of their movements.

'It will be cooler in the conservatory, Roslyn, and I'm sure you'll be interested in it. Lawrence has it filled with some exotic plants you may even recognize.'

She went with him trustingly, lulled by the caring note in his voice. He did not leave her burning with jealousy while he flirted outragiously. Francis was kind and attentive, and she wondered anew if she had made a terrible mistake in marrying Greg. She had accepted his reasons for proposing, but she could never forgive his infidelity.

The air had been stifling in the ballroom. She had danced for most of the evening, and was feeling the tension of meeting Louise, and the folly of taking too much wine in her nervousness. Her head spun alarmingly if she moved it too fast. Francis opened a door that led to a dimly-lit room of large proportions, the walls made entirely of glass. It was warm and humid inside, with a scented earthy smell that reminded her of home.

Roslyn gazed around her. The Judd conservatory was like a miniature jungle. There were huge bushes and plants in every shade of green, so vivid they might have been retouched by an artist's brush. There were brilliant flowers of every hue imaginable. She was instantly enchanted...it was like a sudden sweet reminder of home with the exotic scents filling her senses...she could almost imagine the jewelled colour of a kingfisher darting through the foliage...there was a smarting of happy tears in her eyes as Francis put his arm round her waist...

She realized his hold was tightening and her heart gave an uneasy lurch. They were very close, and she was dizzy with the scents of home and the effects of too much wine. As if her nearness was too much for him, Francis gave a small exclamation that was almost a groan, and pulled her into his arms. Taken by surprise, Roslyn was unable to move as he held her captive, and his lips sought hers.

As she recoiled, he seemed to be pushing her backwards against the wooden frames of the conservatory. With a supreme effort she twisted her head away from him, her senses reeling.

'Francis, are you mad?' she gasped.

His laugh was short and strained. 'Perhaps I was mad to let Greg marry you, Roslyn! It's degrading to know he did so because of the ruby. And now that Louise is back, I fear he will bring you much unhappiness. It has already started, hasn't it? It pains me to see it.'

His words were like knives in her heart, said as they were with reluctant conviction. Roslyn felt as if she would choke as she swallowed back the tears. Francis' arms still held her, his sympathy obvious, and then she realized his hand was sliding gently upwards to caress her breast as she leaned numbly against him.

Whatever the outcome of Louise's reappearance, this was not the answer. Even if Greg turned from her, she could not betray him with his own brother...

'Francis, no!' Her voice was a painful croak. 'I am still Greg's wife—'

'That only saddens me more, Roslyn,' he said mournfully. 'I cannot pretend to enjoy knowing he has everything while I have nothing. And to see the unhappiness in your lovely eyes because of him—'

His voice grew more passionate, and Roslyn struggled to be free of him. His intensity and the humid atmosphere were making her claustrophobic. She could not really be afraid of Francis, and he seemed to be in the throes of some great melancholy rather than anything else. But his arms still gripped her, and his eyes glittered darkly in a way she did not like. He was like Greg and yet so unlike him.

It might be as well to humour him and let him talk. Surely someone would come to the conservatory soon...

'Why do you feel like this, Francis? It's almost as if you seek revenge—' the impulsive word came to her lips, though she did not really believe it. Francis laughed harshly again.

'Perhaps I do.' He sounded as petulant as

a small boy. 'Greg never lets me forget that I'm the second son. Father despises me because I don't give a damn about Radcliffe Manor.'

She felt a swift sympathy, despite his indiscretion towards her. He felt trapped in his life here, much as her own father must have been, with the same longings for adventure. James Darby had made his escape...she pressed her soft lips to Francis' cheek in a sisterly gesture of understanding. At once he pulled her close again.

'We could leave them all, Roslyn!' The words tumbled out with a boyish recklessness. 'Come with me! We'll go to Ceylon! You'd like that, wouldn't you...?'

Roslyn felt a shock at his words. He must be more intoxicated than she'd thought, to speak so to her. He seemed feverishly elated now, and she strove to calm him.

'Stop it, Francis! What you're suggesting is madness. Supposing someone should hear? And besides, I don't want to leave Greg—'

'Why not?' he said sulkily. 'Do you think I'm incapable of loving as well as everything else?'

He seemed to slump as he relaxed his hold on her, and she managed to twist away from him. As if he had relied on her for support, he suddenly went crashing against a wooden frame, sending pots and earth hurtling to the ground. He swore angrily, and for a moment Roslyn was frightened as his fingers dug in her shoulders as he regained his balance. For that moment he seemed to her menacing, and her softening feelings vanished.

'Let me go, Francis!' she gasped.

To her relief, the sound of voices came towards them as other guests arrived to tour the Judd conservatory. Francis swiftly recovered himself, and she heard his stuttering apology as his hand sought hers, his voice beseeching.

'Please forgive me, Roslyn. I had no wish to upset you. I think too highly of you for that, and it's only because I'm concerned for your happiness that I acted so badly. Can you ever put it out of your mind?'

Roslyn still trembled from her brief moment of fear. But he was once more the gentle brother she wished him to be, and so contrite she could not stay angry with him. Her nerves were so taut she was beginning to suspect the most innocent demonstrations of affection. And perhaps she had been foolish to come out to the conservatory with him unchaperoned, knowing he would naturally want to offer his sympathy at the way Greg was neglecting her. She must have been mistaken in thinking Francis meant her ill!

She murmured that she thought they should return to the ballroom, thinking it best to ignore all that had happened.

'And you will allow me to dance with you again, Roslyn?' Francis said abjectly, to which she replied that of course she would.

He looked so wretched she could only feel pity for him because of his lapse. She reminded herself of his previous kindness to her, and even felt guilty that she had sometimes encouraged his attentions too warmly.

Indeed, Francis was so courteous when they resumed their dancing, Roslyn began to wonder if she had imagined the little scene in the conservatory. He was once more the light, bantering Francis of old, and she felt a sting of remorse at her unworthy suspicions of him. Francis had intended no assault on her! It had all been her own imagining...

Roslyn was thankful when it was time to leave the Judds' ball. She remembered little of their departure in her eagerness to get away from the house in York. She was still dizzy with the effects of the wine, to which she was so unused, and she rested her head against Greg's shoulder for the journey home, barely stirring until he moved her gently away from him at the door of Radcliffe Manor.

Presumably she said the appropriate words to Francis and Hester as they sped across the courtyard out of the scudding rain and into the house, but she did not care. She was too unutterably weary and miserable at the tensions of the whole evening, and all she wanted was to lie down and sleep...sleep for ever...

Greg had other ideas. Roslyn had rejected his advances ever since their unfortunate ride to Fountains Abbey, and he had deliberately planned to annoy her that evening by lavishing attentions on Louise. He would force Roslyn to admit her jealousy and, hopefully, her love. She should understand from her life in the East that arranged marriages could, and often did, turn out satisfactorily. And Greg longed for his wife to be the ardent loving woman he knew she could be.

He had been furious to catch a glimpse of her leaving the ballroom with Francis. And he had not expected Roslyn to return to the ballroom with a flush on her cheeks that suggested stolen kisses! He had wanted to storm over to her there and then, and demand that she act more decorously as his wife, but he would not give her the satisfaction of creating such a scene in the Judds' house. Instead, he turned his back on her and Francis, and continued to pay court to Louise, though in all honesty her inane prattle was beginning to bore him.

Now, there were no onlookers and no intruding rivals. Only Greg and his wife, and as he gazed down at her dark hair, flowing loose on the pillow as she lay with closed eyes and relaxed mouth, the desire for her overcame all other emotions. She was his, and as he slid into the bed beside her, his hands pushed aside the cool fabric of her nightgown. The fiery brilliance of the ruby winked up at him. Roslyn's eyes opened slowly. She heard Greg's low exclamation, and then she felt his hands unclasping the pendant from her throat and heard him place it on the little table alongside. She was too drowsy to protest, too much aware that her head no longer seemed to be attached to her body to offer any resistance. And as his hands began their seductive caressing of all the warm pulsating parts of her, too sensually awakened to care...

'These are the only kisses you'll know from now on, sweet Roslyn,' he murmured against her lips. 'The kisses of a lover as well as a husband. You'll need no devil's kiss while I hold you in my arms.'

'No devil's kiss,' she breathed the words on a small sigh of rapture, hardly knowing she spoke. She was in a state of enchantment, warmed by Greg's body, engulfed by the sweet fulfilment of his passion. He whispered words of love to her, and whether they were meaningless or not, she gloried in them and her own true feelings for him spilled out of her in whispered admission as he shuddered against her.

He lay unmoving for a long time, hardly daring to believe that she had spoken the words he had longed to hear from her lips. They had both been playing at the game of life in this contrived marriage, but now the game had become glorious reality, and as he moved reluctantly away from her sleeping face he leaned over and lay his lips against hers for one last lingering kiss. A small pulse beat steadily in the long golden line of her throat and he kissed that too, exulting in the fact that without the ruby's presence between them their love stood a chance of survival after all. He glanced to where its golden chain hung over the edge of the bedside table and turned his back on it.

CHAPTER 16

No devil's kiss...

The words seemed to swim around in Roslyn's brain when she awoke a long while later. She was very cold. The fire had dwindled, and the lamp was turned very low. Unthinkingly she reached out her hand for Greg, and found the bed empty except for herself. Outside, the wind sawed across the moors, accompanied by the lash of rain against the window-glass. Roslyn shivered. Her feeling of foreboding was strong, but the effects of too much wine were still bemusing her mind. She tried to remember.

There had been a ball, and Francis had behaved disgracefully...or perhaps it had all been in her imagination. She had met the cool slender Louise Judd and known searing jealousy when Greg gave all his attention to her. She and Greg had ended the night in each other's arms...she moved restlessly, as the sweetness of that union momentarily drowned all other thoughts. Why then, this unease...this feeling that something was terribly wrong...?

No devil's kiss...it was Greg's voice that had spoken those words! Roslyn's hand went to her throat, and then beneath her pillow to where she normally placed the pendant at night. The rapid pounding in her heart began again, together with an awful feeling of despair. As if she had somehow known of this moment ever since she brought the ruby to England...hastily, she sat up in bed, her fingers scrabbling over the bedside table in desperation, remembering now that Greg had put it there.

She slid out of bed falling to her knees in a frantic search for the precious jewel. She turned the lamp up to its fullest, holding it at floor level, willing the gleam of the ruby to appear in its yellow light. There was nothing. And dimly in her mind she could hear the echo of Greg's whispered words on her lips.

'These are the only kisses you'll know from now on, sweet Roslyn...you'll need no devil's kiss while I hold you in my arms...'

Greg had taken the ruby. It must be so. She couldn't begin to analyze his reasons, but she knew he had resented it as much as he had desired it. In the same way he felt about *her*, Roslyn thought chokingly. Had it all been a pretence after all? Had he and Louise planned this, perhaps, and were they, even at this moment, fleeing through the night with the precious ruby in their possession?

Wild hysterics took hold of Roslyn. She had once had so much, and now she had nothing. She began to shake all over, and was unaware that she was screaming aloud until she heard the sound of running footsteps and then felt the comfort of Hester's gentle arms as she knelt beside her on the bedroom floor.

'There, there, my love, have you had a nightmare? What a night to be sure. To start so cheerfully with the ball, and then to end like this!'

Roslyn stared at her through eyes blurred with tears. The sobs still shook in her throat, and her stomach lurched wretchedly. What was Aunt Hester talking about? Unless Roslyn had been screaming out the truth in these last seconds...she had not been in control of herself...blindly, she spoke Greg's name, the accusation trembling on her lips. Let his mother despise him, as Roslyn despised him...

Hester cradled her to her bosom, rocking her as if she were a small child, pleased that Roslyn's first thoughts should be for her husband.

'Greg has gone out with the rest of the men, my love. It's a wonder you didn't hear the racket when old Wilf from one of the cottages came hammering on the door.'

For a second Roslyn's attention was turned away from the ruby.

'Gone where? What's happened. Aunt Hester?' she stuttered.

'You'll know the stream that runs through the valley where the men have put the new stock? The night's rain has washed half the banks away and there's a danger of it flooding. The new sheep are penned there for the time being, and if they're not moved to higher ground they could all be drowned. It would be disaster after all Greg's efforts to start the stock producing a good wool profit. And the new lambs too expected soon.'

It would be a disaster indeed, after all his pretence at loving her in order to obtain the surety of the ruby, Roslyn thought bitterly. She could hear the worry in Hester's voice, and bit back the damning words she'd intended to say. This was between her and Greg. She let his mother fuss around her and help her back into bed and she made her voice as normal as possible as she thanked her.

As soon as she'd gone from the bedroom, Roslyn threw back the bedclothes. Out on the moors. She knew well the spot to which Hester referred—a normally picturesque little valley between two wide slopes of moorland, its winding stream crossed by several wooden bridges.

Roslyn was consumed with the need to confront Greg and accuse him face to face, and to wrench the truth from him. The thought of his cruel deception all these weeks wounded her immeasurably, and her conviction that he and Louise would soon be together was driving her to total despair.

She could not lie here and do nothing. Nor could she wait to confront Greg when he returned from the moors. If her suspicions were true then it was unlikely he would return.

She dressed with feverish haste, donning her warmest dress and boots and flinging a thick cloak and shawl around her. She turned out the lamp and plumped up the pillows under the covers, so that if Hester should glance in again, it would look as if she were sleeping. Minutes later, she was creeping along the dark corridors of the house and down the back stairs; through the kitchen and out towards the stables.

Her heart was in her mouth. The night air snatched at her face and clothes at once, the icy rain stinging her flesh and making her gasp. It was sheer recklessness to be out on such a night, but Roslyn felt compelled. She must know the truth, now. A convulsive fury gave her added strength. She coaxed the horse she had ridden before out of the stable, and when she had led him some distance away from the

355

buildings, she climbed on his back, slipping and sliding as she did so. There was no saddle or bridle, and she clung to the animal's mane as she dug her heels against his flanks and lay low over his back.

Her teeth chattered together. The moors were a bleak wilderness in the darkness, the rain blinding her, and every movement of bracken and gorse in the moaning wind making her nerves taut.

Once at the top, she was able to make out the dappled flare of torches moving in the valley below where the swollen stream was gushing, and knew that the men would be working desperately to move the new sheep to higher ground. She could hear shouts from the men, and the panic-stricken bleating of the animals. She swallowed, her throat suddenly dry. But she must go on.

She would find Greg and denounce him in front of all of them. Let Thomas Radcliffe know what kind of son he had, and let his labourers scorn him for his ill-use of the daughter of James Darby. Twice in a lifetime the name of Darby had suffered at the hands of the Radcliffes, but *she* had no intention of leaving without her revenge. She urged the horse down the steep slippery hillside, clutching on to him desperately. Despite the mad,

356

tumultuous desire to punish Greg, she was terrified both by the night and the storm.

The flaring lights in the valley were spreading out now, weaving far below like the lure of goblins in the night. The shouts were muffled, lessened by the drumming of her own heart. She felt she was drowning in rain as it soaked through her clothes and froze her face and hands. She could hardly cling on to the horse that was skidding and threshing at her clutching hands...suddenly it bolted with a whinny of fright as a crack of thunder sounded overhead. As a streak of lightning zig-zagged earthwards with a brief flash of yellow light, Roslyn was thrown sideways on to the sodden earth. She fought to catch her breath as the sounds of the frightened horse disappeared into the distance.

Sobbing in her throat, Roslyn moved carefully. Although she felt bruised all over, nothing seemed to be broken. She swayed to her feet. Without the horse's comforting presence, she was now entirely alone. She had screamed out when she fell from the horse...and she knew she had screamed out Greg's name. Dizzily, in that moment, all she had wanted was the haven of his arms. To forget about the pendant's existence and pretend there was a true and abiding love between them. For one crystallized moment, Roslyn had renounced all belief in the ruby's magic. And the premonition that something was terribly wrong had come to her without the ruby's presence. Her own sixth sense had warned her, and her own wild fool-hardiness had brought her out here on the bleak Yorkshire moors, where any track she might have taken was obscured by driving rain and a ghostly mist...

Suddenly she knew she was no longer alone. Someone was nearby. A human sound...

'Greg!' She tried to scream his name.

The sound came nearer, and then she was grasped in a fierce grip. In the grey gloom she saw him towering above her, his black head plastered down with rain. Greg...she realized her mistake as soon as he spoke. It wasn't Greg...

'So you've decided to come to me after all, have you, my lovely girl?' Francis was triumphant.

Roslyn gasped, her hand moving quickly to her throat, and Francis laughed harshly as he saw the gesture.

'The ruby won't help you now, Roslyn *Darby*,' he said brutally.

She stared at him. His fingers were hurting her, his words betraying the truth. Francis had no way of knowing the ruby was missing—

unless he had taken it himself. It would have been so easy. Greg would have been alerted first when Wilf raised the alarm about the swollen river. Francis must have slipped into their bedroom when Greg had gone—and taken the ruby, left so temptingly on the bedside table.

Soaring relief that Greg was innocent flooded through her. But followed swiftly by the realization of her own danger. There was an air of madness about Francis, and Roslyn knew instantly that she had not imagined the scene in the Judds' conservatory. It should have warned her. How incredibly foolish she had been.

'Give me back the ruby, Francis, and I'll say nothing—'she stammered, sensing it was a futile hope. He made no attempt to deny that he had taken it.

'Oh, Roslyn, would anyone give back such a prize?' he taunted. 'But I made you an offer once, and it still stands. We'll go away together—tonight, and you need never see this cold place again. We'll go to the Darby plantation and rebuild it.'

Her rage surged. She thrust his arms away from her and beat against his chest, hating him.

'Go with *you*?' she screamed. She slipped on the wet ground, and he instantly had her in his grasp again. 'I'd as soon be in the clutches

359

of a wild beast as go anywhere with you!'

He *was* a wild beast, she realized, and just as dangerous. His voice was suddenly close to her face, and softly menacing.

'Roslyn, my dear, if you won't come with me, I can hardly leave you here, can I? It's a pity to spoil such beauty, but it seems you leave me no other choice.'

His hands were round her throat. Roslyn knew total terror then, feeling the life being choked out of her.

With a strength born out of desperation, she kicked out and her knee thrust hard. Francis let out an explicit oath and his grip on Roslyn's throat slackened. She wrenched away from him, her feet slithering on the sodden moorland as she tried to run down the hillside to where Greg must be.

She heard Francis blundering after her. He was completely insane, she realized hysterically, made drunk by the power of the ruby in his grasp, and the need to dispose of her. He had been the danger all along. Always Francis, the bland one...the charming one...the treacherous one...

He was shouting her name wildly. Almost frozen with fear, she saw another shape looming in front of her. A hoarse scream escaped her lips as it thrust her out of the way. It was Greg. She could hear the two brothers fighting savagely, both breathing harshly and noisily.

Suddenly she saw that Greg had been knocked to the ground and was lying motionless. Her heart leapt, but as the flaring torches from the valley began bobbing nearer, the shouts of the other men could be heard calling for Greg. Francis hesitated.

'*Go*!' she ground out hoarsely. 'Just *go*, and leave us in peace, Francis!'

For a moment she wondered if he would drag her with him. But the torches were coming nearer, and he must have realized that she would hamper his escape. With a final muttered snarl, Francis twisted away from her and went lurching off into the mist-filled darkness. Roslyn crawled across to where Greg lay so still, heedless of the filth and mud. She cradled him in her arms, terrified that he was dead.

'Greg darling, don't die,' she whispered huskily. 'Please don't die. I love you so much—'

She heard him groan, and went weak with relief. When the other men reached them, in the light from the torches they could see that Greg's head was bleeding.

'He isn't dead,' Roslyn said quickly, her voice catching, 'but he must see a doctor, and

I'm not sure if we should move him.'

'He can't lie here,' Thomas Radcliffe said gruffly, clearly surprised at the sight of Roslyn, filthy and weeping over her husband.

She did not mention Francis. There would be time for all that later. Greg's well-being was all that mattered for the moment. And she had meant what she said to Francis. All she wanted was for him to get out of their lives and leave them in peace. If it meant he took the ruby with him...for some reason there was a great calmness now seeping into her mind whenever the ruby came into her thoughts. She looked dumbly into the anxious faces, rain-soaked and weary beyond words, as the men stood around Greg like the watchers in a wake.

'There's a shepherd's hut a little way from here,' Wilf offered. 'We could carry him there and send someone for a cart to take him back to the manor, and someone else for the doctor. What do you think, Mrs Radcliffe?'

Roslyn's throat filled suddenly. He was asking *her*— Greg's wife. The lady of the house ...she nodded quickly, fighting back the little rush of tears. Wilf would never know what dignity he had restored to her ragged feelings.

'That would suit very well, Wilf—and when we reach the hut I will stay with my husband, if you will all attend to the rest of it, please.'

She could not speak above a whisper for the bruising of her throat, but she looked directly into Thomas Radcliffe's eyes as she spoke, daring him to argue with her. He did not, merely barking out the orders as if they were his own.

The men carried Greg carefully. It wasn't far, but it seemed an eternity before they laid him gently on the earthy floor of the hut and went to do Roslyn's bidding. By now the rain had stopped, and an unearthly yellow-grey light was beginning to lighten the dawn sky. Roslyn knelt beside Greg in the dimness of the hut, chafing his cold hands with her own, and willing him to stay alive.

At last he opened his eyes, staring at her blankly for a moment, and then recollection rushed back to him.

'Roslyn—what in God's name was happening out there?' He winced as he put his hand to his head and felt the congealing blood. 'And what were you doing there in the first place? You and Francis—'

The sudden suspicion crept into his voice, and she shook her head quickly.

'Oh no, my darling! Never me and Francis! Oh, I hardly know how to tell you—'

She realized his hand was gripping hers.

'Am I still unconscious and dreaming, or did you just call me your darling?' he demanded with something of his old spirit. 'Your voice is so soft, my sweet one, I might almost believe you meant it!'

She leaned forward and with an impulsive movement touched her lips to his. She smelled of earth and rain, and he had never felt so sure that she was the only woman with whom he wished to share his life. She was as unkempt as when he'd first set eyes on her, the proud daughter of James Darby, yet Greg realized he had begun to fall in love with her at that very first moment.

'I love you, Greg,' she whispered simply. 'I always have.'

He realized she was fighting back the tears, and that she was unbearably tense. And she still hadn't explained her presence on the moors on this filthy night. She looked as fragile as if a breeze would waft her away from him, but he was in great pain and couldn't pull her into his arms as he'd have wished. Instead he held her hands tightly in his own.

'Tell me what happened, Roslyn,' he said gently. 'It has something to do with Francis, doesn't it?'

She looked at him mutely. The dawn light was filtering through the cracks in the wooden hut now, and the door swung gently to and fro. His face had lost its usual colour, but his eyes were as demanding as ever, demanding to know the truth. She pulled back the cloak from her smooth throat, and his eyes hardened as he saw the tell-tale bruising on the golden skin.

'Francis tried to kill me, Greg.' She shuddered as she said it. Even now it seemed unbelievable. 'He wanted me to go away with him. He made me believe you were still in love with Louise and would continue your association with her despite our marriage.' It hurt to say the words, but she ignored Greg's angry exclamation and went on quickly. 'He was angry when I told him I could never do as he asked. He wanted us to take the ruby and go back to Ceylon. He used my longing for home to try to persuade me—'

Her voice broke, and Greg sat up too quickly, gritting his teeth at the giddiness as he did so.

'Roslyn, I have never loved Louise Judd, nor did I ever have the desire to marry her. As for continuing our association—there's none to continue. She's a friend. No more than that. Do you believe me?'

She nodded. She had to believe him because all her instincts told her it was true. She had been a fool to listen to Francis' poisonous insinuations. She licked her dry lips. She hadn't finished telling Greg everything yet.

'Greg, I came out on the moors tonight because of you, to accuse you.' She could hardly put it into words, and they came out haltingly, knowing how wrong she had been. 'When I awoke, I discovered you had gone—and so had the ruby.'

There was only the sound of their heartbeats in the little hut now, and the conviction in Roslyn's mind that she should never have suspected Greg. It wasn't in his nature to go like a thief in the night.

'Greg, I'm sorry,' she said softly. 'I should have known it wasn't you. I must have been mad not to realize how devious Francis was, beneath all his charm. You should have warned me!'

'Would you have believed me?' Greg said grimly. 'But if Francis has the ruby, we must alert the authorities as quickly as posible. He must be stopped—'

Roslyn restrained him as he struggled to stand. The strange feeling of calm she'd felt earlier was still with her. It was as if the words were put into her mouth by someone else...a young, dark-skinned Indian prince...or James Darby...she spoke them slowly, as if repeating a lesson that was half-forgotten.

'Let him go, Greg. If the ruby is stolen it will only bring disaster to the thief. In time it will be restored to its rightful owner. We only have to wait. I did not part with it voluntarily, and I truly believe its protection is still with me.' She gave a sudden shiver, remembering the moments when Francis had almost choked the life out of her. She had been badly in need of protection then...but she had survived, and she was here with Greg's arms around her...standing unsteadily, but together. Hope soared in her heart. 'Greg, there have been moments lately when I wished I had never seen the ruby,' she admitted slowly. 'Instead of binding us together, it only seemed to push us apart. But I can't forget that it was part of our marriage bargain, and until its brought back to me, what will happen...?'

He put his fingers on her soft mouth. 'The bank insisted on insuring it, my darling. Never to its proper value, of course, but there will be no problems there.' He couldn't have her faith in the ruby's return, and something basic in him hoped he would never see it again. It had served its purpose, and with the night's threat to the new stock averted, and the insurance money that the bank would honour, Greg had no need of reminders of the way he and Roslyn had sealed their marriage pact. No need of superstition in which she believed so implicitly.

The sound of the men returning with a horse

and cart to take Greg back to Radcliffe Manor stopped further talk between them. He protested irritably that he could quite easily walk, but both Roslyn and his father would hear no arguments. It was the first time since she had known Thomas Radcliffe that they had been in accord, Roslyn thought with a glimmer of a smile on her lips.

It was a long while later that Greg Radcliffe and his wife were finally alone again. The doctor had been waiting at the house, and insisted on examining them both, though Roslyn was obstinately reticent about the reasons for her swollen throat and the bruising there. The doctor suggested they should both spend a very quiet day in their room to recover, but he could see no permanent damage to either of them.

Hester fussed round them, sending up hot food and brandy and ordering the fire to be made up. It crackled and glowed, throwing a welcoming warmth into the room. Bathed and relaxed, they had gone through the painful process of reporting to the authorities the theft of the ruby and Francis' disappearance. It had to be done, though by now Roslyn was sure he'd be well away from Yorkshire. And making his way to the coast to find a ship that would take him to Ceylon. She knew it as surely as she breathed, but she said nothing to anyone.

There was no need. Francis would be caught, and the devil's kiss restored to her. Its description would be circulated; its own legendary powers would do the rest. If Francis tried to sell it, he would only incur the wrath of the gods even more. The mysticism of the East would never fully lose its hold on her, even though she knew she would never go there again. In some ways it was beginning to seem like a fabulous dream, all the glitter and pageantry, the elegant Darby mansion gleaming among the grey-green slopes of the tea plantation, the scorching heat and exotic colours. And James, striding like a king in his own little empire...her eyes were suddenly damp, for James had been real, and so had her dearest Nadja, and everything in her past life had fashioned her into being the woman she was today. The woman Greg Radcliffe loved...

Roslyn bit her lips. He still had not said he loved her, only on those other occasions when the heat of passion had made the words come easily. But now...when she had made the terrible accusation against him, could she really expect him to forgive her for that? He sprawled out in a comfortable armchair in front of the fire, and she sat on a soft footstool beside him, her head resting on his knee as the flames leapt in the hearth. She wanted to say so much...to ask so much...but she was somehow tongue-tied. She felt the touch of Greg's hand on her tumbling hair, and looked up into his eyes.

'We've come a long way, you and I, Roslyn,' he said slowly. 'Until now I didn't realize quite how much I asked of you in marrying me, nor that it might be too much to ask.'

Roslyn's eyes filled with tears. Was he saying that it was all a mistake after all? That he regretted it so much? The devil's kiss was no longer touching her skin to bring her love or warn her of danger, yet she tingled all over. She couldn't bear it if she were to lose him now. She swallowed back the lump in her aching throat. The ways of pleasing a man were various, her nurse had said softly...sometimes subtle, sometimes frank...and only you will know which one to choose at the appropriate time...

Now was the time for frankness. Roslyn caught hold of his hand and gently kissed the split knuckles.

'I love you, Greg. Didn't I tell you?'

'You also spoke of your longing for home. Is Radcliffe Manor so very alien to you, Roslyn?' He sounded troubled.

Her cheeks reddened. In the last hours she had discovered the great and glorious truth, and was burning to share it with him. She spoke so softly her voice was almost inaudible and he had to lean his face close to hers to hear it.

'My home is wherever you are, Greg. I think I always knew it, even as a child when I fell in love with the handsome Englishman I never expected to meet. You were always my destiny. Laugh at me if you will, but if you will only love me a little, then I'm home...'

He pulled her on to his lap, gently and carefully. Their bodies were bruised and aching, but there was a great need in each of them to be close in body and spirit.

'Don't you know I love you more than life itself, my darling?' He whispered the words against her lips, where she had thrilled to his kisses so many times. But never more so than now, when his mouth was touching hers in a kiss almost devoid of passion, but alive with tenderness. It was all she asked...all she wanted right now. The time for passion was later, for they had the rest of their lives to savour its pleasures.

'Oh Greg!' His name was no more than a sigh of pure happiness on her lips. She leaned against him, feeling the steady beat of his heart and the warmth of his arms holding her.

'The ruby was both a curse and a blessing,

371

Roslyn,' he said slowly. 'It will always be somewhat shaming to me, like an accusing eye, because of the way I used it to my advantage. I thought I was right in being so honest and practical, but there was always the barrier between us because of it. It stopped me admitting that the real reason I wanted to marry you was because I loved you too much to go on living without you. I'm not a believer in magic, beloved, except for the enchantment you bring to me. That's all the magic I'll ever need in my life.'

He went on kissing her and holding her, and Roslyn gloried in his words. A curse and a blessing...she no longer needed the ruby's presence to cast a mirage into the mind. She was already whispering goodbye to time past that could never come again. Welcoming time present with open arms and a loving heart. And time still to come..? If this was a mirage of the mind, Roslyn thought dizzily, as Greg's arms tightened more urgently around her slender waist, then the future was a promise of happiness that exceeded even her wildest dreams. The future with Greg was all she ever wanted, and nothing else mattered. It was more glittering than all the fabulous jewels of the East...and infinitely more precious.